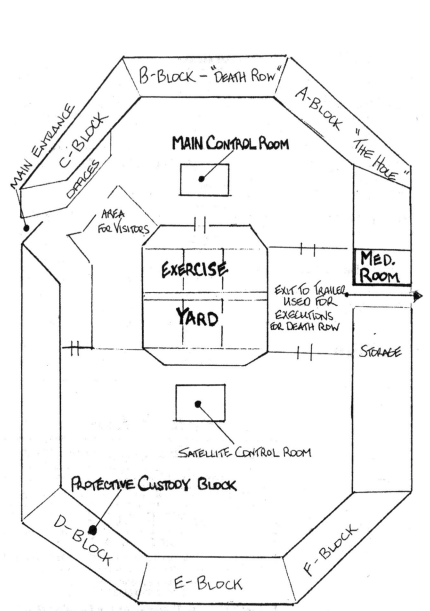

THE MONTANA Department of Institutions says 68 inmates were housed in the state prison's maximum security unit when a riot erupted Sunday. Five prisoners were housed on death row, 10 prisoners in an area designated for protective custody inmates, and 53 prisoners were in cellblocks for regular maximum security inmates. A hand-drawn diagram of the unit is shown above.

Hot, Sunny, Bloody Sunday

by

James M. Powell

DORRANCE PUBLISHING CO., INC.
PITTSBURGH, PENNSYLVANIA 15222

Dorrance Publishing Co., Inc.
701 Smithfield Street
Pittsburgh, PA 15222
Visit our website at *www.dorrancebookstore.com*

ISBN: 978-1-4349-1848-2
eISBN: 978-1-4809-0588-7

A hot, sunny, bloody Sunday. This is a true story about the prison riot that happened on September 22, 1991, when Montana State Prison was engaged in the bloodiest takeover of the prison's history. The author depicts, through a dramatic verbal description, what transpired that day, including: Giving the history of the prison, stories obtained from staff, inmates and community; showing the devastation and destruction that years of relaxed security and not keeping up with modern technology can create. How inadequate salaries, unsuitable leadership, and lack of morals and behavioral stability of the staff affect the outcome of the way the prison is run.

In everyone, there is a con lurking to get out. For the majority of us, the con man stays inside, while the prisoner acts on his emotions over and over again. What is worse: A person who gets caught and goes to prison or a person who commits a felony but never gets caught?

The average person on the streets has no clue as to what goes on inside a prison.

What is learned inside the prison is generally how to perfect their crimes and to teach the wannabe gangster on the street. The government, accompanied by each state in the Union, has done an extensive study on gangs and criminals. The findings show that longer sentences, three-strikes-you're-out, and bringing back the penitentiary system where they are punished for their crime, is the best way to keep crime off the streets. Being punished in prison means to take away things they have on the streets, but it does not mean to be cruel or inhumane, which prisons today are neither.

With an unusual twist in the story there are two brothers: one an inmate that other inmates are trying to kill; the other, a correctional officer working at the prison and caught between family/ blood and loyalty to his fellow comrades. Having a brother in prison brings down your family name, let alone siblings that depend on the person who gives in to his or her own desire. For the officer, it was confusing learning to do the appropriate things while watching the oldest brother get into trouble doing things the wrong way. Then again, it is hard growing up in any lifestyle.

They say the road to hell is paved with good intentions. Each one of us experiences good works and bad thoughts. The ones who have bad morals, bad discipline, no religion, and low self-esteem are generally the ones in prison. There is good in all inmates; for me, having my brother teach me the right way by not allowing me to do the wrong things. His giving in to sin himself but explaining to me the right way had a big effect on me.

My brother has a saying about sin: Each time you sin, you are doing a dance with the devil. At the end of your life, the devil tallies up the sins that you committed and if you have too many sins, the devil takes you down to hell with him for eternity. As Christians know, this is not true. It is God that you sit at the white throne of judgment with. It is He that sends you to hell if you do not confess your sins, believe in Jesus Christ, and follow Him. Not confessing in your sins only makes sins double, and you progress to prison or a life of unrest. Most inmates will say: "I'd rather follow the devil than be around pious people."

Well, so be it!

For the ones who wear the badge, hiding behind it does not make doing wrongs right. Just because you get away with doing wrong, does not mean you don't have the same chance of going to hell as one who gets caught and is in prison. A plain and simple fact is the United States would not need prisons if there were no Christian faith to stop people from killing the people who committed the crimes; something to contemplate.

September 22, 1991

Waking up with no worries. No kids to start planning the day for; no wife to snuggle up to in a queen-size bed. Realizing the pillow that I was hugging was the same pillow that I fell asleep with and the only security I was getting after six months of being divorced. But it was Sunday, my second day of rest after enjoying Saturday with friends in the Rocky Mountains east of Deer Lodge where my father was raised.

I am James Powell, thirty-two years old, five feet seven inches, about 190 pounds, in good condition. I had to believe in myself, because getting bad grades in school and being hyperactive was not a good start in life. I didn't find out what being dyslexic was until out of school for ten years. I had good hand and eye coordination, was fast on my feet, and a good athlete; a running back in football, second-best short-stop at baseball during the summer of 1977. Took third in the Mid-West Karate Championships at full-contact sparring in 1989 at Omaha, Nebraska. I don't smoke, have never done any illegal drugs; drank alcohol maybe five times when I was young. But the biggest influence in my life is I try to be a good Christian. I handle myself with an air of confidence that cannot be broken.

My biggest weakness is women, not that I have ever been unfaithful. I am attracted to the bad girl, the girl of rock and roll, who is good looking, not a Christian, and who is good in bed. They say opposites attract. Well, they are right. I am shy, co-dependent, and have been married four times because I was afraid of being lonely and it is a sin to have sex when not married. In my teens and twenties, I was the center of attention no matter where I was. Then I found out that if I was not the center of attention at a gathering, there was no reason to be there.

Being raised in a family of five siblings with only my father working at the old rock-walled Territorial Prison in Deer Lodge for low wages, we were considered a middle-low class family. Education was not important; you could find a good job after high school in the '70s. There was always good money working on the railroad or in mining or the sawmill. Nevertheless, I took after my father, working for the prison with a steady income.

I am a fourth-generation Montanan with cousins who were pioneers of Montana in 1864. My grandfather arrived in Montana the year it became a state in 1889.

Deer Lodge is a beautiful town that sits in the county of Powell, around 4,000 people residing, and is reigned over by the majestic Mount Powell to the west, that was named after a cousin, John Powell. Deer Lodge was put on the map by having the first college in Montana, the first hardware store in the state, and having the first large cattle ranch in Montana, as well as the rock-walled territorial prison that was built in 1881. This massive prison still stands on Main Street, converted to a museum when the state closed it down in September of 1979. The present prison is two-and-a-half miles west of Deer Lodge. So as you can see, I am your basic middle-class person with your basic thinking. I am your upper-class person who can't leave the small-town life because I know that I would be a nobody outside of nowhere, no how.

I have two daughters that I think the world of, the oldest girl born the summer I graduated from Powell County High School in 1978. I got married to her mother and we had the second angel three years later. I tell myself that my daughters are the reason for not going on further in sports. We were separated on my birthday ten months after daughter Sarah's birth for trying to convince my wife that I knew everything; I was never wrong. My ideology should be how to raise a family. This got me a divorce and three more divorces after that. Yes, I am bullheaded and with a confident spirit that can't be broken. I started working for the Montana State Prison in May of 1979. I worked a year before the Milwaukee Railroad before they abolished their lines in Montana. I was a second-generation correctional officer (guard). Starting pay was $4.85 an hour, a cut in pay from the railroad at $7.00 an hour.

After working at the prison for twelve years, I came to this conclusion: that majority of the people who work at the prison are only one step higher than the inmates, with inmates lower than a **bum on the streets**. Do not get riled up yet; this might take a little explaining. You see, inmates are in prison for getting caught doing horrendous things, not once but numerous times. Prison is a breeding place for the Devil leaving no stones unturned. Prison staff, from the warden down to the guards, while working there, have done everything imaginable—from killing another person to stealing, robbing, taking illegal drugs, rape, child molesting, writing bad checks, driving under the influence of alcohol, being unfaithful to their spouses, and on and on.

For example, here are stories that happened during the time I had been there: A teacher from out of state was working at the prison for two years when charges arose from Colorado. He molested a couple of his students in Colorado. When asked to talk with the sheriff's office in Helena, Montana, he left the state and went to California and committed suicide. Another example involves a correctional officer who, while drunk and driving a motorcycle, killed a pedestrian. He left the scene of the crime and the next day was hauled to jail. Later, he was found guilty of murder and also of stealing valuables out of the houses of his friends who worked at the prison.

Another officer, with his brother, went to the small town of Whitehall. While drinking, they got kicked out of the bar and started shooting up the town with a gun they had in the truck. Driving away as fast as the truck would go, they turned a corner and hit a lady walking down the street, running over her and killing her.

Drinking parties were an everyday occurrence with staff during the '70s and '80s away from the prison. A sergeant was fooling around with the ladies at Conley Lake west of the prison site and on prison property. His wife came to the party with a .38 pistol tucked away. I reiterate, *this was on prison property*. While the carousing was going on, the sergeant and his wife were having choice words back and forth, until she pulled a pistol out and shot him in his stomach. She left the party and everyone sobered up fast, looking at the sergeant on the ground thinking he was dying. There was no blood and no hole in him became she shot him in his belt buckle. There were no charges brought up on her because no one said a thing, but the rumor was that he kept his pants zipped for a couple of years.

Another incident was a classic: A first-shift captain was responsible for all the contraband taken from the inmates, and he had the only key to the contraband room. Items of contraband were always missing from the locked room. This went on for years, and the captain would blame the guards. He would say that they never brought the contraband, just the paper work to the office. I, myself, at different times, found illegal items in inmates' rooms, like money, drugs, finished hobby items that the inmates never had a hobby permit for, and shanks. So, I would write the inmate up and, if necessary, bring the inmate to max if it was warranted. More and more contraband was being stolen from the so-called secured room. Prison officials went to the captain's house and saw his garage was filled with inmates' contraband—items like televisions, stereos, and some hobby items, but the expensive hobby items like horse hair belts that cost $350 and horse bridles that cost $1000 were never found. This captain got his hands slapped by putting him on night shift as captain, and stayed there until he retired with honors.

This was not the shocking thing about this captain. He raised a brood of daughters and each one of them grew up with secrets that they held from the public. The prison has a fine ranch and dairy during the 1960s and '70s, and probably before that time. The commissioned staff and higher officials would go to the slaughterhouse with the keys; not alone, but in teams after it was closed at night, stealing beef and pork. It was cut and wrapped, feeding their families the choice cuts that were to be served to the population of inmates. Another example; each Thanksgiving, the state would purchase enough turkeys for the whole prison population event. One Thanksgiving, the turkeys made it to the kitchen the morning before, but by the next day, forty-five twenty-pound turkeys were stolen. So, Thanksgiving that year was served with pressed canned turkey because they couldn't give half the inmate population fresh turkey and the other half canned turkey. There was no way the inmates stole the turkeys, so it was from the same person who had the only key to the contraband room.

Deer Lodge is like every other small prison town in the USA, where the prison is the major industry; the town thrives on the prison. All you hear is gossip about the prison, like the staff never make enough money; the inmates' wives and children cause all the problems in town. The second part of that is a fallacy, but it makes for a good conversation. Before the 1990s, Deer Lodge had a big population of inmates wives. This has changed for different reasons, one being that the families were on welfare taking advantage of Powell County, making a small county's taxes too high. Also, many of the crimes were from the inmates' families. Do not forget about the retired people that will tell you story after story, incident after incident until you are telling their stories back to them word for word.

The Montana State Prison (MSP) has quite a history behind it. In 1869, the original prison was built by inmate labor on the Main Street of town. The perimeter wall fence came from a nearby rock quarry. The stone wall is sixteen feet high and three feet wide at the top. The prison was one of the original Western Territorial Prisons, along with legendary institutions such as the prison at Florence, Arizona, and Colorado's Old Max in Canyon City. The old MSP ran well throughout its 100 years except for two major crises that I will briefly tell you about.

Four men took Warden Frank Conley and Deputy Warden John Robinson hostage in 1908.

Inmates George Rock and William Hayes killed John Robinson; they were hanged inside the prison walls less than a year later. Warden Frank Conley saved his own life even after they slit his throat. The Deer Lodge newspaper, *The Silver State Post*, stated, "The fact that Warden Conley had heavy jowls was the only thing that saved his life."

The other major incident was the riot in April of 1959, when inmates took control of the entire prison. The Montana National Guard was brought in and thirty-six hours later, the prison was commandeered back, with another Deputy Warden, Ted Rothe, killed. The penologist, Warden Floyd Powell, took back control of the prison and broke up the "Con Boss" system, which changed the way the prison was run.

To give you a brief description and history of the new MSP that sits on a prehistoric glacier bench two-and-a-half miles west of Deer Lodge, the land was owned by my cousins, the Evans family, in the late 1800s, with the remains of their foundation that can be seen at the place called "the bone yard" west of the prison compound. In the early 1900s, the bench was known as the Deer Lodge Farms; later, Warden Frank Conley was buying up the land. He contracted with the state for the inmates to work the land, with Conley paying a fee to the state for inmate labor, then keeping a profit for himself. Conley was also the mayor of Deer Lodge and the warden of the prison from May 1895 to May 1929. The land around the prison was sold to the state in 1952, and it is known as the Prison Ranch and Dairy, spanning over 33,000 acres from Deer Lodge to Gold Creek on the Old Stagecoach Road. In about 1960, the state built a two-story dorm building, known as the Rothe Hall, that housed the low-custody inmates working at the ranch and dairy on the future site of the new prison west of Deer Lodge. While the old prison was still being used in town, three more units were built in about 1976, facing east of the Rothe Hall building, to house more of the lower custody inmates. By 1979, there were two high-side units and three low-side units, and a refurbished industries building made into a max unit.

This brings us back to September 22, 1991, when MSP included three primary compounds within the perimeter fence. They were referred to as the Low-Side Security Compound, called A, B, C, and D units, all of which are 96 to 98-cell buildings. The High-Side Security Compound included three 96-cell housing units called Close I, Close II, and Close III. The Maximum Security Compound included but a single building which was divided into two sides (east and west), and both sides included a Unit Control Room (cage) and three 16-cell, 2-level-pod living units, referred to as A, B, and C for the west side, and D, E and F for the east side.

(Refer to the picture of the inside diagram.). There were fifty-eight acres inside the perimeter fence. The institution included 838 cells. There were an additional forty inmates in dormitory housing, all in one dorm called the dairy dorm.

A double fence topped with razor ribbon secured the institution's perimeter.

There are two towers staffed twenty-four hours per day, with three other towers staffed sixteen hours per day. The Industries Area was outside this double-fenced perimeter, enclosed by a single fence. Only low-custody inmates were approved for this area.

The Reception Building was adjacent to the Wallace Building (Administration building), but within the double-fenced perimeter.

Presumably, inmates did not leave their own compound except to go to the infirmary, religious activities center, to gym, to work, or to eat three meals a day. The high-side food service building had the institution's main kitchen and bakery. Most food was taken to the low-security compound kitchen, ready to cook.

Max inmates were subsisted in their cells with food taken to the Max compound on insulated carts.

Staff, official visitors, and inmate's visitors all used the same single entrance to the Wallace Building. Each was searched at the front of the first floor of that building. The on-site count of the institution that September morning was 1,169 inmates. The total number of staff positions authorized at MSP was 428, including 404 inside the main institution and 24 positions at the ranch or at the industries. The inmate-to-staff ratio in 1990 was 2.76 to 1 correctional officer. The staff turnover for the fiscal year 1991 was just over 19 percent. The beginning salary for a correctional officer was $15,563 per year, which was at least 15 percent below national average.

* * * * * * * * * * * *

0600 Hours

The day started the same as any other day. But then again, if you get lucky to wake up alive in a 6 ft. x 8 ft. cell on the PC block in the Maximum Security Unit at the Montana State Prison, you would think that every day would be the same. *Ha! ha! ha!* with a sarcastic laugh, inmate Powell was thinking. Every day is like dancing with the devil. At the end of the day, the devil tallies up how much you owe him.

His day started out at 0600 hours with the banging of electric doors, a humming sound of the doors opening and shutting. Plus, the men in gray uniform whispering; footsteps coming toward inmate Powell outside of his cell. When the footsteps stopped, a flashlight would shine in his eyes through the small door glass of UD-6 cell, where, adult offender AO 00325 resided. It was count time, the same routine taking place every two damn hours—all night long, seven days a week, 365 days a year, a flashlight would shine in his eye.

Inmate Robert Powell came into prison three months earlier, serving fifty years plus five with a "dangerous" label tacked onto his record for being stupid, acting like "What can America do for me" instead of "What can I do for America under God." This was not his first time in prison. He was doing the rodeo circuit at Stillwater, Minnesota, and Vacaville, California. Inmate Powell was thinking he was getting too old to spend the rest of his life in prison, so he was trying to play it straight this time because if he fell one more time, he would get the "Big-Bitch," or in other words, 100 years without parole.

Inmate Powell was thirty-nine years old, 5 feet 10 inches, receding hair line. But the hair on the side of his head was long down to his neck. He was 215 pounds, with a slouch and a chip on his shoulder. He grew up in Deer Lodge, Montana, in the '60s with long hair, drugs, free love, with rock and roll music changing the lives of a whole generation, virtually with one big peace sign.

At 0715 hours, a voice came over the speaker in the day room outside of his cell said, "Powell, time to go to work!" It was an unfamiliar voice coming from the satellite cage on the outside of the block. His chain-driven door hummed open with a loud clang at the end, telling him that the door was locked open. As inmate Powell stepped out onto the upper tier, the door proceeded to close. At the same time, he heard, coming from his right, three cells down on the same tier, over a speaker, "McFarlane, time to go to work!" The door opened to UD-3 cell, and inmate McFarlane stepped out; the door closed and locked shut behind him. McFarlane, 6 feet tall, around 165 pounds in his early '40s was what you call an Old Con. He had been in trouble his whole life, in and out of prison, learning the con game to a tee. A con is an inmate who got his education inside the prison; getting his illegal contraband by talking correctional officers, other inmates, or other staff into bringing in things that he needed and or could sell. An old con was so good at his game that when the trouble caught up to him, he would most of the time be not be indicted to the offense because he surrounded himself with fools. Inside prison, being called an "old con" meant a high status, a privilege wherein all the rest of the inmates respected you. The guards also had some respect for a con because they knew that they were up to something, but it was hard to pin anything on them. McFarlane was a smooth talker, sly, and, even on the streets, if you gave him enough time, he could talk a preacher's daughter out of her panties.

Over a year ago, inmate McFarlane was working outside the double fence, called the tag-plant. In the prison industries single-fence area, another one of McFarlane's grandiose ideas got the tag-plant supervisor fired and other inmates sent to max.

McFarlane was caught bringing in drugs from the back gate. The investigator, Robert McNally, talked to him, and inmate Chuck (McFarlane) slyly convinced the investigator to set up the supervisor, with Chuck signing a plea agreement keeping him from serving more time in prison for drug trafficking and selling.

Well, for the reason I told you, Chuck did not make it to max that night. He was back to work the next day, setting up plans with his supervisor, Lowell Bird, to bring in drugs for him to distribute inside the prison. In return, Staff Supervisor Bird would get money that was marked with invisible ink. The money was traceable, able to be seen with a blue light.

Coining the phrase, in prison, a "low-bird," is a low-flying bird whose motives conveyed misery and shame; an officer or staff who brings in contraband to inmates for any kind of gain. After the tag plant supervisor, Lowell Bird, was caught, the low-bird was placed in jail in downtown Deer Lodge. The news spread around the prison about how McFarlane ratted off the supervisor and for a short time, the marijuana was in short supply to the inmates, so the inmates wanted to kill McFarlane. That was how Chuck made it to max and on the PC block. If you felt that Lowell Bird was caught unaware, that he was taken advantage of from an old con, then you were very mistaken.

Lowell Bird came from Butte, Montana, and worked at the prison for maybe fifteen years. He was married and had two or three daughters. Bird was a nice guy and had a nice home with a beautiful family. The low-bird lost everything he had going for him in Deer Lodge, so he moved the family to Walla Walla, Washington.

He started a new life as a guard at a new prison. Sometime later, he was arrested and sent to the Walla Walla Prison for molesting his daughters. So, as you see, folks, the devil keeps track of your sins and tries to make it so you won't make it out of the Abyss.

So, that gets us back to this Sunday, September 21, 1991 where inmates Powell and McFarlane were walking down a flight of stairs to the sally-port from the protective custody (PC) block. The PC block was located in the max unit on the designated D block. A swamper's (prison term for janitor) job was to break down the food cart, clean any spilled coffee or milk off the carts and floor. After the officers picked up the breakfast trays, the swamper put all utensils and trays back in the lower part of the cart, then wheeled it out the front door so the kitchen staff could take it back to the kitchen, then got it ready for lunch in order to feed the max unit. The swampers never touched the food in the cart because the inmates in max would always be paranoid that the PC would spit in the food or do even more disgusting things to the food like put human feces in it, to get back at the regular population of max from threatening them all the time. So, the officers always served the food while the inmates in their cells watched from their door windows, each meal the officers served during chow. The swampers cleaned the trays and bagged up the garbage, placing it on top of the cart to get rid of it. Next, it was time to prepare the clothes for showers. All towels, socks, undershorts, and if it was the block's day to get clean orange overalls, they were rolled up and placed on a metal cart by sizes. Later in the day when there was no food cart to attend to, in the summer, two swampers would go outside. They would water and mow around the max building. Basically, the job was from 0715 hours to 2030 hours doing laundry, mopping floors, and putting up with a lot of bullshit. Being an inmate swamper, you were put right in the middle between the guards and the inmates.

You saw and heard things, but you couldn't tell anyone else, because it meant losing your job. You could not go to the guard and tell them anything that the inmates were doing wrong or you would have the inmates wanting to kill you.

Likewise, you could not tell the inmates what the guards were doing wrong; but what the hell, they were PC swampers, up in max for being rats. So they told whatever they figured would give them an edge over both the max inmates and the guards.

Let me explain what a maximum security unit is in laymen's terms. Max is a prison inside of a prison. It houses the worst of the inmate population, including the death-row inmates, disciplinary inmates, and inmates who have a lot of years to serve inside the prison. They were placed in max to see how they would react. Then, with good behavior, an inmate even with 100 years can see the low side of the prison in ten or so years. So, a protective custody block is to house, quoting the inmates, "rats/cheese eaters breaking the first of the inmate code of ethics; never inform on another inmate for anything, anyhow, or anyway." An officer's point of view is that PCs are the misfits of the inmates. The inmate who complains more requires higher maintenance than other inmates—basically, a person who cannot live in society or in prison. At the end of the day, the prison administration found out how ludicrous an idea it was to house PC inmates and max inmates in the same unit.

Walking inside the ¾-inch protective glass sally-port—like the rest of the corridors, the blocks also have glass windows facing the cage. So the cage officer, seeing that inmates Powell and McFarlane were in the corridor, closed the door, opening the outside door leading to and around the cage. The satellite cage was on the east side of the building with two ways you can get to the cage. One way was from the south hall that comes from the outside sally-port, past two offices and a staff restroom on the left. On the right, in the center of the building was a storage room and three of the dog-runs accessible through a metal yard-door about 25 feet from the cage. The west corridor leads down the back hall to one of two electric chain-driven security doors to secure and divide the building in half. On the other side of the door to the right was a back door with a corridor, and then another door leading to the outside back of the building. There were always two doors in a prison. You open one door, go through it, close the same door, then open the next door; as you can see, it was for security. Next, on the right side going down the hall was another storage room, and past that, an infirmary exam room.

The infirmary was only for small things like aspirin, bandages, and small items—no knives, hammers, wire cutters, or hard drugs. So, the infirmary was a safe place to check out a max inmate for minor illnesses without the nurse or doctor getting hurt as long as two officers were present. The inmate would have belly chains and leg irons on. To the left was a door leading to the middle of the six-man dog-runs, where an officer could go to watch the inmates inside the metal chain-link fence.

Three runs on the right and three runs on the left with metal chain-link separating the runs. Last is a room on the right that was for storage. Next was the second electric door which secured the west side of the building from the east side of the building.

The cage was a hexagonal room made from cinder blocks, about 6 ft. x 6 ft., with three separate electrical panels with toggle switches to open every door, sally-port, block doors, and emergency block doors. The emergency doors led from one block to another block, from D, E, and F blocks. The cage had no bathroom.

Inside, the cage had a metal ladder leading to the roof with a metal lid that could be locked so no one from the outside could get into the max building from above. Inside the cage, you can see out in every direction—inside all three blocks, down both corridors, and into the yard through the window of the yard door. The windows were on all sides of the cage, waist high and amazing. There was no need to put bars on the cage windows because they were inmate proof. I was one of the staff members who tested the new type of non-breakable windows before the max unit and close three units were built.

About thirty-five staff and officers went out to the rifle range to see a demonstration from a manufacturer of their windows. The first attempt was to try firing different ballistic weapons at a window, and found out that smaller-caliber bullets bounced off the window, while larger-caliber bullets stuck inside of the window with no cracks around the bullet. The next test was taking firemen's axes to the window, to no avail; three officers, including myself, struck at the window until tired, and only put a hole in the window as big as an oval egg. Last was a test of fire; the salesman put gas on the window with not much damage. He tried a torch to the window and that did go through but like he said, there will not be any gas pressure torch in any unit, especially in a max unit. Also, on the outside of this plastic window would be a glass window to stop the torch problem and any scratching of the Plexiglas.

The max building was about 200 yards away from any other building. It was fenced away to keep it isolated from being involved with the rest of the units in the prison. The max building was built with the newest and most modern ideas, making it one of the most impregnable buildings for the money at the time.

So, inmates Powell and McFarlane were out of the D block sally-port walking down the hallway to the west-side cage. They did not have to wait for the two security doors to open because they were already open and stayed open to make the officers' job easier. It made it easier on the floor and in the cages. Getting to the other side was the kitchen cart to clean up. Plus, cleaning the floor from spilled coffee and milk that had to be mopped up. After that job was done, inmates Powell and McFarlane went down to the sergeant's office to talk to the officers while they were finishing eating breakfast left over from the cart. The officers and the two swampers (janitors) generally got along because the inmate swamper would do whatever the officer asked them to do without complaining. If the swamper was a complainer, then the sergeant would find another inmate who wanted to get out of his cell and work. It wasn't uncommon for the officers to call the swampers by their first name, but it was never appropriate for the inmate to call the officer by his first name. They are called 'officer' with their surname or just officer, or "Yes, Sir, No, Sir."

The sergeant saw the two swampers and said, "Powell, you can clean the staff restroom while we are taking a break," with inmate Powell replying, " Yes, Sir."

Powell headed next door while Officer Dale Browne opened the door with a key and said, "Bob, it is going to be a hot day today, in the high '70s, so it would be a good day for you and Chuck to mow the front of the building this afternoon."

"Sure we will, Mr. Browne. It would be cool to get outside and get some sun," Powell stated happily.

Next to the sergeant's office was a room with a mop tub and drain. At the back of the room was another door, a room big enough for a toilet and sink. It took five minutes to clean with the bleach and toilet brush and rag in the corner. As Powell left the bathroom and went back to the sergeant's office, McFarlane was leaning against the door, laughing and joking with the officers. McFarlane, seeing that Powell was back, picked up the officer's trays. Then the sergeant said to the officers that it was time to pick up the rest of the trays. So off they all went one block at a time.

"McFarlane," one of the officers said, "would you bring (not a question, it was a command) the officers a cup of coffee to both cages."

McFarlane said, "Sure, I would be glad to."

Heading out of the office down to the cage on the West side, McFarlane nodded his head and showed the officer in the cage that he had a cup of coffee for him.

The cage officer went over to the door, unlocking it from the inside. The cage officer said, "McFarlane, why didn't you bring me a bigger cup, this will only last a short time." McFarlane said, "Sorry, this was all the cups that were in the office." He then left and went over to the other cage.

The officer unlocked the door on the inside, but the cage was not locked on the outside of the door. Each time the inmate gets the door open, they make a mental note, looking at the panels and figuring the cage out. An inmate never knows when he might need the information about the cage or other important information; an inmate can sell their information or blackmail an officer when the time is right. These were common mistakes happening a lot in max—leaving the outside door unlocked, opening a cage door when an inmate is not locked behind another door; never opening the cage door for an inmate for any reason.

The officers would go to each cell, look inside the cell before opening the slot in the door with a Folger Adams key, called a jailor key in the old prison. The Folger Adams key is a big brass key that fits in the palm of your hand. You would turn the key with your wrist to the right to unlock and to the left to lock. The inmate in the cell would hand the officer the tray and then the officer would lock the slot back up. This was the routine for each level, picking up the trays then giving them to the swampers. The swampers banged the trays in a fifty-gallon plastic garbage can with a plastic liner in it, then stacked the trays on a cart. This went on until all the blocks on both sides were picked up. Tray passing and pickup was a sweaty, galling, and long job. On first shift it was done twice—breakfast and lunch. When finished with the trays, everything was put back on the hot cart.

Inmates McFarlane and Powell started back to the main cage side pushing and pulling a cumbersome cart, with the sergeant and officer leading the way going back to his office. As they started down the hall, the first electric door closed behind them, then through the last electric door, it closed. They proceeded down the hall past the sergeant's office to the sally-port door, heading outside with the cart; the cart went back to the kitchen. The main sally-port opened with the sergeant and inmate Powell pushing the carts through the sliding door. The door closed behind them. Waiting for the main cage officer to pop the outside door open, the sergeant opened the door and then helped pull the carts out the door, pulling the carts away from the building so the kitchen staff could bring a gas- driven Cushman vehicle to max to pick up the carts. Inmate Powell went back inside, closing the door. The sergeant walked down the cement quarter-mile walk to the captain's office to turn in the count sheet.

Powell, back in the sally-port, waited for the main control officer to open the inside door. Both inmates McFarlane and Powell walked down to the laundry room next to the electric door on the same side of the main cage. It was time to do laundry while the officers brought C-block inmates out of their cells to the yard in the middle of the building. The yard period was for an hour and a half.

Powell said to McFarlane in the small laundry room away from any other ears, "Chuck, did you see the rookies in the cages and the old men on the floor?"

"Ha," Chuck laughed, "the old man Olson, I think we are going to have to wheel him around or find a coffin to haul him around, and I found out that his wife is the sergeant of A-Unit. Rumor has it that she is twenty years younger than him and she will spread her legs for anything that can keep it hard except for an inmate, for now. That will be my next project when I get out of max. Miller is a good officer but in his late forties. He might have to get the oxygen bottle for him and for Sergeant McPhail with all the cigarettes they smoke," Chuck said, telling another story as Bob started to laugh.

"Browne is the only officer that has been here for over six years and is in his early thirties," said Bob Powell. He continued,

"Yeah, Browne graduated with my younger brother. They grew up friends. Browne is a good officer. He does his job without causing trouble to us or any inmate and he is smart enough not to play any con games."

"Boy, you are right there. I tried to get him started in baby steps and he wouldn't even bite at that," frowned Chuck.

Chuck kept talking. "The two officers in the cages I have only seen once and I have never seen the other rookie in the main cage."

Bob commented, "They must be short on officers because I thought you had to have six months in at the prison before they could work in max, but I guess not. The old saying in the Territorial Prison in Deer Lodge was when the bums got off the train in Deer Lodge, the training officer would go down to the yard, ask the bums if they wanted a job and would give them free room and board and a badge to go with the new uniforms. I think those days are coming back again," laughed the both of them.

"Oh," Chuck was thinking out loud, "Warden McCormick is a good warden but I think he has his mind on other things than the operation of the prison."

Powell asked, "Why do you say that, Chuck?"

Chuck answered, "Because there is a good-looking lady that works in the administration office, the name of Colleen Fine. And let me tell you, she looks real fine in tight pants or dresses. Us low-life cons get to see her walking through the yard sometimes on her way to the chow hall.

"Whoa, Chuck, is this a story that I want to keep in my mind for later tonight when I am all alone in my bungalow?" replied Powell.

"Yes, it might help you out on those interminable nights with your pillow by yourself," laughed McFarlane. "Well, it was getting back to the inmates that McCormick and Fine were seeing a lot of each other, and they were seen coming out of a Deer Lodge house together and no one else was there at the house. I'm not saying that anything was happening between them, but only their hairdresser and God knows what was going on in that house. All the guards would say is that it must have been a Fine lunch," he said, as they both were laughing.

McFarlane was on a roll now. "If you think that was funny, Bob, then you will get a kick out of this. The Warden before him was Riesly. He had a beautiful wife and a good-looking tall secretary. Well, this story has a turn in it; Riesly and his secretary were both married, and the two couples would be seen together in surrounding cities. Well, it was only about a year and a half later, the secretary came up pregnant. And then after Riesly left the prison to be the warden or something back East, I think New Jersey, the secretary was letting it known that her child was Riesly's. To make the story better, Riesly, some years later, was flying to Hawaii, and the plane went down and killed him. I guess he paid off his debt dancing with the devil that day," Chuck concluded, thinking about what he just said. "Bob, I never told you about some of the funny stories that happened during the years I've been here, have I?" asked Chuck.

Bob answered, "No, you haven't. We have some time, let's hear some."

"Well, I guess I will start with some stories before my time and about ghosts that have haunted the new prison. These are stories that the guards tell me," said Chuck.

"You mean the officers and you talk about things that are going on around the prison, and they tell you stories?" muttered Bob.

Chuck said, "Yeah, there are some nice guards all over the prison that, to pass the time, will talk. That is how the inmates find out almost anything that is going on at the prison and outside the prison. Plus, it is a way to find out information about the prison guards who slip up and tell things they shouldn't be telling us.

"Give it some time, and you will get into conversations with the guards. You will see, Bob."

"I will tell you some ghost stories first." Chuck began his story. "The Rothe building was built in the early '60s and was a dorm for the inmates that worked on the ranch and dairy. The inmates' dorm was upstairs in the two-story building."

Bob butted in, "Yeah, in the '60s my family would drive by the building going to Conley Lake to go swimming. Rothe was out in the field to the left of the road.

"It looked out of place, that big building all alone. Conley Lake was just up the road about a mile. The townspeople could go to the lake and swim. There were boat docks and a nice sandy beach to lie around on. Also, there was a big log cabin that was open to the public."

Chuck interrupted, "Do you what to hear my stories or reminisce?" Not waiting for a response, he started in. "The guards tell of a story that…. Did you see the tower on the hill when you came to the prison, Bob?"

"Yes," Bob replied.

Chuck kept talking. "Guards would say when they worked in the tower in the evening and at night, they would get a glimpse of an inmate wearing pin-stripe clothes running away from the prison. At times, they would hear the steel door open and close, and hear footsteps coming up the metal stairs. The guards would yell out, 'Is anyone there!' but no answer. And at all times, the guards would have the hatch door closed. When they heard noises, they would stand on the wood door in case somehow, something could get through the steel locked door at the bottom, so if the sounds were coming up the stairs, then they would not get through the hatch."

"That sounds like the other guards were playing a joke on them," Bob stated.

Chuck said, "No, to get to the tower on the hill there is a half-mile road to get up the hill to the tower, and the guard can see all around the tower for miles. Plus, I was told that two guards, years apart, shot their .357 pistols off from inside the tower, putting a hole in the window and into the cement floor," proclaimed Chuck.

Bob said, "Whoa, that does sound a little spooky!"

McFarlane added, "But you have to remember, Bob, each time I hear the stories, they get better and better every year. It don't matter who tells it, the guards or the cons. And when a con or staff left the prison for good, they were always the meanest, baddest person to ever leave the prison. It doesn't matter how nice they were inside the prison, from guard to sergeant to warden or from con to con, they were the meanest bastard alive in their stories.

"Here are stories during my time in prison," Chuck was boasting. "In '80 or '81, there was an inmate drug ring inside the prison, which there always is inside a prison, but this time, it was getting pretty bad. The head inmate was Dunster, big guy and he was handsome, looked like the Marlboro Man on the commercials on TV. He lived in A Unit, I think 240 cube. Well, there was a young dumb kid that lived in cube 340 and I think room 345. The kid was being punked out, and...."

"What do you mean, 'punked out?'" Powell asked.

"Oh, I didn't tell you," laughed Chuck. "It means that he was getting screwed in the butt without him wanting to. The inmate's name was Rosier. Two days before he was killed, he was up in the Rothe Hall building going to school, and the teacher, Wallace, was talking to him. Rosier was crying, telling the teacher that his mother was going to get him out of prison and that he didn't belong in prison. Wallace told him that he was in prison now and it will take more than his mother to get him out."

"Bob Wallace lives behind my parent's house, and they are good friends," said Bob.

Chuck continued, "Rosier was going to snitch Dunster and others off, so Dunster and the others went up to 340 cube during the day and taped Rosier up with tape given to them from a guard, but the guard didn't know anything about what the tape was used for. His hands and feet were taped and Rosier still was going to snitch them off. So Dunster cut Rosier's head off, and I mean all the way off. Dunster and the others didn't know what to do with the body, so they started cutting him up and flushing pieces of the body down the toilet drain. But they ran out of time because it was getting close to count time. The killers cleaned up the blood with a wool blanket and sheets which I was told was a mess with more than a gallon of blood on the floor. Then they put the rest of the body under Rosier's bunk. Finally, the guards came up to count and couldn't find him so a search took place and they found him. Dunster took the blame for everyone that was involved.

"He went to max and was in one max escape attempt where Dunster was going to get killed by some death row inmates. They got a gun into max through the max visiting room. They were going to kill him and kill some guards, so Dunster ratted them off. He told the guards where the gun was and how the other inmates were going to escape."

Inmate McFarlane kept on talking. "To get back to the ghost part of the story, inmates and guards at late evening and at night under the bright lights in the compound yard, and only on the low side, have seen a figure walking on the grass after lockdown. The figure stands by the tree in the middle of the yard. Guards have checked it out but when they would start over to the person, the figure would go behind the tree and somehow disappear. This started happening after the young inmate was killed."

"Whoa, I like that story the best!" said Bob.

Chuck said, "I have time to tell you one more story if you quit interrupting.

"Back in the 1960s, I believe, the Rothe dorm was built for the inmates that worked on the outside of the prison. The building was built after the riot of '59. There was a con name of Falcon and he was a strong, big, hefty man. Got his muscles the hard way by lifting bales of hay on a farm, not like people today lifting weights to make them big. Weight lifting wasn't even done much in these parts of the country, maybe on TV you would see them. Well, what I am saying is Falcon was a heavyweight, and he wanted to run the prison inmates and the guards if he had a chance."

"You better get going with the story or lunch time will be here," said Powell.

Chuck kept on talking, "I am if you will give me a chance to tell the story right.

"Well, Falcon had his stuff rolled up a couple of times and brought inside the wall because he was fighting with other cons. He told his side of the story, that he was The Man, and he wasn't going to back down to anyone for no reason. Well, there were two main cons running the Rothe dorm back then, and they were supplying the drugs inside the prison by having them brought to the dorm road at night by family that lived in Deer Lodge. Then the drugs were picked up from a con on the ranch. Falcon told Fitzpatrick, Baldwin, and Gardner that he wanted part of the profit. Well, Fitz and Gardner and others were not going to let

Falcon bulldog them, so they were going to tune him up, just give him a shave, nicking Falcon here and there. So, downstairs in the basement of the Rothe Hall building was a recreation area with pool tables, cards, dominos, and things like that. The group of cons were to only rough Falcon up and let him know who was running the show. But Falcon was outshining them, so the weapons came out and Falcon's neck was cut almost off by Fitzpatrick. The gang left the room and each one tried to make up an alibi before Falcon was found. Gardner and Baldwin came back and carried the body up the stairs and out the door, setting Falcon on the mail bags, with a note saying 'first class idiot on board.' After that, they say the Rothe Hall downstairs in the basement and the hallway up the stairs is haunted. The guards and staff have seen and heard someone walking up or down the stairs."

"That was a good story before lunch. Now, I don't think I'm that hungry for meat anymore," said Bob.

McFarlane cackled and said, "If that was all it would take to keep you from eating, Bob, then I would have told you these stories before." They both started laughing.

"I have one more story that will take only a few minutes, and I have to tell you because it happened while I was here," said McFarlane.

"Boy, you really like telling stories, don't you, Chuck? But I don't have anywhere to go right now," stated Powell.

Chuck started his story, "Well, it happened in the summer of 1979 at the new prison. At that time, there was only the letter units. The high side and max were still at the old prison in Deer Lodge. There was two cons, one was Buckley, and the other was an old man name of McLean. Well, Buckley was in the service, did his time in Vietnam. He was supposed to be a badass in karate and killed a lot of Gooks in the jungle. He came back to Montana and went crazy; killed someone with his bare hands, I guess. I am not sure what his crime was and it does not matter because it does not have anything to do with the story anyway."

McFarlane kept talking. "McLean was living in the same cube as Buckley, A unit 140 or 130 cube. Buckley was a wacko from the service, and the old man kept him sane by talking to him and being his only friend. Other inmates were afraid of him, but the guards got along with him fine as long as they left him alone. Then when the old prison moved to the new area in September of 1979, Buckley had to move to Close II Unit on the high side. McLean was trying to tell the guards that Buckley was going to go off, but no one cared or didn't have enough pull to do anything about it. Plus, they didn't believe the old man because Buckley was a good, clean, and neatly kept person and respectful to the staff. It was Close II library time in the late afternoon. Buckley went to the library and at that time, the library was on the low side of the prison by A Unit. Well during library, Buckley was to meet another inmate that had a shank that was sharpened from the cement floor. It was time to go back to the unit and the guard was walking the group of inmates back. Well, the guard was walking in the middle of the group of inmates instead of walking behind the group were he was taught to walk. He was talking to the inmates when Buckley came up behind him with the shank. He held the guard close to his body with his left arm and the shank across his neck with the right hand. He told the guard to go back to the Rothe Building and he was going to kill him if they did not let him out the front door."

McFarlane, getting into his story, kept talking. "The front door to the prison at this time was in the Rothe Hall. Buckley wanted to walk right through the two electric doors with the guard as hostage, and down the hall past the warden's office and out the door. I guess he was going to take the guard's car from the parking lot if he thought that far ahead. The main control officer would not let him out the doors, and the warden was called to take care of the problem. Well, they tried talking to Buckley, but he wouldn't listen so to buy some time, the control officer was told to open the visiting room doors. This was to give the warden some time to think. A lieutenant at the time, the name of Ruwon, was the best shot and was working during this time. A plan came together and it had to be soon because Buckley was threatening to cut the nuts off the guard."

Powell had to comment, "Boy, Buckley sure had some balls or he needed two more."

"That was good, Bob, I liked that one," said McFarlane. McFarlane kept on talking, "The plan was that the old nurse that was here for a hundred years and looked like it, was to run back to the visiting room screaming and yelling. That would get Buckley to stand up and wonder what was going on, and leave the guard alone for a minute. Ruwon was outside the prison with a .308 sniper rifle. When Buckley stood up, Ruwon put a bullet in Buckley's chest that dropped him like a hot potato. The guard and the nurse ran back out the visiting room doors. The prison had its own ambulance that had to be from the early '60s, if it was a day old.

They walked Buckley out the back door of the Rothe Hall and put him in the ambulance. He got his wish to go out the front door but he died on the way to the Powell County Hospital."

Powell had to get the last word in because the guards were on their way to the yard. Powell said, "I remember when that happened, Chuck. The siren was going off and you could hear it from town. I was on one of my smoking a bong parties but it was all over town before Buckley made it to the hospital."

McFarlane added, "I don't think anyone has seen Buckley's ghost, but if you go to the visiting room on the low side, at times the hair will stand up on the back of your neck and you will feel a weird cold feeling come over you."

Powell said, "I've got to admit, Chuck, your stories are interesting and they make the time go by fast."

＊＊＊＊＊＊＊＊＊＊＊＊

0500 Hours

His day started early waking up at 0500 hours, taking about fifteen minutes to put his uniform on, brush his teeth, and shave the hair that was growing sparsely on his face. This was a routine Dale Browne had done for six years, five days a week. The routine was old hat, shower before bed and wake up before the alarm goes off. In the prison system, Dale was known to the inmates as an "apple," red on the outside and white in the middle. Montana's state prison population was one-third American Indian and Dale was an Indian. So the Indian population thought Dale was a traitor, thinking that his heart was for the white man who put them into prison under white man's laws.

Another Indian term for Dale was a scout for the white man. Dale Browne was thirty-two years old, six feet tall, 225 pounds, with a strong build. He grew up in Deer Lodge, his father being French and his mother being American Indian. Both of Dale's parents were very well respected in the community. Growing up in Deer Lodge, you did not know what being prejudiced was. But for Dale, being an Indian was confusing. He was proud of being an American Indian, but living in a white man's world, learning the white man's ways instead of his native heritage was daunting. Dale's personality was a likable guy, easy going, will do anything for anyone until he believed you have used him for his talents too often. Then a dark side came out in Dale; then it was time to back away from him for awhile because you didn't know if he were going to scalp you. Of course, only a few people ever have seen his dark side.

Dale and I grew up together in Deer Lodge, sharing something that neither one of us knew why back then, but later finding out it was our own heritage and love of the mountains around Montana. Going through grade school and high school together, I was always competing with Dale. I never could outdo him in getting better grades, or working with my hands like in industrial shop. The girls and teachers liked him more so the only thing I could compete with him in was sports. Dale lettered in wrestling his freshman year, which took a special talent, making me work harder trying to better him in football and baseball. Dale, during the summer of our junior year, decided that Deer Lodge was too small for his open-minded ways, so he joined the Army. We stayed friends during the time he was away. When he came home on leave, we would go hunting and take rides in the mountains, learning about nature and always wanting to be a part of it, somehow. So, Dale got out of the Army and came back to Deer Lodge, with the town and the people changing. He did not know what to do with his life. Within three months, he was back in the service in the Navy Seabees for another four years. After seeing the world and growing up faster than the rest of us in our Class of 1978, another four years was up. Dale decided to try working at the prison in about 1985. Things were going along fine for Dale, learning the ins and outs of the prison system; giving respect to the inmates as long as they gave him respect. Dale never gave in to lowering his standards by being manipulated into giving in to the inmates and their games.

Six years went fast, and now he was on his way to work just like every other day, day in and day out. The job can get so monotonous doing the same thing every day, never seeing that you have accomplished anything in a profession like a contractor, carpenter, miner, teacher, or any other job. Each day, you see the same inmates, day after day, year after year. An inmate gets out of prison and comes back in, so you don't see that you are helping any one of them or accomplishing anything. You go to work, do your job, go home, and every two weeks you get a paycheck for babysitting convicts.

Dale walked out of his house lighting up a cigarette and got into his truck. He drove from the east side of Deer lodge in the dawn of the morning, heading west of town the three miles to the prison; driving past Main Street, looking at the time and temperature that was on the marquee hanging on the Deer Lodge Bank, seeing that he was on time, 0530 hours. It would be a hot day, with the temperature already at 5 degrees. This fifteen-minute drive for Dale was relaxing as he smoked his cigarettes on through town to the west side past the cemetery to the top of the hill where the state prison's land began. He drove on the bench road looking at the ten-acre garden, knowing it was getting time to harvest in two weeks. The inmates would start digging up the potatoes, carrots, and other crops during the fall harvest. He turned the 90-degree corner to the prison ranch. At the ranch office, he lit up another cigarette, relaxing before he got to work. The next 90-corner was the checkpoint. Dale stopped briefly as the correctional officer checked to see who was in the small Chevy truck, waving Dale on by after the checkpoint officer recognized who was in the vehicle. Dale finished the mile drive to the parking lot. He finished the cancer stick before going inside the personnel building, called the Wallace building.

Ironically, the Wallace building was named after the death of Richard Wallace.

He was killed when tower 1 was blown up during construction of the personnel office building, later known as the Wallace building. Wallace was the supervisor of the MVM (Motor Vehicle Maintenance) in the industrial building. A new warden of the prison came to town; Warden Hank Risley, from back East, was elected warden by the bureaucrats of Helena, Montana. The people of Deer Lodge and surrounding towns wanted a local gentleman; he was Deputy Warden James Blodgett, at the prison under the previous Warden Crest. Before Risley came on board, Richard Wallace and others started a petition to Montana's Capitol to overthrow their decision on hiring Hank Risley. They wanted to give the warden's position to Blodgett. That never happened, and all it did for the prison employees was Warden Risley would show his authority by ousting some supervisors. Mr. Risley did this by making the job qualifications higher than the nonconformists' qualifications. This left Richard Wallace out of a job, and he was close to retirement age. Warden Risley offered Wallace and other jobs as correctional officers for, probably, half the pay. Wallace needed the job to finish qualifying for a state retirement, so he had to accept the job. Weeks before he was to retire, the construction of the personnel building was coming down to its end.

Wallace's job was quite simple, working in tower 1 watching over the everyday repetition of prison life. He just had to look for something out of the ordinary and report it. The tower, at the time, was entered through a tunnel from the personnel building. To finish the tunnel, the cement walls of the tunnel had to be painted.

The construction crew put a propane gas heater, called a space heater, in the tunnel to dry the paint because it was during the winter and cold. At about 2140 hours, Wallace was about to be relieved for the day. The heater was left while the crew went home. The air in the tunnel was used up like in a vault. The space heater needed oxygen to keep burning while the heater was still on, but the heater was still pumping out gas, making the tunnel a bomb with only a match to set it off.

The officer on night shift went in the tunnel and there was no light in the dark hole.

The switch to turn on the lights was in the middle of the tunnel. After locking the door to the personnel office, he walked to the middle of tunnel, about sixty feet, and turned on the light switch that makes a sparks when turned on. That ignited the gas that exploded out from both directions, making the light switch the center of the explosion; this caused the north end of the two-story personnel building to blow up. The other end of the explosion caused tower 1 to blow like a missile, taking the cement top off the tower and blowing Richard Wallace out from the 90-foot tall tower. He was blown into a field more than fifty yards away from the tower. The sound of the bomb was heard from Deer Lodge and was on the national news.

Gary Barris was the officer coming to work that night. He was in between the explosion at the light switch. It was miraculous that he lived through the ordeal. His clothes were burned to his body, with the face being burned also. Gary Barris went through many different skin grafts and never has worked again.

Richard Wallace's family received an unknown amount of money. Randle Chase was the officer who found Barris that night, Barris still on fire. He helped him put the fire out from his body and brought him to safety.

Up on the second floor, Dale went to muster himself; Lieutenant Struble was running the prison on that Sunday.

"Morning Dale," said Lieutenant Struble, then giving Dale the scoop on what was going on during the shift.

"Morning Erv," Dale replied. "I see we have some fairly new officers working in max today," said Dale, looking at the roster sheet.

Erwin Struble answered, "Yeah, two new officers in the cages. You are working with three older men on the floor, so you are senior officer today. Help the cage officers with their questions. We are short staffed today as we are every day. So, wait for the other officers that are going to max. Get me the count sheet ASAP after you have done the 0600 count," Lt. Struble demanded in a nice way.

Struble was still informing, "Oh, by the way, Sergeant Morani worked max yesterday. He told me that things were too quiet in max, that the inmates were acting unusual, not the norm. So, be alert taking inmates out of their cells and putting them back in, okay, Dale?"

"Okay," came the answer from Dale. Then after instructions, Dale and Erv's conversation turned to hunting, talking about their hunting stories, asking if either one had seen any elk so far while out scouting the mountains for the upcoming hunting season.

Lieutenant Struble was a big man, 6 feet 5 inches tall, 285 pounds. A damn good lieutenant and probably, as the years go by, would go higher in the system.

Dale was well liked at work; always did his job to the best that he could. He liked to listen in on conversations and join in the conversation to make the day go by faster. The rest of the officers were coming to work sporadically and in droves.

It was now 0545 hours. Five out of the six officers with one sergeant were ready to take the quarter-mile walk up to max to relieve the third-shift officers. Heading down the stairs to the main floor of the administration building, the talk was casual, talking about hunting and who was going to win the NFL football games today. They came to the Main Control door and it started to open with about fifteen officers grouping up inside the first electric door, waiting for that door to close, then waiting for the inside door to open to the courtyard. The wait between the doors was for sergeants and officers to get their keys with other equipment. After Sergeant McPhail gave a chit to the main control cage officer, the cage officer gave back the sergeant's keys for the max unit through a key slot that was built into the wall under the window. The door opened to the courtyard. Officers were heading down three different sidewalks to eight different units. Down the walkway to the left went the max officers to the max gate. The five men waited at the gate entrance to max. They were chatting about winners and losers in football, as the season just began in the NFL. While waiting, the main control officers were opening and closing gates to the high-side and low-side yards. Finally, the max gate opened and the officers walked through, still talking bullshit back and forth.

About a three-minute walk up to max, two of the third-shift officers were waiting inside the max door for the relief officer so they could go home. The max door popped open and the third shift officer said, "See you guys later. Have a good day in hell." This comment was only taken lightly because it was said everyday on every shift when the officers were relieved.

Inside the max building, the two cage officers went to their assigned places, while Sergeant McPhail went into his office and started to make a thirty-two-cup pot of coffee in the coffee maker. Officers Browne and Miller hung around the sergeant's office for a few minutes, talking about football until all of third shift was out the door. Then it was time to count the inmates who were in their cells. This was done twice on first shift, once at 0600 hours and again at 1100 hours. So, Browne and Miller went down the hall to C block. The officer in the cage opened the electric door to the sally-port, and the day was about to start. Inside the port, they waited until the door closed. The C block door opened, then one officer went to the upper tier and one officer went to the lower tier, counting all eight cells with a flashlight in the door window as they went. To do a count the proper way, you would look inside the cell from the door window. If it was dark, you would shine a flashlight by the person that was in the room. If you could not see skin, you would tap lightly on the door window to let the inmate know to move or uncover his face so you could get a live count. A live count was important because if the inmate was trying to commit suicide, the officer would see the blood on the floor. The officer would stop the count and would get help to the inmate. Plus, each cell you checked, you would have to sign your initials to a sheet of paper on the outside of the cell door. This represented that you checked the cell and the inmate was alive at that time of day. That was implemented about three months earlier because of two inmates who killed them-selves in their cells by hanging off the air vent. This was how it went, counting cell by cell, block by block. After each block was counted, the officers would yell out the count off their tier, letting the cage officer hear it from the block speaker. A reply came back to the officers on the block, "Good" or "Recount."

After counting all three blocks on the west side, it was time to go over to the east side of the building to help count that side. So down the hall, through the electric door, past the infirmary, past the back door to the east side electric door. Talking into a speaker, Browne said "East door" and about a minute later, the door opened after waiting for the cage officer to let in the last two of-ficers who were working on the floor. The two officers, Boggs and Olson, went on to D block.

They entered the east wing down the other corridor from the main sally-port and front door. Browne and Miller went to F block to count and after that, they were finished counting be-cause Officers Olson and Boggs counted the last block, called E block.

After count, all four floor officers walked down the hall back through the electric doors to the west side of the building, back to the sergeant's office for a ten-minute break before they had to serve breakfast. The high-side kitchen would bring the food to max with a small gas-powered truck called a Cushman. The Cushman was pulling a metal wheeled cart that had an electric heater to keep the food warm. The food cart was brought out to max about a half hour before the meal was served, to plug it into an outlet to get the food back up to serving temperature. Serving meals was probably the hardest job working in max. On first shift, you served two meals and on second shift you served one meal a day. Once you got started, you did not stop or slow down until you were finished, about a half hour later. The carts are brought over from the kitchen the same time each day to keep the officers on schedule. After bringing in the hot cart and drink cart, sometimes there would be other carts that came with the specified meal that morning. The floor officers and sergeant wheeled them down the corridor to the main cage and plugged in the hot carts.

The officers took off their gray uniform shirts and put on a white smock coat to serve chow so they would not get the food on the uniform. Sergeant McPhail served the food from the hot cart so he was preparing the so-called continental breakfast that they served every Sunday morning. This Sunday consisted of hot oatmeal, a glazed roll, and some grapefruit pieces that came packed from a can. With juice, plus condiments, packs of sugar, salt and pepper, butter, and a plastic spoon-fork that was called a spork. The condiments came wrapped with a napkin around it.

It was routine to feed the blocks from left to right, C, B, then A block; so Officer Riggs went on C block first. He was opening each slot in the doors of the cells with a Folger Adams key on both upper and lower levels, while Browne and Miller were filling metal coffee and milk pitchers that would hold two gallons at a time.

They would tote them onto the block and serve the inmates who wanted one or both beverages. Officer Olson was to help put the food on the trays with the sergeant. They would bring the trays to the outside of the block through a slot in the wall for each block. The slot had a hinged 3 x 12-inch door, the same size as the slots in the inmates' doors. You would open the slot with the same Folger Adams key. So, Olson would bring the trays to the block and hand them through the slot to the officers on the block. Officer on the block would take the trays from Olson, then they would carry the trays three or four at a time up and down the stairs to each inmate until finishing that block. Browne and Miller would be the first to finish on a block so they would go to the next block. They would open slots and pour coffee and milk until they had all the slots open and poured the drinks on the west side of the building. Working as a team, they would help run trays to the inmates. The officer in the cage would open and shut the electric doors to the sally-ports. In and out of the blocks, the floor officers would go at their command, keeping the cage officers busy. After the west side was completed, the team would do the same thing on the east side until the whole max building was fed. It was a good system, and worked well that way for years.

It was time for a short break after feeding the east side. The max staff would sit down for ten to fifteen minutes, eating breakfast and to smoke a cigarette. Then it was time to pick up the trays. That was a messy job; an inmate swamper from each block was let out of their cell to retrieve the trays. He would take the trays to the block landing and bang the trays against a fifty-gallon garbage can. Then the block swamper would stack the trays. He would then go back into his cell; after that, the door was locked. The officers would go onto the block. The floor officers would shut the slot if it was not their day to go to yard. Starting like for serving the breakfast, the officers would start on C block, working their way around the building until the trays were cleaned up.

Approximately 0730 Hours

All four floor officers walked onto F block and yelled out, "Yard out, who wants to go to yard!" The inmates on the block would stand in their door window, letting the officers know they wanted to go out. Two officers would go to the room where the inmate was in the door window. One officer would open the slot in the door with a Folger Adams key. The 3 x12-inch door flopped down on the hinge. Each officer carried a set of handcuffs, so the inmate turned around with his back to the door. The inmate puts his hands out of the slot behind his back through the door.

Browne put the handcuffs on the inmate. Then Browne lifted his arm to the top of the door, slapping the door where the cell numbers were stamped. Then the new cage officer opened the door. Browne did a pat-shakedown of the inmate, Wild, after he came out the opened door. Inmate Wild knew the routine, to turn around facing the door. A pat-shake is when an officer sweeps his hands over the inmate's body and clothes; this is to find any contraband (i.e., any item or thing that an inmate is not allowed to have) the inmate may have on him. Officer Miller and Officer Boggs brought two more inmates named Kenny Allen and Nevens.

They pat-searched those two in the same manner that Browne did. So now it was time to take the three inmates to the yard, escorted by the four officers through the block sally-port. The officers would walk the inmates past the cage, then over to the yard where there were three cages called dog runs. Browne opened the middle run with a different Folger Adams key. Miller took off the cuffs as the three inmates went to the middle run of the three dog runs. After the cuffs were off, they sat down and started to talk to themselves until the rest of the inmates made it to the yard. So as you can see, this was a monotonous process.

For the next trip, the officers went into E block and saw only three more inmates who wanted to go out to the yard this morning. Each of the officers went to different cells and proceeded to get the inmates out of the cells by themselves; only one officer on one inmate, breaking a max rule of two officers on one inmate. Each door opened; inmates Cox, Turner, and Gollehon came out of their cells. Walking them over to the sally-port with an officer behind each of them, not much was being said between the inmates, unlike every other day when the so-called brothers would exercise their mouths along with their muscles.

Maybe it was too early in the morning or they stayed up too late last night watching a good movie on TV. The inmates were too quiet and too good, wanting to get in the yard with blank looks on their faces. This was what officer Browne was thinking to himself. Things were not normal, but this was going on for the last week or longer. Browne did not discuss this with the other officers because they were only filling in that Sunday in max. The inmates were escorted to the yard with no problems. Cox, Turner, and Gollehon were placed in the last run to the left.

The dog run on the right was empty. That completed the east side of the building.

The yard door was locked after all the officers were out and headed to the back hallway through the electric doors as it was opening. The electric doors stayed open to make the officers' job easier, both on the floor and in the cages. Walking past the back door and past the max infirmary, the officers were joking about different things, except for Browne. Through the west hallway door, the officers did not have to wait because it was already open. Inmate swampers McFarlane and Powell were close by the laundry room, folding towels as the officers walked past them on the way to C block.

Browne was the only officer wondering what was going on in the max unit, thinking to himself, *None of the inmates are acting their normal selves. Why?*

We got to go back to basics, do everything by the book. Walking to the west side talking to the other officers, Browne casually said, "Yeah, let's take our time getting C block out to yard because we have only a handful of showers to do. We are ahead of schedule." The other officers didn't think too much about Browne's request, only knowing that they respected Dale and knew he had a reason for saying it.

It was no different taking the inmates out to yard on the west side of the building. The inmates were no problem bringing them to yard. There was not much talk between inmates and officers. They put three inmates in each of the three runs, except for the last run where the officers placed only one inmate, name of Ray. He was an old man who cannot stay out of max; but while in max, he was a good inmate, staying by himself. Ritchson, Gleed, and Cook were in the run to the right. In the middle run was Daniels, Linn, and Castro. Then C/O Olson closed and locked the yard door after all officers were out.

0810 Hours

Time to start showers. Getting the shower cart ready to go, the officers wheeled the metal cart that was filled with clean towels, underwear, and socks. The cart was stocked by the two inmate swampers, Powell and McFarlane. Officers Browne and Miller went on C block to shower the inmates on the upper level, while Officers Boggs and Olson went on the detention A block to do those showers. On C block, there was only one inmate who wanted a shower that day.

So Dale went up to UC-1 and unlocked the food slot door, then locked the inmate's hands up through the door slot. Browne called to the cage officer to open the door after he put his hand above the door, making a loud bang on the metal. That was a sign letting the officer know that he wanted that door open. Walking the inmate to the shower, he opened the grill gate so the inmate could go inside the shower.

Then Dale locked the gate shut with a padlock. Next, he took off the cuffs so the inmate could shower.

Officer Miller was at the other end of the tier, talking to inmate Bobby Close.

They were talking about NFL football, who would win the games today. Close, as usual, was calm, cool, and collected while talking to C/O Miller. Inmate Close was pleading his case that the Atlanta Falcons were going to beat the Chicago Bears.

"Charlie," Close started the conversation. "The Falcons are going to have a good season this year and Chicago is not going to stop them. Their second-string quarterback, rookie Brett Favre, is going to take them places. During the preseason games he looked good. You wait and see, in years to come, he will set some NFL records."

Miller laughed and said, "Yeah, to the cleaners or maybe to an early shower or maybe to an early vacation because they won't make the playoffs."

"Charlie, put your money where your mouth is. I'll bet you a bottle of pop that the Falcons win," Close made a bet.

"Close, you know I can't bet with you," Miller laughed.

Browne was on his way over to Close's cell and said, "Close, Charlie doesn't want to take your money because he feels that he would be taking advantage of a handicapped person."

Close said, "Thanks, Browne," as they all laughed. "Lay down your money instead of your mouth, guys."

Browne, changing the subject a bit, asked Close who he thought would be in the Super Bowl this season. Close replied, "Buffalo and Washington or maybe the Giants again after winning the Super Bowl last year against the Buffalo Bills.

"These teams have the best defense and offense this year."

Miller and Browne both nodded their heads, and Miller said, "Yeah, you have been doing your homework, Close, they do look impressive so far this year. But the year is just beginning."

Inmate Close said, "Sometimes a beginning is all it takes to rally the troops, to weather the storm to the end, guys."

As Browne started back to the upper shower, Miller and Close were still discussing football. Browne handcuffed the inmate who was in the shower up behind his back, ready to be placed back in his room. Opening the grill gate to the shower was easy to do—just unlock the padlock, turning the bolt to the back of the door, which was secured in the pumice block by only drilling a hole in the block that is hollow inside. As the door opened, the grill gate made a squeaking sound from the moisture on the hinges. Browne backed up far enough to let the inmate by him so he could get back into his cell. The shower was right next to the cell.

After the inmate was past him, he turned and shut the grill door and locked the padlock closed, but not locking the door.

Showers were finished, so Browne and Miller left the block and went down to the sergeant's office for a break. Sergeant McPhail was sitting behind his desk doing paperwork. As the officers lit up a cigarette, they were discussing the rest of the day as the other two officers came in the room.

Olson said, "There were only two showers to do on A block, and we are finished."

Browne started a conversation in the sergeant's office while everyone on the floor had a break. Browne said, "Things just don't seem right today in the unit, Pete." Sergeant McPhail was addressed by his first name by most of the officers.

Sergeant McPhail said, "I know what you are saying, Dale. Everything is going smooth today, but something is wrong. The hard part is just putting the yard away, then it is a cakewalk from there," Pete explained.

Dale was thinking out loud. "You know, with all the things that have been going on recently, like the full box of .22-caliber cartridges that was found in the high-side kitchen; the shells were under the serving line a couple of weeks ago.

And two guys committed suicide about two weeks apart. Inmate Ost was a different person after he was transferred back from, I think, New Mexico prison. I heard he was someone's bitch down there. And when he got back here, he never caused anyone any problems. But his eyes looked like they looked right through you when you looked at him. They think Ost was trying to get the .22 shells into max to kill as many staff as he could before he killed himself."

"Browne, what are you trying to do to us, scare the hell out of us? But keep going," said Boggs.

"Just over a month ago, inmate Brown hung himself in his cell also," Dale said, "and night shift officers said he was kicking the wall. The whole block could hear him dying. The officers came on the block while he was still alive but couldn't go into the cell until they had the shield and the scissors to cut him down.

By the time they got back, Brown was dead, with his tongue sticking out of his mouth. They tried to give him CPR but it didn't work. One of the officers had to go home after that, stayed home for three paid days off."

"Boy, I sure hope I don't have to do any of that!" said Officer Olson, with everyone else nodding their head and saying, "Yeah."

Browne kept talking. "Yeah, inmate Brown wrote two kites to staff members, telling them that inmates in max was going to kill him, that there was going to be a riot last month in August before he hung himself. It was going to start in the yard. Last week, there was another kite written to the second-shift sergeant. He took it to the Deputy Warden, Gary Week, and the kite said a riot was going to take place sometime soon, and it was going to start in the yard."

Sergeant McPhail said, "Plus, it even gets better than that. Two days ago on the twentieth, an officer which I will not give you his name, but he was working RAC Church building, and one of the outside sponsors came up to him and asked if he was nervous about the riot that was coming during the next week, and asked him what days off he had, and the officer replied Sunday and Monday, and the sponsor said, 'Good, you won't be here.'"

"So what is going to happen, is the whole high side going to riot?" asked Boggs.

McPhail just put up his hands and said, "I don't know."

Boggs said, "Maybe max will be the safest place to be because they're not getting in here," The rest of them just nodded their heads, thinking.

McPhail spoke up again with a smile on his face, and said, "Guys, don't you remember that all these rumors were coming up after we went on strike last April for six days. We got only 1.5 percent raise each of the next two years. We wanted the Hazardous Duty Retirement benefits but they would not give it to us. The majority of the staff couldn't stay out any longer, so we settled. Now, you hear the guards starting the rumor that there is going to be a riot, telling the inmates that so they will tell everyone, and that way we will get the Hazardous Duty Retirement benefits."

Browne butted in and said, "But don't you remember that Oldhouse and I were on the block when Ritchson wanted the block swamper, Herman, to take his tray and a paper sack. I thought that it was a little odd, so I went over to the trash can and picked it out of the trash, and found two pieces of fence wire with the diamond pattern of the cyclone fence clearly visible in the pieces found. That tells you something is going on up here, because that was on the fourteenth of this month." McPhail said, "It's time to get the kids out from the yard; be careful and make sure that the cuffs are on tight behind their backs." All five started to walk out of the office, thinking to themselves.

* * * * * * * * * * * * *

0830 Hours

After the yard was out, the swamper's job was back to more re-laxed and running smoothly. Inmate Powell told inmate McFarlane that he was going down to mop the hallway from the cage to the sergeant's office. McFarlane went over to the officers and would hand them clean cloths through the block slot for showers.

Powell started mopping the floor down by the outside sally-port. Inmate Powell was looking from the inside of the building, and could see Sergeant McPhail coming back from the captain's office, so he left the floor dry from the door to the sergeant's office. Powell took his time, waiting for Sergeant McPhail to get in his office.

McPhail commented, "Powell, thank you for waiting until I got in my office before you made the floor slick."

Powell, with a smile, said, "No problem, Mr. McPhail." Powell was playing the inmate game of being polite, but in his heart, he would never change from believing that no man is better than any other man. He blamed all officers and staff and society for him being in prison.

"Powell, you and McFarlane can mow the front yard today after lunch trays are picked up," McPhail spoke.

"That will be cool. The weather is sure staying warm this fall in the Rocky Mountains. Man, I sure can remember these September days, getting fire wood and looking for game before the hunting season so I would know where to go," inmate Powell answered.

McPhail stopped the conversation with a 'yes' nod from his head, and then moved into the office. Inmate Powell kept mopping the floor to the cage. When he got to the cage, he looked in the yard at the inmates, noticing that none of the inmates in the yard was exercising. They were not playing basketball, running circles in a square pen, not doing pushups and sit-ups, not even walking in the pen.

This behavior was out of the norm. All the inmates were sitting in groups, just talking back and forth with other inmates in the pens next to them. This had been going on for over a week. None of them getting exercise in the exercise yard; just talking, sitting on the cement floor giving no problems to the officers. This was an eerie feeling for inmate Powell because this behavior had not happened before.

But, since he had only been there a short time, he would take a mental note of this.

Another thing that seemed out of place was two of the inmates in the yard, Turner and Gollehon, were going to trial at the beginning of this coming week. Instead of being hyper, nervous or mad, the two were sitting in their groups, just talking.

＊＊＊＊＊＊＊＊＊＊＊＊＊

Inmates Gollehon and Turner were going on trial for the baseball bat killing of another inmate in the high side yard one year before. Both were juvenile misfits in society who wanted to be leaders. But they can only be followers, making it to the Big House in Deer Lodge by killing innocent people in two separate incidents.

They met each other on the juvenile block of low D, in Close Unit I. At first, they were scared kids. Working in Close I and in the gym while they were there, you could talk to them and they would listen to you. But after about six months in prison, they started hanging around the problem inmates, until their personalities changed back to how they really were. Both of them got a job in the kitchen. They were not good workers, so one of them got fired. An inmate named Pillegi took over the job. Pillegi, about thirty-five years old, looked like the identical twin to our warden at the prison, Mr. McCormack. Pileggi was a model inmate (good inmate who follows the rules). He just got off the PC block for having an inmate jacket put on him for molesting a child. Pileggi did not molest a child, and was not going to live on the protective custody block looking like he did. So he went to Close Unit II and took some beating. He gave out more beating than he got for standing up for himself.

Turner and Gollehon thought that was the last straw, after getting beat by Pileggi fairly, like men do with their fists. Turner and Gollehon realized the reason they were in prison was because they could not do anything civil. It was time to get rid of Pileggi by setting him up. One afternoon while the officers were changing shifts, the tower officer was coming down from Tower IV while Close Unit I and Close Unit II yard were out. Pileggi was walking alone on the walking track outside the softball back-stop during a softball game. There were probably 100 or more in-mates in the yard that day. Turner came up to Pileggi from his front. He started a confrontation with swinging fist and mouth a-running, while Gollehon was sneaking up behind Pileggi. Other inmates were lookouts for Gollehon, making sure there were no officers or staff witnessing what was going to happen. As Turner kept Pileggi's mind on him, Gollehon sneaked up behind him. He hit Pileggi in the head with a metal baseball bat. This knocked Pileggi down to the ground. Then Gollehon hit him three or more times to make sure he was dead. Pileggi's face caved in, his cranium cracked opened like an egg on a skillet, with brains, blood, and pieces of bone matting the hair around the open hole in the back of his head. Pileggi's mind was gone but a gurgling sound was coming out of his mouth. He was still alive, which was not a blessing but was his sentence dancing with the Devil. Pileggi's face was broken with the nose flattened to his face. His eyes bulged out of his head from the force of the bat hitting his face, the pressure pushing the eyes out of their sockets and blood splattering all over Gollehon and Turner. Pileggi was life-flighted to the hospital in Missoula; he was pronounced dead on the flight to Missoula. The ironic thing about it was Pileggi was airlifted to the county where he committed his crime.

With all the inmates in the yard, at least a third of them had to see the killing. None would say anything in court because of the number one inmate code of ethics. There were a lot of inmates who gave the investigators all the information they needed to bring it to trial this coming week, but a year later, only two inmates would testify. One inmate was being housed on the PC block in max. Inmate Chip Davison was housed in lower D1, ready to testify on Turner and Gollehon on Monday. That was the reason all the inmates in the max yard today and for the last week were grouping up; talking over how they were going to get their bloody hands on Davison, to stop anyone from testifying against them. The information about Davison testifying was handed by their lawyer to one of the two inmates who were going on trial. That information was passed from one inmate to another until the max population was all informed. Hence, that nice lawyer can say after the end of the day that he has blood on his hands.

* * * * * * * * * * * *

0930 Hours

Back on C block, inmates Bobby Close and Paul Allen were talking between cells on the upper level. They were two cells away from each other and were talking through the cracks of the doors. The conversation started out nonchalantly, just a conversation to break up the day. Inmates talked away the seclusion of being in their cells twenty three hours a day.

Robert Dee Close was thirty-seven years old, about 5 feet 11 inches tall. He had a strong lanky and wiry build. With long hair past his shoulders, mustache, dark sunglasses that he wore most of the time, Close was considered a handsome guy. He was sentenced to prison in 1976 to 100 years for aggravated kidnapping, murder, and robbery in the shooting death of an Oklahoma carnival promoter, Billy Joe Hill. Bobby Close escaped from the prison twice; the first time leaving after dark from Close I, climbing the fence that separated the high side from the low side. Then they climbed a low-side fence between the old max building and Rothe Hall building and then breaking out the window of the front entrance building. Then, there were two of them who ran away, getting a ride from a friend on the back road of the prison. The next time, inmate Close escaped from the visiting room, September 1981. He came to the visiting room as a man and left that day as a woman. He shaved his legs and mustache, put on a dress in the bathroom of the visiting room, and left with the visitors. It was rumored that he got a ride from a lady in Deer

Lodge who left with him out of state. The lady was said to have died in Arizona.

Also, when a priest was found dead, it was figured that Bobby Close had killed him. He was captured a year later, August 1982, in Great Falls, Montana.

Bobby Close started the conversation, "How are things going over there, Paul?"

"Oh, just hanging out, waiting for lunch to come around," Paul answered.

Bobby asked, "How many more days do you have before you are set free?"

"It's 361days and a wake-up, if Janet Cox has the same figures that I do," Paul thought out the figure from the top of his head. He had already marked it off his calendar this morning.

"Did you fly a kite to Janet Cox yet, to find out when the state said that you were getting out?" Bobby questioned.

Paul responded, "Yes, but she wrote back and told me to send her another kite after I had less than a year left. I am getting tired of sitting in this cell and nothing going on, just the same routine day in, day out. The only thing to look forward to is when the guards bring us something on their schedule or yard time or once in a while, a visit from my mother," Paul rambled on, singing the blues.

Bobby Close asked, "You don't have an old lady out there waiting for you? Just your mother out there waiting?" Bobby laughed out loud.

"Well, I have fine-looking ladies in Billings that want me to stay at their crib and bang them night and day. But I think I am going to Butte and see what the smack is like there."

"Yeah, I believe you about the two ladies in Billings, right," said Close, "but did you hear that some bloods are trying to get members in the Aryan brothers in Montana?"

"Yeah, my ladies are out recruiting with their legs open wide to catch any bees with the honey," laughed Allen.

Close said, "Well, if you are looking for a little excitement, then wait until our bro's come back from yard. There will be more excitement today than when you did your crime on the streets," Close said, reflecting back to the night he was doing his time. Close kept talking, "I only wish Fitzpatrick was here to lead us into this fandango, to be a part of raising hell. That Fitz knows how to party."

Allen asked, "Who is this Fitzpatrick you are talking about, Bobby?"

Close said, "Fitzpatrick is one of the most coldblooded killers this prison has seen. He has laid bodies to rest on the streets and the same inside the prison.

"When he was here, there was nothing that went on without him approving it beforehand. Fitzpatrick ran the prison. If Fitz was here today and we take control of the building like we hope to, then anyone that doesn't help in the riot would be dead. And that will include the guards and any blacks and Indians." Close did not care whose ears were listening.

Inmate Nelson's ears perked up. Nelson was the inmate who was in the cell between inmates Close and Allen. A young twenty-year-old inmate who was small in stature, he was in max today because of walking away from the dairy dorm with another inmate, making their way through the mountains east of Deer Lodge. They made it to Montana's capitol city, Helena, where they were caught and sent back to prison. These two mixed-up young kids learned the hard way about prison that day. Listening close to the conversation now, he heard inmate Bobby tell Allen that a riot was going to happen right after the inmates were brought in from yard. Nelson was thinking, *How can this be when all the inmates were locked down except for those in the yard?* He had no way of knowing how it was going to be done, but he heard they were going to tear up the max unit; he thought probably take the guards hostage.

Bobby Close was thinking to himself that he was glad he never went to yard today because this way, he could play both sides, looking like he was not a part of the plan to riot. If the brothers in the yard got out and somehow took over the cages liked planned, then opened the cell doors on the blocks, he would enjoy the rush that he would get from destroying the unit and maybe even more.

Things got quiet between the two inmates, Close and Allen, as they both just stared out their door windows looking at the two PC swampers by the laundry room, Powell and McFarlane enjoying, as usual, getting out of their cells spending the day. Bobby Close was thinking McFarlane was going to be dead before the day was over. He would never inform to the gray-suit guards anymore. Powell will be caught up in the rush with the flush of his blood on the floor with the rioting brothers taking everything to extremes. His thoughts formed in his head, thinking that the PC Powell had not done any wrong to him or to the other brothers. But, Powell's brother works in the transportation office at the prison and that was enough to place him on the PC block; even though Jim Powell is a friend to his brother, Jim Close, down in Deer Lodge, playing on the same team during softball this summer.

Bobby Close was still contemplating in his mind how the chain of events got to this day. Plans to riot were started back in the summer, when he and some other inmates were going to cause a disturbance and try to escape from the high-side yard. Days before the scheduled escape, someone informed the staff of the plans. The same day, inmate Chip Davison was sent to max. Guards went out to the high side yard and found the stash of homemade weapons behind the backstop of the ball field. A ladder was also found in the yard. The plans were that while the young dumb kids, Turner and Gollehon, were killing Pillegi in the yard with baseball bats, Close and others were going to escape over the fence with the ladder and wire cutters. When inmate Davison went to max as a PC, he snitched off Close and others for formulating the plan. So, inmate Close's property was rolled up and sent to max population. Turner or Gollehon's attorney told them that Chip Davison was on the PC block, and was going to testify against them in the trial that was going to start in a week. Just a couple of weeks before today, a former brother inmate, William Brown, hung himself in his max cell with strips of bedding. It was on third shift, and the guards on duty in the unit called for help on the phone. The officer could not enter the cell alone because of strict guidelines against it. The reason against going into an inmate's cell without proper help and equipment is in case an inmate could be setting the guards up to injure them.

By the time they had enough help to cut William Brown down, he was dead.

Close recalled that night, the inmates on the block were yelling and screaming, but not to get help there faster. They were yelling to make the problem more complex so Brown was sure to die. Brown was a known informant, writing a kite to the officers on August 3. He warned the staff that the prison was going to riot, and it would start in the yard. The staff found out that the locks in the yard could be opened from the inside. So the staff installed new deadbolt locks. The inmates on the block kept taunting Brown because, somehow, the inmates on the block found out that he wrote a letter about the locks and them planning a riot. Close and his buddies were taunting Brown, letting him know that he was a dead man, no matter where he went in the prison or out of the prison. So after that plan failed, they started with a new plan.

Concentrating on the twist in the chain link fence where the mesh is woven together in the yard, whoever was in the yard would sit by the fence and talk while one would work the fence and the others would be the lookouts for the officers or the swampers. It was a simple matter to remove the whole stand, which allowed the mesh to pull back like a curtain. A week ago, as Close was still thinking, Officers Miller, Oldhouse, and Browne found bits of the fence wire hidden in Stevie Ritchson's cell. The yard was closed and shaken down, but nothing was reported out of order, or where he got the wire.

Inmate Close was smirking to himself and thinking, *Those naïve officers reopened the yard some days later with Ritchson not getting his yard privileges revoked, so we kept on working the fence.*

The fence was softened over a short period of time by taking a cloth bandana that was bought from the canteen. The bandana was wound around the wire. As the inmate put his feet on the fence, he would be sitting on the concrete floor pulling the wire fence to him. Then another inmate that was in the dog run next to him did the same as the first inmate. He sat on the floor with his feet on the fence, taking the bandana and placing it under the first bandana. As one inmate pulled on the bandana, the wire would bend to him. Then the other inmate pulled his bandana to him and that bent the wire his way. This went on until they saw that the fence wire was soft and pliable to break. They stopped because if they broke the wire, then the guards would have spotted the break in the fence. The fence was pliable enough that they were able to pull pieces out by kicking at the wire when the time was right. Today was that day that the inmates in the yard were waiting for.

* * * * * * * * * * * *

0935 Hours

In the far corners away from the yard doors, the inmates in the yard were sitting cross-legged on the cement floor. The temperature was already hitting the high fifties, making it comfortable to talk about their plans on taking over the max unit. All twelve inmates were at whispering distance from each other, with the one old inmate, Ray, in the dog run by himself. His job was to be the lookout for any guards or swampers trying to listen in on their conversation. The six runs in the yard were divided in half by a walkway between the two sides. It was designed so that a correctional officer could walk back and forth, entering from a door through the back hallway. If there was an officer to watch the yard, then he would have gone through the door in the back. Then, climbing a metal ladder that brought the guard up above the inmates, the guard could walk a metal walkway called the "catwalk." This catwalk ran the length of the yard between the six runs. If an inmate was to get through the wire fence, it would be a major compromise to the max unit. At the end of the catwalk was another shorter ladder leading to the top of the max building, to a flat roof. The delegated inmate lieutenant in the max yard was given the rank from a rating process involving his age, his crime coming into the prison, what crimes he did in the prison, along with the respect he got from other inmates and how he could defend himself with a level head.

This was the inmates' last chance to meet in the max yard before they started havoc on the prison. They were all focused and united, wearing bandanas on their heads over their long hair. Some were wearing mirrored sunglasses, and gloves on their hands; most of them wearing sweat pants and tops.

The lieutenant said, "Let's go over the plans for the last time. After the guards take you three out first (talking about the three inmates who were in the middle dog run) because you will tell them that you have to go to the bathroom very bad and can't wait until the next trip, I want you guys also to talk their heads off, keeping the attention on you. While the guards have left the yard and passed the cage, the rest of you will take the broken fence wire out of each run. Don't leave your run until the officers are on C block. Then spread the fence apart like you have seen each piece spread apart before this last month. At that time, go as fast as you can through your run over to the middle run. Take that piece of fence apart and then run to the different places you have been told to go. So, each of you tell me what your job is."

A voice spoke up and said, "Us two are to run out to the cage, grabbing the fire extinguisher off the wall," pointing to his bro in the run with him. "He is going to grab a portable telephone that is welded on the dolly cart, and start bashing at the windows of the main control cage on this side. We know that the bulletproof glass will not break but the glass on the outside of the bulletproof glass will shatter, scaring the new guard inside."

The next two inmates started talking. "We are to run down the hallway to the sergeant's office, and start throwing things like the office desk and chairs, out of the office into the hallway, blocking the entranceway to the front door. Also, keeping anything that can be used as a shank, any matches or lighters. Go through the swamper's closet; throw that stuff out into the hall. Next, come back to you and see what to do next."

Two more inmates spoke up, "We are to run down the back hallway. I am to threaten the two rat swampers with my shank made from the fence wire; wrap this extra headband around the bottom end so when I do use it, the shank will not go through my hand. I will tell them rats not to try to get into our way or they're dead. Then I am to place the laundry cart in the open back hallway door after my bro runs through the door."

The bro spoke up. "I am to run through the first back hallway then run through the other back hallway door down to the outside of the yard door; grab the five-gallon cigarette bucket that is full of sand; run it back to the back hallway electrical door; run it into the doorway before the satellite-cage guard in the east cage can shut the door. Then we both will grab something and start pounding on the windows of the east cage.

The lieutenant said, "What are you guys going to grab?"

"I am going to grab the fire extinguisher that is on the wall." The other inmate who was muscle-bound in the arms and in the head spoke up. "I am grabbing one of the rat swampers and beating his head on the window until one of them breaks," he laughed.

The lieutenant spoke up with a fierce look in his eyes and said, "You touch one of those rats before we get control of the building, I will cut your head off and throw it out the front door to negotiate with the warden and the press. Do I make myself clear?"

"Yes," with a pause, "I am to find something and keep hitting or throwing it at the windows until the guard leaves the cage up the ladder," said the muscle-bound brother.

The lieutenant said, "If we can get the new guards flustered in the cage enough, and if we can burn a hole in the door, get all the brothers out of their cells. Then we can cause helter-skelter, brothers. Then if we can get into the cages, take all the belly-chains and leg irons. Then chain all the doors shut to the outside and the cage escape hatches."

The next one of the two inmates who was sitting cross-legged in the group, spoke up. "We are to go to the back hallway, take the cart out of the door, hold the door from shutting, go through it and put back the cart so the door won't shut. Then go to the infirmary door, ram the door until the latch breaks, then look for anything that would be a shank and pry-bars to open things up."

There was a moment of silence. Then the lieutenant spoke up again, "I am going to the laundry room. If the two rats are standing there pleading for their life, I will tie their hands up, bring them over to the yard door and tie them up to the bars on the window, leaving them there for anyone to take a shot at them.

"Next, I will pick up all the clothes, clean or dirty, and throw them by the cage door.

"Then I will start a fire at the door, smoke the guard out if he is still inside.

"Hopefully, the fire will melt the Plexiglas in the door. If the two PC's get the laundry door closed, that won't be a problem with a window in the door. We can either burn them out or break down the door; either way, they are our main dead hostages." The lieutenant was still talking; "When you two are done with barricading the entrance way by the sergeant's office, I want you two to come back in the yard, go to the guards' catwalk right here." He pointed to the middle of the yard between the six dog runs. He continued, "Go up the ladder, cross the catwalk and over to the short ladder leading to the roof. Wait there and don't go on top of the roof, but look for the guards to come out of the escape hatch on either side. Run as fast as you can to the guards, grabbing them before they can close the hatch. Then bring them down to me. If they fight with you, then just throw them over the side. That will take care of them for good. But, if possible, bring them down; it will be good for negotiating with."

The lieutenant delegated more authority to the inmates in the yard. "One of you, in each run, work on the chain link fence between each run. The rest of you watch out the windows in the hallway and the door window. Let everyone know if there is an officer coming around. Also, let everyone know if the two rat swampers are around the laundry room or around the hall where they could see something they shouldn't in the yard. The fence is about ready to break open, so be cool and don't blow it by getting excited or making a stupid move."

* * * * * * * * * * * *

0700 Hours

So, to start this blessed Sunday, I got out of bed at 0700 hours and headed to the bathroom. I did the three S's, dressing casual for church, wearing gray dress pants, a polo overshirt with a blue sweater on. Almost always wearing a pair of tennis shoes. I walked over to my mother's house that was a block away. My father died in 1986, so visiting my mother was for comfort and a chore, but mostly to get fed. My mother would start breakfast, having it ready for me when I got home from Mass at church. We would talk about anything, but mostly gossip about things that were going on around town. That was my mother's favorite thing to do, gossip. Visiting for about an hour, then it was time to walk back home.

I would drive down town to the church and attend the morning Mass. I had a weird feeling this Sunday as I pulled up to the parking area in front of the church.

It was as though I forgot something or my mind was far away on a matter that was inconceivable. Walking up the stairs gave me a sense of peace, that a weight was lifted off me. As I entered the foyer before the pews, dipping my two fingers into the Holy Water and making the sign of the cross thing became routine. I found my normal pew to the left in the back of the church, five rows up. Then kneeling, I looked to the front where, on the wall to the right of the tabernacle, a life-size statue/corpus of Jesus on a cross was. I lowered my head and again gave the sign of the cross and said, "In the name of the Father, Son, and Holy Spirit. Amen." Next, I got up, entered the pew, and knelt down on the padded kneel board, before I was home saying prayers. Today, the soft pink rose color that shone on the white walls, coming from the stained glass window from the front of the church, was more soothing than normal. The stained glass was an original Tiffany and was made to give you the effect to calm the parishioners.

Time had passed by fast. At the end of Mass, an announcement was made that there was trouble at the prison and everyone who worked there should call to see if they were needed. As we all stood up waiting for the procession out the front of the church to pass by, people started to talk and already, there was information about what was going on at the prison.

The adorable lady beside me started talking to me saying, "Jim, Bill's family next to me said that the trouble at the prison is in the max building, saying that the two guards are on top of the building. Smoke is coming from the top of the max roof. How could the inmates take over the max building?"

I said, "Elizabeth, how did you get that information when it was just going on as we speak? The inmates cannot take over the max build. It is one of the most secure buildings in the nation with all the newest technologies at this time."

Elizabeth proclaimed, "An officer working at the kitchen called home, telling his wife what was going on at the prison. She was the one who came late for Mass, informing everyone around her of the story." As the double doors opened, the sound of the emergency siren was blowing from the prison. It gave out a constant bellow throughout the valley, with the prison being more than four miles away.

Elizabeth, still rambling on, said, "They can take over the building, Jim. I heard that the inmates can take over any building at any time because there are 100 inmates to 1 correctional officer. Inmates are so strong that they can break two pair of handcuffs by just turning their arm, twisting and turning their arms."

I was smiling as I said, "Elizabeth, that can't happen; there are no inmates at our prison that can break cuffs. I am sure that things are not as bad at the prison as everyone is thinking." I was trying to ease her mind, at the same time thinking to myself, hoping, praying that things didn't get out of hand.

It was my turn to exit the pew where I was standing. I took a side step, then genuflected, facing the front of the church looking at the large corpus of Jesus on the Cross. As I bowed my head, taking my right hand and going from my head to my chest, then from left shoulder to my right shoulder, giving the sign of the Cross, I was saying in my mind to God, "Please, God, let the problems at the prison be not as bad as it can be."

Getting up from my knee, I turned around and started talking to the people who were also being ushered outside. I smiled and nodded my head as I said my hellos to the people around me. Getting closer to the doors, I placed my two fingers in the bowl of Holy Water and made the sign of the Cross one last time, my mind slipping away from the church to the problems going on at the prison.

Last, I shook hands with Father _____, remembering the words that he said to me, "James, go in peace. Things will be all right!"

As I said, "Thank you, Father," I walked down the stairs and got into my car.

I started driving away, thinking of everyone's worst fear—the unknown. What could have happened? Are all the officers okay? My friend, Dale, was working in that unit; could things have gone wrong for them? Is my brother, Bob, okay; he was in that unit. At this time in my life, I figured that my brother, Bob, was the worst brother anyone could have. An inmate in prison was a low-life scum who citizens had to pay high taxes to keep people like my brother in prison, keeping inmates off the streets so innocent people could live.

I was thinking, "Why can't they just get rid of the low-life inmates, then we would not have to pay for them?" But that is what the homily was preached about today, having mercy on the prisoners; praying that some inmates will follow Christ before they die in prison. Plus, being Catholic, I cannot believe in the death penalty. That one I still have problems with, knowing how evil some of the inmates are. But I guess it will take more studying and praying before I understand, and the choice is not mine to decide.

Back at the house, I called the prison, a phone number that I knew by heart, a number that I have been calling for the last eleven years—684-0020.

Twenty, I thought to myself. *Oh, how I wish I was twenty again. I would have chosen a different career, like working at the mines or going to California and stayed working for the railroads like I was doing for the Milwaukee Railroad before working at the prison.*

The prison Main Control answered the phone. As the guy started saying, "Montana State Prison, Offi...," I interrupted and said, "Jay, what is going on out there? Do you need me to come out?"

Jay replied, "Jim, we need everyone to come out to work, max inmates are rioting."

"I will be right out," I said. "Do I need my uniform on?"

"No, Jim, just get out here."

After saying, "See ya," and hanging up the phone, I started to the back door when, seeing the picture of my daughters, Jaimie and Sarah, sitting on the coffee table, I picked it up, staring at the three of us smiling. I was thinking about the day the picture was taken; Jaimie was five and Sarah was two. Not a care in the world was on their faces as long as they were with their dad. Putting the picture back in place, I started out the door. Turning back, I remembered not feeding my stomach. I went back to the kitchen and made a peanut butter and jam sandwich, then back to the car, headed for the prison about 2½ miles away.

As I started to drive away in my decade-old 1981 Z28 Camaro (the car has seen better days), I was thinking of my brother, Bob, being housed in the max unit.

Knowing that he was a unit swamper, reality hit me, thinking that he was in a lot of danger. Mixed emotions were going on inside of my head. I started daydreaming, thinking back to when I was a child, and my oldest brother took care of me.

I was watching TV lying on the floor beside Bob, my head in the crook of his shoulder.

Heading down the Oregon hill and taking a left to the prison, my mind was on cruise and slipping back to the past; thinking about Bob's track meet when he was in high school; I watched him take first in the high hurdles. After the track meet, in the locker room he introduced me to his friends. He draped his cleats over my shoulder as Bob smiled, saying "You pack the cleats, Jimmy. Someday, it will be your turn to run, and I will pack your cleats. Let's go home."

Driving past the cemetery, my mind was still daydreaming, reflecting about when he was on leave from the U.S. Marines. He was taking time to be with his sister and brothers. When the time came for him to go back, Bob wanted to take me with him. He started to stuff me in his duffel bag, but Mom stopped him. At that time, I would have gone anywhere with my big brother. Weaving around all the potholes in the road that had not been fixed since the road was paved, probably in the 1950's, give or take a decade, I started up the grade to the prison onto the dirt road, thinking back when I was in high school playing football. I was a junior, starting for the Powell County Wardens as their defensive safety. We were playing the town of Laurel, and it was a tough defensive game with neither team scoring any points. It came down to a Montana playoff in overtime. Each team got the ball on the five-yard line and had four plays to score a touchdown or kick a field goal. Laurel got the flip of the coin, so they went first; we stopped them from scoring. It was the Wardens' turn; four downs went by, and no score. So, it was time for me to get back on the field. We stopped them for the first three downs, and it was fourth and three yards to go. I lined up on the wide receiver. The ball was hiked to the quarterback. My receiver ran to the inside, into the end zone. I took a look at the quarterback and saw a running back coming my way, with no teammate of mine on him. I could anticipate what the quarterback was going to do. He rolled out to his right and had two receivers on me. There was no time to think; I let the wide receiver go past me and I went for the running back. It was too late to intercept the pass. The receiver caught the ball on the 1-yard line, starting for the end zone. I hit him hard at the one; stopped him dead in his tracks.

He crumpled at the half-yard line, and it was our ball again. I watched on the sidelines as the Wardens scored a touchdown in the next three plays, winning the game. I was on cloud nine that whole night and the next day, when the paper told about the game, "'Jim Powell and John Bignell saved our bacon many times during the game,' said coach Thomas."

Still ruminating on the daydream, I was thinking about after the game that evening, going over Bob's house. I had my varsity school coat on, thinking I was cool. I drove up to the house with my newly painted green metal-flake-color car that had two black racing strips down the middle of the 1969 Chevy SS. My brother, John, showed me how to spray paint. Walking up to the house, I could hear the music of Pink Floyd blasting through the walls with the door shut.

Coming to the door, before I got there, my bother met me as the door opened before I rang the bell. I looked inside at the people around the coffee table, inhaling smoke from rubber tubes coming from a glass bong. Most of the peace-loving people had a beer in their hands and were just lying around, mellowing out. The front room was smoked-filled, with fluorescent lights glimmering around the room.

"What do you want, Jimmy" said Bob with an angry voice.

"Bob, I stopped the Laurel Locomotives from scoring a winning touchdown. We won the game after two overtimes!" I explained. "It's time to party hearty, Bob. Let me...."

Bob butted in excitedly, "So you think you are going to celebrate here and ruin what you have going for yourself?"

"It won't ruin my game, it will only enhance it!" I exclaimed. I tried to brush by him to enter the house. He grabbed me by the back of the coat and threw me up against the outside wall, then grabbed me by the ear and the hair with his left hand, forcing me up onto my toes.

"I am saying this one time and one time only, Jimmy," Bob, looking straight into my eyes, started. With a stern voice, he said, "If I catch you smoking any pot or drinking any beer, I will beat the hell out of you in front of your friends, and will tell our dad." Then he threw me down on the porch toward the sidewalk. "Get out of here and go home, Jimmy! You don't belong here," Bob stammered. He waited on the porch until I drove away.

I was now on top of the hill, driving past the garden the inmates planted last spring, then driving past the hayfield before the 90-degree turn that leads to the ranch 1 office. I was back to daydreaming again, thinking about the karate meet I was in last month, taking third place in the Midwest Full-Contact Tournament held in Omaha, Nebraska; thinking, *hope I didn't need to use what I learned*. At the turn to the ranch office, there were some staff members stopping traffic, with a highway patrol officer overseeing what was going on. It was not a familiar face that stopped me.

I rolled down the window and I said, "Hi, I am a transportation officer working at the prison. I called Main Control to see if you needed any help. They said you need all the help you can get."

Another person came up to my car and said, "He is cleared to go through. Sorry, Jim, go to the Command Post. In the big meeting room, they are telling everyone what is going on."

"Thanks, Linda," I said as I started off. Down the prison road at the next turn, was the check point building with an officer there, waving people through. Stopping, I said, "Hi, Fred." He was the officer who I would normally see coming to work at eight o'clock on Monday. "What is going on out here?"

Fred said, "There is a lot of smoke coming from the middle of the building where the yard is, and the rumor is that all five of the staff members are on C block. We don't know if they are all right or not. All the highway patrols in the area are around the outside of the double fence around the perimeter. There are snipers on the high-side kitchen roof and as you can see, a sniper on top of Riesly Nob that is high enough to shoot over the top of the fence looking at the back of the max building. That's all I know for now, Jim."

With a deep sigh and then saying, "Thanks, Fred," I started down the road, seeing all the cars around the fence with highway patrol officers, their shotguns sitting on the front of their cars. As I was passing by the max building, I was looking through the double fence. The hair on the back of my neck was standing up as I drove by. I kept driving, making it to the parking lot and walking inside the Wallace Administration Building. There were many staff and correctional officers standing around talking to one another. As I greeted everyone with a nod of my head, I walked to the main control doors. The door opened and, walking in, I said, "Hi, Jay," through a key slot at the 3-foot level below the window. Jay was the officer I talked to on the phone at home. The electric door closed and the next door opened. Away I went through one more door that I pushed open to the courtyard. The yard separated the high-side from the low-side inmates, with another gate in the yard leading to the max building. To the right was the command post door, with groups of people standing around talking with one another. The disturbance team was waiting in the yard for the next orders to be given. I went to the door and looked through the window, seeing that the command post was just standing-room-only. Opening the door, I went in. To the right were the captains and lieutenants from all three shifts. I stepped over to the door and I could hear, on a speaker-phone, the voice of someone filtering their voice, talking. With everyone concentrating on the voice, they never even had a clue that I was there, listening.

The unknown voice was saying, "You guards are getting too close to the max building! I want you to move them back and get the press in here to talk about the way you pigs have been treating us. We have a list of demands and if you don't start fulfilling them, we will cut the head off of one guard that we have as a hostage, and throw it out the front door. Plus, as a bonus, we will throw out the head of one of the rats that we have killed. But I can't tell you who's head it is because it was beat so bad that, through the blood and missing eyeballs, it can't be identified!"

A voice from the command post responded, "Don't harm anyone. We are trying to get the press here so they can listen to your demands. Please give us the rest of the day to get this organized so you will get the best TV and news press here."

The muffled voice came over the speaker loud and excited, saying, "You don't have all day, you have two hours, then heads will start flying. You can start by shutting off the water that is flooding the building. Bring us 100 meals from downtown, we're getting hungry. And bring fifteen or twenty cigars, and they better not be cheap ones, either. Get that stuff here, then call us in the main cage." The phone speaker made a humming sound.

I decided to exit and go to the left where the big meeting room was. More correctional officers and staff were grouped together talking. I looked around and by the tables across the room, staff was signing a sheet of paper that was to verify that you were there. After signing, I went back outside because it was getting stuffy inside. I walked over to a group talking, nodded my head to the group as they kept on talking. Randle Chase was talking. He grew up in Deer Lodge and graduated around the same year. Randle was working that morning as high yard man. As things started to unfold in max, he was ordered by the lieutenant, with one other officer, to go on the outside of max and investigate what was going on. Anxiety was setting in, but Chase was telling the story to all that would listen, saying, "We went up to max and looked around, going to the left side first, seeing the five officers in the lower level on C block locked into cell Lower 6 or Lower 7.

They said that they were all okay at the time and that the officer in the cage locked them in the cell to protect them. They told us to bring something to break the window to the cell, and to hand them an AR-15 rifle with a lot of shells. We tried breaking the window but couldn't break though the inch-thick glass; we could only crack it. Then I told Dale Browne that Joe will go back to the Command Post to let them know where they are and to get a gun. I went over to the other side of max to see what was going on over there. The PC inmates were asking for my help, saying they were burning the cage door and trying to melt the Plexiglas in the door to open the cells. The look on the inmates' faces burned a lasting image in my head, seeing how scared they were. Their eyes looked like they knew what was going to happen next."

Randle Chase stammered, with a sad look on his face as he was looking down at the ground, and said, "I told them I will get them some help. I left the inmates to go back to the west side of the building where the officers are. There were no officers, couldn't find them. I thought I was not in the right place, but I looked around, and was sure enough, this was lower C block 6 or

7. After looking through all the cells that I could see, not finding them, I ran back to the command post, telling them that I can't find the officers. Didn't know where they were. The doors were all open on all the blocks, so I think the inmates got the officers."

Shortly after 1100 hours, the pace of staff actions accelerated sharply, and a number of initiatives were underway at the same time. Warden McCormick asked for blueprints of the max building. He also directed Associate Warden Mahoney and the lieutenant of first shift, Mike Micu, to pull together his team leaders. Other necessary staff had arrived at a preliminary plan for ////preempt commandeering//// the Maximum Security Building. After retrieving the blueprints and bringing them back down to the Command Post area, Micu and Mahoney with others went across the hall to the parole board room that had plenty of room to lay the prints on the tables. It was primarily quiet inside the room.

After studying the prints for minutes with the door closed, Mahoney spoke up and said, "If we think the worst, that the whole building has been compromised, that all cell and doors are open to the inmates, then we have, as I see it, four basic ways to reenter the building. One, through the front door." Pointing with his finger on the blueprints. "Second, through the back door, and third, through the top of the building, through the yard or down the control hatches, one on both sides of the building. We think the officers are still on C block in the lower right shower, locked behind a metal door, hopefully still safe from the inmates. We think they are going after the PCs on D block as we speak. The officers that have been looking around the max building said that inmates are blocking the hallways to the front door for a frontal attack. I would imagine the back door will have debris blocking the door, but the door swings out. Through the top of the building, the yard doors will probably be locked from the inside with a Folger Adams key. And the door from the back hallway that leads to the yard and the catwalk opens with a Folger's key also. The door swings to the inside of the building. I would believe it to be locked also. If we try to bring the DCT Team marching through the front walkway down to the front of the building, that will get the already excited inmates nervous. They might take it out on the five officers inside. So what do you guys think?"

After a long pause, Lieutenant Micu spoke up, "If we go through the back door with keys from the armory and had people to hurry to get whatever debris from the door away, throw a canister of gas both directions to disperse the inmates back from us. Then take most of the team to C block. Leave some of the team with shotguns along the way to protect us. Find the hostage officers and get them out through the front door."

Mahoney commented, "That sounds good, but we need a diversion to get the DCT team to the back without exciting the inmates."

Carl Nelson spoke up and said, "What if we take the fire truck to the back of max in route of the guard station, then behind Close Unit III through no-man's land?"

"That is a good idea," said Mahoney. "What would we have to do to get the fire truck ready?"

Carl answered, "Take the hoses off the back and there will be room for the DCT Team. It will take over an hour to unload the truck."

Mahoney said, "Carl, get some guys and get started with that. We need a tarp to put over the team while en route to max to surprise the inmates in max. And take a radio." Carl nodded his head and out the door he went.

Deputy Warden Garry Weer spoke up, "We need a backup plan. What about problems that could come up inside of max? Like what if the inmates have the hostages under knife point or we get resistance on a block? Or if there are dead bodies on the PC block, and/or do we handle the death-row block different than the rest of the blocks? Last, what do we do with the inmates when we get them out of the building?"

Mahoney saw the warden come to the door. The warden gestured to Mahoney to follow him back to the command post.

Mahoney, as he was leaving the room, said, "Keep on thinking about it and come up with some answers to those questions.

Micu spoke up, "If the inmates have the officers at knife point, the team can take the inmates that are not involved with the hostage situation and get them out of the building. This will eliminate a lot of the problems. Then we will know what to do next. If there are bodies on any block, we get the rest of the inmates out of the area, then check to see if the bodies are dead or alive. Then we seal off the area as a crime scene. The death-row block we can handle the same way as the rest of the population. As we go on a block, we can order the inmates to come out of their cells, order them to strip all their clothes off and get down on the floor in front of their cells. Then have a first team member with flex-cuffs tie their hands behind their backs, with another team member with a pistol pointing at the head of the inmate in case the inmate tries something. Your last question on what to do with the inmates after we get them out of the building will have to be discussed with the warden.

Weer spoke up. "Does anyone have more questions that can be handled at this time?" No one spoke for a short while.

A sergeant spoke up and said, "If we have someone to climb a rope from the outside of the build to the top of the roof and put some gas canisters down the control cage hatches while the team is going through the back door, this would disperse the inmates before they were in the building."

Weer said, "That sounds like a good idea. Do you have anyone that can climb a rope to the top of the roof, Mike?"

Micu replied, "I do, but I think we should use an extra man to do that because the Team will be needed on entering the building. I will go out in the courtyard and find someone to climb a rope and put gas down the hatches."

Mr. Weer adjourned the meeting by saying, "Well, guys, I guess that is all for now. Get your team together and wait for further orders.

＊＊＊＊＊＊＊＊＊＊＊＊＊

The command post door opened and out came the lieutenant on first shift.

He was the assistant commander of the Disturbance Control Team or DCT.

Lieutenant Mike Micu was asking everyone outside if there was someone who could climb a rope to the top of the max building. Micu was another person I grew up with, graduating the same year in school. Throughout grade school and high school, Micu never played sports. I did not remember him in any school activity. He was around 5 feet 5 inches tall and about 140 pounds. He had what you would call the small-man-syndrome; small in stature but tried to be bigger than he was with his mouth. He would belittle people in front of other people to make himself look bigger, or use his status to cause problems for others. Micu lowered himself by lying to make an appearance of being right. Micu was hated by most of the people in town who knew him. He is sharp-witted, has many talents, but did not believe in himself enough to let his brains get him to this point. He did more ass-kissing than anyone at the prison, which was an endless list above him.

One season, Micu went hunting in the Fall, taking a walk back in the Rocky Mountains. When he came back to his truck, all four tires were flat, someone cutting holes in them, trying to get even with him playing the Devil's advocate.

In another incident, Micu was a sergeant at the prison and working as a relief officer downtown for the sheriff's office at nights. He worked all night in town then he came to work on first shift at the prison. It was well known that he would come to work and go down to Close Unit II where he was sergeant of the unit.

Entering into the unit, he would go upstairs, lock himself in the corner office and sleep all morning. He would have the floor officers doing all the work. If there was a problem, the floor officers would inform him if someone or something needed him. One time, Micu saw an officer sleeping in the perimeter vehicle as he came to work, and went over to the vehicle and woke him just to take him into the Command Post to file paper work on him to get him fired. Micu had a smartass mouth, belittling anyone when he could get away with it. It was said he would have even picked up his mother for going over the speed limit by one mile an hour if that would get him a higher position at the prison.

Later on, Micu was a lieutenant and got his captain's position by informing on his captain for using the copy machine to copy papers for the Montana National Guard. You would think that copying papers for another State agency and having the Guard pay back for the copies, that everything would have been all right with the prison. But Micu needed a new job, so out goes the old captain and in with the new.

Today was different from the past for Micu. He had to find people to back him in order to take back the max building. That would not be hard because there were fellow officers who had to be saved, so any hard feelings would be put aside for now. Coming out the door, Micu looked around and said, "Is there anyone that can climb a rope to the top of the max building?"

There was a pretense for a minute, then I said, "I can climb a rope to the top of max. I taught rope climbing in high school to the younger classmates." Micu and Sergeant Wolfy came over to me as I turned around. "We need someone to put the chemical agent down the two hatches to the cages. We need this done before the DCT team goes through the back door. Can you do that, Jim?"

"Yes, I can do that," I spoke up without even thinking about it.

"You need to go over to the armory building and get on the fire truck with the DCT team. Walk around the back way with the others. They're getting ready over at the accounting building right as we speak."

Saying, "I will head over there right now," I gave a nod with my head.

Leaving Chase's group, I went back through the double electrical doors of main control. Back out of the administration building I went. Walked over to the accounting building where the north half of the building was the prison armory. On the other side of the road was tower 1. As I reached my deployment area, I looked around. All my co-workers had sober looks on their faces, standing around talking to one another. The talk was about what each person would do as a group. They were thinking of backup scenario plans in case there were different obstacles to diverge from plan A. Plan A was to get all the max building duplicate keys that were on one big ring from the key control office in the armory; take the keys and go through the back door of max with guns drawn, secure the area to the west side of the building.

Staying in a group over to C block where the officers were last thought to be held hostage. If the officers were there and alive/unharmed, they would take them out the front door. If the officers were being threatened by inmates with shanks and clubs, then the team would make a decision right there if they could take out the aggressors with a bullet to the head, or if they had to leave some officers there. Other team members would finish clearing out what was left of the inmates in other areas in the building. They would handcuff each inmate and bring them out the front door, with help from officers on the outside of max escorting the inmates over to no-man's land. No-man's land was a fenced-in yard between Close Unit III and the max building. If there was anyone killed, the team would clear the area of inmates, then secure the area for investigation.

The DCT team wore black uniforms. The team was holding or had close by them on the ground a bulletproof flack vest that was too hot to have on for now. They also wore a helmet with a face shield on it, and a .357 or .45 pistol in a holster on a belt, with a gas mask and plenty of rounds to kill twice the number of inmates in the unit.

If this was a different situation, the guns would be armed with defensive bullets like salt rock, or blanks that would go under the skin but most of the time, would not kill a person. But this situation had changed over from a defensive team taking control, with the quarterback on the sideline making decisions over a handheld radio. Each DCT member had a radio, and broadcast on an emergency frequency that was not transmitted over the daily channels. Some of the DCT team had different equipment like crow bars, fence cutters, hand-held shields, defensive batons or clubs, medical kits. One person had a video camera recorder. I was still wearing my blue sweater and gray pants to look like I was no threat to the inmates. As a matter of fact, I was not even given the gas containers yet. I was not worried because I saw canisters of gas put in a box and then put in the back of a truck.

As I was in a group listening to their conversation, I heard my nickname called out behind me. I was known as Boog or Boogie to anyone who knew me. That nickname was started back in grade school when a pro baseball player was in his prime, named Boog Powell. They were not calling me to come over to them. They were discussing my affairs between the three of them.

One of them was saying, "Do you think Boog should come with us on the fire truck? You know that his brother Bob is a PC inmate in Max. The reports from the Command Post said that he and McFarlane were out of their cells as swampers."

I didn't turn around because I wanted to hear what was being said without them knowing that I could hear them.

The staff member kept on talking. "It's not that I don't trust Boog, I am sure he wouldn't do anything against his friends, but I was told there wasn't much hope for the two swampers being alive because they were out working by the laundry room.

Micu spoke up. "I understand what you are saying, but we don't have anyone that can climb the rope to the top of the roof and put the canisters down the escape hatches. Tell you what, if when we get inside and find out that his brother is dead, then we will get him off the roof and get him out of there. Make sure that he doesn't get a gun because who knows if that would start him shooting inmates for revenge."

Thinking about what was said and visualizing what would I do if he were dead, I knew after a couple of minutes my job came first over any feeling that I had for my brother. I was not going to leave this day with any regrets, so at that time, I knew I would leave vengeance to the Lord, my God. It is hard being an inmate's brother because I did not want my fellow friends and officers to not trust me, or have them even think that I would bring in con-traband into the prison to betray them. So I tell myself, *You do not have a brother in prison*. That he was just as good as dead to me, wanting nothing to do with him; auspiciously not to let new of-ficers know that he was related to me. Semantically, I was just like my brother, raised by our father and mother with our idiosyn-crasies being basically the same. I was afraid that if I made a mis-take in life, I would be in prison with my brother. That was the last place I wanted to be. But deep down, I knew that blood was thicker than water. I was thanking God once again that I did not turn out like him; maybe thanking Bob, as well, that he helped keep me on the straight and narrow path. But none of that mat-tered right now. I had a job to do and nothing was going to get in the way. Once more, in my mind, thinking if they had someone to climb the rope instead of me, it would have been better for all, maybe.

"Men, listen up," said Commander Micu in a high tone of voice. As we all stopped talking, Micu gave a speech. "We have been training each month for years in case this day would come, and that day is here now. Remember, take care of yourself first by staying together and watching each others' backs. Then take care of the staff that has been taken hostage. Then we will go from block to block, securing each block. If an inmate is coming at you, command him to stop.

If he does not, then shoot him until he stops. Remember, if the officers have been taken hostage, they may be dressed in only their underwear or even dressed in an orange jumpsuit. So you all know who the staff are and have seen pictures of them in an earlier briefing at the armory, so be sure who you are shooting.

Likewise, if a person is coming up to you in an officer's uniform, have him stop where he is and identify himself. IF, and I mean if, he keeps coming at you, command him to lie down. Then IF he does not stop, wound him, and carry on from there. So, let's all watch each other's back and look for the unexpected. We can head around back to the fire truck."

The DCT team started walking the perimeter fence road with a couple staff workers from the maintenance office. Everyone seemed to be talking about what their duties were, each trying to think of different scenarios and what they would do in different situations. Myself, the order I was given was with no scenario; just climb a rope to the top of max and drop the canisters down the hatch. But if…well, I guess, there was no 'but if.'

* * * * * * * * * * * *

0930 Hours

The two inmate swampers, Powell and McFarlane, had time to talk back in the laundry room.

"Bob, did I tell you about the escapes that took place in the twelve years since the prison moved from town?" asked McFarlane.

Inmate Powell answered, "No, but I seen the news reports on TV."

McFarlane said, "Well, then, I will only tell you the best part of the stories. The first escape was, I think, in 1980, when the wire fence was not tested out yet. The administration was still thinking it was a rock wall to climb over, I think. After moving from the old prison, there was a lot of kinks in the new prison to fix.

"Well, there was an inmate from B unit, I think cube 210 or 310; he wanted to leave the prison to go back home. I think he was a wetback from Mexico, and he wanted to see his family. It took about a month to get all the supplies needed; smuggled them in from the warehouse and industries and the hobby store.

Plenty of inmates knew about the plan, but didn't rat him off because they wanted to see if he could pull it off. His plan was okayed by the inmates running the prison at that time. A week before he escaped, the night shift inmate cook that was living in the same cube was asking the guards on night shift questions like, 'Has there been any escapes from this new prison?' Guard's answer was 'No.' 'Does the perimeter guard get a break to come in to eat, and what time?' Guard's answer was 'Yes, the perimeter gets a break, and he is relieved between 11:00 and 11:30.' 'Can the tower guard on the hill see us in the kitchen dining room at night, in case I wanted to wave at him?' 'Yes, the guard has a spotting scope and can see what is going on inside the kitchen and around the front of the prison.'"

McFarlane was still talking, "A manikin head was made with pillow down stuffing and a white pillow case for the head. He had help putting the down feathers on top of the head for hair. Made an ear to put on one side of the head. Then winter coats were used to make the body under a blanket. It was after midnight count when the guard brought up the count sheet. The con left through the sliding glass window from 210, went down the outside stairs to the concrete wall between B and C units. He climbed the wall and jumped down the other side to the ground. Then he walked behind C unit and to the back gate where there was no guard on duty at night."

Powell asked, "How did he get past tower 4 guard at the back gate?"

McFarlane explained, "Oh, I forgot that at that time, in the late '70s and early '80s when this took place, there wasn't no tower 4. That came later, I think in '82 or '83. So, getting back to my story, the con went over to the big long drive-through gate, pushed at the bottom of the gate, and he squeezed through the first gate then again through the next gate. Then the third gate was open because at nights, there are no cons at industries so the gate is always left open. The con ran down the back road and was picked up and driven away by a paying costumer. He wasn't caught for years, and he said it was the biggest rush he has ever had; running away was better than whisky and women."

McFarlane had all day, and he was going to pass the time away by telling stories. He kept talking. "The cons liked the idea of a galvanized metal chain link fence. It was better than the old prison that had a rock wall. The chain link double fence was a challenge that seemed doable. I mean, it was a challenge but there was a lot of flaws to be worked out by the guards. You have to remember it was a new prison, and the cons were doing their part to find the problems." They both were laughing and folding laundry as McFarlane passed the time away.

McFarlane said, "First, in August of 1980, not even a year after the two Close Units were built, there was a disturbance in Close Unit I. Prisons called them disturbances back then if the problem was handled in less than a day. There was a riot in the summer of 1980 in Idaho, and they lost a couple of housing buildings in the riot. So Montana said that they could send their problem children to us. There were about forty-eight cons that went to lower C and D blocks in Close I. The guards sent two of the Idaho cons to max for something they did on lower C block. I can't recall what it was about, but the Idahoans were mad. They told Sergeant Beeson that their block would not lock down until they brought back the two cons from max. Well, Bob, as you can imagine, Warden Crist was going to show those spud pickers who was the boss. After the warden went down to Close I to talk them out of causing problems, the cons just started more problems. The Idahoans made makeshift shanks from metal on the day-room block. By the way, all the cons were out of their cells on the block for day room. They soaped up the dayroom floor so when the guards came in to get them, they would fall on the floor. So Warden Crist locked down the prison at that time. Tear gas and guns were brought in, with guards on the kitchen roof with guns. I found out that day the guards don't play fair. I was watching from upper C block that day. On each block is a door to the outside. Tear gas was thrown in the front door of C block and through the back door of C block. The front door was closed but the back door was left open. The cons were told to come out the back door and to lie on the ground, face down. Most of the cons stayed on the block for some time, so they just threw in more gas. Then the cons came out one at a time, lying on the ground, coughing. That was the end of the bad Idahoans; they were good until sent back to their spuds.

Powell asked, "Did anyone get hurt?"

McFarlane answered, "No, it was handled pretty well. My next story is the Close Unit I, cons building a wine cellar."

Powell's ears perked up as he straightened up in his chair. Powell said, "No, you're telling me some tales now, aren't you, Chuck?"

Chuck replied, "Well, wait until you hear the story then. I would say it had to be the best escape plan that I have ever heard of around here, Bob. I thought when it was happening I was back watching the TV show, *Hogan's Heroes* or the *Great Escape* movie."

McFarlane started his story. "Well, back in July of 1981 in Close Unit I, lower C block again, there were four cons that wanted to escape. The four were Faarasen, Hintz, Sudbury, and Shurtliff. They found out that the bottom bunk was made of a concrete slab. One of them was getting curious, hitting the top of the slab with his hand; it sounded like it was hollow inside. So two of them lifted the cement slab off the cement shelf that supported the slab for the bed. After lifting it up, there was a hollow place big enough to hide in, so it was about 2 feet by 6 feet by 3 feet high. Their plan was not to hide inside of it, but to pound away at the cement floor under it until they had a hole as big as a person's shoulders. Then they would take turns digging out the dirt and flushing it down the toilet or pushing it back from the tunnel."

"Wasn't there no rebar in the cement floor?" asked Bob.

"Yes, there was, but the rebar was two feet apart and running the same way as the bed. So the four cons dug it out between the two rebars, and three feet wide the other way."

Bob asked, "Is this a true story, Chuck, because it's not sounding like that?"

Chuck replied, "Yes, it is a true story; just ask some of the old guards. So the four cons came up with two problems. One was how they were going to get the two cons from lower C 8 and lower C 10 cells when the tunnel was finished, and how were they going to get over the two perimeter fences without getting cut to shreds by the constantan wire. They were digging for at least seventeen days to figure that out. Plus, they were taking dirt to the yard and dumping it on the track each day when they went out to the recreation yard. But not a lot of the dirt was dumped out in the yard because it was a different color than the dirt on the track. They figured how to take the bars off the door window by paying a guard to bring in a screw driver that fit the security screws. So, they did not have to mess with the door until the day of the escape. To keep them from getting cut up on the razor wire and fence, they wore extra clothes and coats. So the day of the escape, they finished the tunnel and loosened the screws in the door windows. At about 3:00 in the morning, all four cons escaped over the fences. When they caught them and brought them to court, they said they were digging a wine cellar."

Bob asked, "What happened in court; what did the judge say about the wine cellar?"

Chuck replied, "Everyone in the court room had a good laugh, including the judge. I think each one of the cons got three years for escape and they were told that they will have to drink their wine warm."

Bob replied, "That was a clever one, and no one got hurt in the escape. That sounds like a fun time to be in prison."

Chuck answered, "That wasn't fun during that time. There was more problems then just staying out of people's way. If you were not into trouble, then someone was causing you trouble. But I guess that is the way it is in prison. If I was you, I would rather be with my two daughters in town than in this joint."

There was no response from Powell. His head just sunk to his chest.

Without hesitation, McFarlane changed the subject, starting on another story by asking a question. "Did you know that your brother caught an escaping inmate by himself?" asked McFarlane.

"No, I didn't. My brother quit coming to see me when he started at the prison," said Powell.

McFarlane said, "It was about 1980, when Jim Blodgett was Acting Warden.

"Blodgett took over when Warden Crist left for a warden's job down in, I think, New Mexico, after the big New Mexico riot. But, to get back to my story. Your brother, Jimmy, had taken a trustee con over to the old folks' home across the street from the hospital. From the way I heard the story, the trustee con was singing and playing a guitar for the old folks. Jimmy was looking out the big day room window in the direction of the hospital.

Out the front door of the hospital ran a young twenty-year-old inmate. Seconds later, came a guard just watching the inmate run away towards the highway. Well, your brother, I guess, told the old folks to watch the trustee for him, that he would be right back. Out the door he went, running to the six-foot fence that the inmate had already climbed. Your brother was catching up fast on the way to the fence. He ran to the fence and with two climbs with each foot, he was to the top of the fence. I guess he ripped his shirt and cut his stomach on the top of the fence as he jumped down the other side. The inmate was at the double-lane highway, waiting for cars to stop going by; the cars were going at least 65 miles an hour. Jimmy was right behind him when the inmate crossed the first lane of traffic, and Jimmy told people that he had to wait for one car and he was off again. The two crossed the last lane together with cars coming fast their way. Then your brother yelled, 'Stop, or I will shoot!' The young inmate was out of breath anyway, trying to outrun your brother, and stopped. Then Jimmy shook him down for weapons, then escorted him back to the fat guard that lost him. Then your brother went back to the trustee at the old folks' home and said, 'I told you I would be right back!' I guess Jimmy got four hours of overtime for capturing the inmate, and a citation from Warden Blodgett."

"What was the inmate's name?" asked Powell.

McFarlane said, "I think it was Gutenberg, but I'm not sure if I have it right.

'Oh, yeah, and when the cons at the prison was talking to Jimmy, they were kidding him that if it was them running away, when he caught up to them, they would have just put Jimmy under their arm and ran away with him. As you have seen, there are a lot of big cons, so they were having fun with him. Then I guess Jimmy said, 'If it was you that I ran down, then after seeing you, I would have ran the other way.' They all got a laugh out of that."

"This is the last story before lunch that I will tell you," McFarlane said as his stomach started to growl. "This story made me wonder if I was going to be involved," said McFarlane. As Chuck started the story, he said, "The disturbance happened in March of 1982, again in Close Unit I. A con name Fed Perry was running the prison at that time, and for as long as he was in prison. Perry's story is an interesting one, but I will tell you about him some other time, Bob. There was a problem that Perry wasn't getting his way. So when Fed Perry was upset, then the prison administration would come down to the unit and talk to him. Believe me, Bob, this doesn't happen anymore like that. Today, if you have a problem, then you are sent up to see them, where they have the upper hand on you, if you know what I mean, Bob. The admin could not get anywhere with him, so they left. Fed Perry was in the sergeant's office, talking to Sergeant Jones, yelling and complaining. The whole unit could hear him from each block. The counselor, Mike Thatcher, went in the front door to try talking to Perry. Sergeant Jones told the cage officer, Bud Bohling, to open the door and let Thatcher in. Fed Perry took a shovel and jammed it in the door so it was all the way open. Then Perry told the cage officer to open all the block doors but, luckily, Bolhing didn't. Then Perry went over to lower B block and raised his hand and lowered his hand. That was a sign for the cons on all the blocks to start rioting. Fed Perry went out the front door and over to the gym. This is where I learnt to have dummies under you to take the fall for you.

"Then all hell broke loose; lower A, B and upper A, B started destroying the day room tables. They were concrete tops. The tops were lifted off the concrete base that was anchored to the cement floor. They took the round table tops and broke the cement pillars that were anchored to the floor. Now they had battering rams to break windows and doors. This went on for a long time, about an hour. In lower A and B blocks, the block door was rammed until the cons got the doors open. They were also ramming the doors from the block to the outside doors. Alarms were going off in the cage. I was watching from the block window, saw that two staff in the cage were getting frustrated. Cons were running all over the building. The staff that were on the floor at this time locked themselves into the sergeant's office, which was upstairs in the northeastern corner of the building. They were a bunch of scared people. They were Sergeant Jones, Salle, Rundle, Officer Jones, and Thatcher. The cons were trying to smoke them out of the office for hostages. They broke out the window in the door like the one that is in this door of the laundry room, and then stuffed a mattress in the window area and lit it on fire."

McFarlane said, "Then I found out later that Deputy Warden Weer called Bohling in the cage to throw tear gas out the cage hatch into the lobby. Bohling was nervous as he pulled the pin to the gas, and the gas canister was smoking in the cage. He tried to pick it up but the can gets hot, so he took another canister and pulled the pin at the hatch and dropped it out of the hatch into the lobby, then closed the hatch lid."

"I bet that was funny seeing the smoke in the cage," said Powell.

McFarlane replied, "It was only a little funny because I was watching the riot from upper D block. I was more worried about myself during this time, but now it sounds funny."

McFarlane was back on the story saying, "There was two in the cage that day, Ted Hiltz, the electrician, and Bud Bohling. Ted went up the ladder to the roof after the gas was filling the cage. Then Bud went a few minutes later. Then the fun began; gas projectiles were shot into the back doors and through the front doors. The gas was so bad that your eyes teared up and you couldn't see across the day room. All the inmates went in their cells and waited for the guards to come in.

"We had to lock our doors; then and only then did the guard take us out to the yard two at a time. There were gunmen on the roof of the kitchen and in the towers and on the Rothe building. We had shotguns in our faces when the guards took us out of the building. There was so much lead around that one would think that somebody would have died of lead poisoning, but no one got hurt.

* * * * * * * * * * * *

1000 Hours

At approximately 1000 hours, the two swampers, McFarlane and Powell, heard one of the officers ask for the yard keys. Anytime there was movement on the max floor, the swampers were to be out of sight. As the two swampers went into the laundry room, McFarlane leaned against the dryer and Powell was leaning against the door edge. They were still talking about women working in a men's prison.

There were sounds that were normal at this time; hearing inmates coming from the yard talking to the officers; the electric door opening and then shutting, then the next door opening onto C-block.

All of a sudden, inmate Powell heard the sound of feet running towards them.

Inmate Powell's coffee cup hit the floor. The infirmary emergency table (gurney) moved as inmate Wild placed it in the back hallway door, keeping it from closing. Wild looked straight at Powell in the laundry room, with a shank made from the galvanized wire. The handle was a scarf wrapped around the part that was in his hand; Wild was trying to protect the hand from the wire penetrating into his own hand when thrusting at a body.

Inmate Wild said, "If you get involved in this, you are dead." As Wild left, inmate Powell grabbed the door and tried to close it; it would not close all the way because of a mop head on the knob. Inmate McFarlane came into action, opening the door enough to get the mop head off the door handle, then shutting the door.

McFarlane then put his weight against the door to keep it shut. Powell went over to the lower shelf of the clothes rack, looking for something to defend themselves with and handing a squeegee to Chuck. Chuck was wondering why Bob handed him a squeegee. It might be used as a poker, but it was not much good other than that. Powell, finding a toilet bowl brush, took the metal brush away from the wooden handle; hopefully, this would stop a marauder from coming in the door by stabbing at his hand or even at his head, looking for an eye. Would inmates Powell and McFarlane have the killer instinct to save their own lives by gouging out someone's eye? Would it came to that? And if they had to kill someone, would that keep the cycle going, proving that human nature is that one crime leads to the next crime of a reprobate on the State of Montana. Or, would the PCs just give up, hoping that the marauders would have pity on them because they did not do anything to them?

It seemed, almost instantly after the door was shut, like a herd of inmates rushed the door. Chuck could not hold the door closed with his weight. The marauders were pushing from the outside of the door, trying to get in. The door kept opening a little at a time. The PC swampers were stabbing the inmates and shoving at the door with their made-up shanks. The PCs did not have the killer instinct, stabbing at an arm and a shoulder of a marauder who was winning the battle to squeeze in. Next, the marauder showed his face. It was inmate Gollehon.

Gollehon had his chest, head, and one arm through the doorway. With other inmates pushing at the metal door behind him, Powell or McFarlane lacked the killing mentality that it took to take Gollehon's eye out. The two PCs were thinking, maybe if they did not try and mar the marauders, then they would take mercy on them. When they finally got through the door, Turner was behind Gollehon. He had a box of matches that came from the sergeant's office in his hand. That only meant he was going to burn them out if they did not get through.

Seconds later, Powell saw the blood on Gollehon's face and arm. This gave Powell an idea. Behind him on the shelf was a gallon bottle of bleach. Powell grabbed the bleach bottle and started splashing beach in Gollehon's face, plus splashing it past Gollehon in the faces of the other inmates trying to open the door.

This stopped the attack at once, leaving the inmates temporally blinded. The marauders had to leave for a short time, getting water to rinse away the bleach. The door was closed and blocked it with both of their shoulders. Chuck yelled, "Dryer, I need to get the dryer, Bob. You stay here and keep your hand on the handle, and shoulder against the door."

McFarlane turned around and unhooked the dyer. Dragging the dryer on its metal studs on the bottom of the dyer, that were for leveling, it was scraping across the cement floor. He was pushing and pulling it to the door. Powell was looking out the window in the door. He could see inmate Cox rubbing at his eye. That brought a slight grin on Powell's face. He could see that the rest of the inmates that were trying to break in were doing the same. Powell identified inmate Cox because he was the only one that was wearing thermal underwear top and bottoms; he thought that wearing thermal underwear for a workout suit was weird even for an inmate. As the dyer's destiny was to be placed in front of the door, Powell moved out of the way as McFarlane shoved it home. Powell sat down on the floor, putting his back to the dyer. Then, stretching as far as possible, his legs were too short for his feet to brace against the washer that was in front of him.

McFarlane was looking at Powell's toes touching the washer and said, "Bob, do you want me to trade with you?"

Powell replied, "You noticed, Chuck, my legs are too short," as they switched places. Powell got up and turned off the light. Then he looked out the window in the door. He could not identify any of the inmates but Cox. Another inmate was taking cloths off the rack that was just outside the door. They were throwing them on the floor in front of the laundry room door. Cox started a torch on fire, then threw the torch to the laundry room door.

McFarlane said, "Bob what are they doing outside the door?"

"Chuck, they are going to smoke us out of here, putting cloths and fire at the door," said Powell.

"Bob, whatever we do, don't give up and don't open the door. They will kill the both of us because we are their only hostages at this time. So even if we die in here, it will be better than what they will do to us. So do we have a pact, Brother?"

McFarlane asked.

"Yes, to the eeennd," Powell stuttered.

McFarlane said, "Bob, take the hose off the washer and spray down some of the towels so if we need to breathe through them, it will filter away the smoke."

The smoke started coming through the cracks in the door and under the door, making it so smoky that Powell could not see the clothes rack outside the door.

"You okay, Chuck?" whispered Powell.

"I'm okay; the smoke is going more up than staying down here," McFarlane whispered.

If the air vents were not working in the laundry room, then the two trapped would have succumbed at that time. The air exchange was still working, letting the smoke go out of the laundry room to the basement. For now, the inmates left the two PCs alone.

It did not take too long for the uncontrolled inmates to break the latch on the door of the infirmary. The infirmary was on the other side of the back hallway electrical door. They concentrated on ramming their shoulder to the door, taking turns. After breaking through the door, they found locked cabinets that you wondered why they were locked because it only took a matter of minutes to break the doors with any kind of pry bar. But then again, a lock is only to keep the honest person honest. There were hardly any drugs in the infirmary; mostly aspirin or items of that sort. But what were in the infirmary were more weapons like surgical scissors. At that time, the smoke was so bad that no one could see a foot in front of one's face, all through the max unit. During that timeframe, the water was starting to come in under the door of the laundry room; the sprinkler system was flooding the entire building of max. Each hallway and every cell block had sprinklers going off.

* * * * * * * * * * * * *

1000 Hours

"Time to get the yard in, guys." Sergeant Mcphail slowly got up as the four floor officers started out the door before him. They walked down to the control cage, asking for the 75 and 76 Folger Adams keys. One unlocked the yard door; the other unlocked the electrical box that opened the yard gates. All five officers were still wearing the white smock that they put on at the first of the shift, wearing them all shift so that their clothes would not get dirty from serving the chow and different jobs. McPhail handled the keys, opening the yard door then walking over to the electrical box to open it.

Two inmates from the middle dog run spoke up, "I got to go to the bathroom real bad, boss." The inmates were hamming it up. They kept talking, "Can you take us out first before I piss all over myself and the floor? We have been yelling for you for the last five minutes to get us out of here; where were you, guys?"

Officer Miller spoke up with a smile and said, "We were waiting for you guys to say 'Please.'"

One inmate said, "Please, please, please hurry!" So Browne went over to the yard door and handcuffed one inmate's hands through the handcuff slot, cuffing the inmate behind his back; he was stirring a little, showing that he had to take a piss. Browne left no room in the cuff but didn't tighten it too tight, just snug.

Boggs was right behind Browne, and handed him a set of cuffs for the next inmate to be cuffed up. It was the same process for Browne on the last two inmates, taking only seconds to hand-cuff them. Sergeant McPhail hit the button in the box to open the middle run. Out they came to the front of the officers, and stopped.

Three of the officers pat-searched the inmates who were in front of them, from head to toe; putting their hand on the inmate, running their hand on the inmate's clothes, searching for contraband. After the search was completed, you heard, "Okay." That was a sign from the officers to have the inmate start walking to the yard door. The gate was left open because there were no inmates in that dog run. After the three inmates and five officers went through the yard door, the yard door was left open because they would be right back picking up three more inmates and so on, until the last six were on C-block. The three inmates, as they went by the cage, looked down the back hall as they yapped their jaws; saw that the two PC swampers were standing inside the laundry door talking to each other. The three cuffed inmates had a smile on their faces as they went to the sally-port of blocks C and B with the five officers right behind them. The cage officer was looking straight ahead on C-block, using the panel to open the door. After everyone was in the sally-port, the door closed and simultaneously, the door opened to C-block. Inside, they all headed to each of the cells the three inmates lived in, with the whole block looking out their windows in the door, anticipating the checkmate coming from the pawns in the recreation yard.

The nine inmates who were left in the yard cages broke off the pre-stressed pieces of fence that was worked on for who knows how long during the last two months. It took only a matter of moments to break the wire. Next, they took the piece of wire out of the fence to make a hole, ranging from 1foot by 2½ feet to 1 foot by 6½ feet.

Browne climbed the metal stairs to the upper tier with the inmate who was going to upper C-8 cell. The inmate living between inmates Close and Allen yelled out to Browne as he was going by his cell.

Inmate Nelson said, "Browne, pick up the note that I dropped on the floor for you, it is really important."

Browne said, "I have to put Castro away first, then I will get it."

"No, you don't need to get it now," Close interrupted. "He's just being pushy, Dale. It can wait until Castro is put away."

As Browne was putting the inmate in his cell, you could hear all three doors shutting at the same time. Browne turned around and, out of the corner of his eye, he could see inmates running around by the cage and headed to the back hallway.

"Oh, shit, guys, the inmates are out of the yard!" Browne said as he started back for the stairs. "Get all the officers together!"

Inmate Nelson, who wanted Browne to pick up the note before, said, "Stop, Mr. Browne! Get the note on the floor, it's important."

Browne picks up the note and reads it to himself. "The inmates in the yard are going to start a riot. Almost all the max inmates know about it. Please help us who will not take part in it." Browne threw the paper down while shaking his head, and started running down the stairs thinking, *What good did it do to write a note after it already started?*

"All five officers were trapped on the block," McPhail said to the cage officer over the block speakers. "Close the back hallway and call the command post. Tell them that the inmates in the yard are out running around the building and that we are trapped on C-block." At the same time that McPhail was talking to the officer in the cage, the cage officer was trying to shut the hallway door that was not going to shut because there was a cart in the way. The cage officer called the command post.

Captain Struble answered in a relaxed voice, "Command post, Struble."

That was all Captain Struble got out of his mouth with an interruption coming over the phone, saying, "It's going down, we need help!" The phone went dead.

Back on the block, one of the officers said, "Let's go out there and stop them! There is only about four marauding inmates that came from the yard."

Browne spoke out of turn, "No, we don't have any idea how many inmates are out. There were nine inmates left in the yard when we left. Who knows if there are more from the other side that got out. That is too many with us not having any protective gear and no weapons to defend ourselves. Right now, if all the inmates are out in the yard, then they have us outnumbered two to one. At this point, we are only isolated on C-block, we are not hostages yet. I don't know about you, guys, but staying alive is important to me." There was not another word said about leaving the block.

* * * * * * * * * * * * *

Struble was a seasoned captain, big burly man about 6 feet 3 inches tall, pushing 280 pounds. He has all his ducks in a row and was respected by the troops. As the phone went dead, Struble told the officers hanging around the command post to use other phones to call all different units to find out where the problem is coming from, how bad the problem is. As two officers went to call, Captain Struble got out the emergency handbook, ready to go down the list of things to do after he found out how bad the situation was. Struble called up all available officers over the base radio to come to the command post.

Back in the max unit, the east cage was being attacked by one inmate, seeing another inmate running to the yard door and picking up the five-pound bucket of sand. McCaughey was the officer in the east cage. He was pressing the control button to close the back hallway door while the other inmate kept pounding on the windows with a fire extinguisher that he grabbed off the wall by the cage. It sounded like the inside of a metal drum vibrating, loud banging noises on the glass.

McCaughey's finger was on the door switch with one hand. He was trying to call the command post with the other hand. The door was two feet from closing with an inmate running to the door. It was too late for him to get the bucket in the door so the inmate stopped. Lowering his head in dismay, the inmate envisioned that everyone was cut off from one another. Anxiety was lessening for the officer while the door kept shutting until he saw a mop handle stopping the door from shutting. The mop came from the back hallway. The motor above the door kept humming as the cage officer was still trying to shut it. McCaughey finally gave up on the door closing; the humming quit after he took his finger off the switch.

McCaughey's phone call got through and before the officer on the other end could say a word, McCaughey said, "We need help in max. They're starting to riot, help us!" Then he hung up the phone. The phone number that he called was not the command post. With McCaughey's heart pounding and stress building, he called the wrong number, calling the back guard station officer. The officer at the back gate did not think too much about it because officers would joke around, actually trying to get someone's goat. It kept the officers awake, playing practical jokes.

The window of the cage broke, making a loud crash, with glass from the inside and outside of the cage breaking. McCaughey jumped back towards the side of the cage, hitting the ladder to the escape hatch. He thought he saw the inmate coming through the window after him. He heard a loud horrifying voice coming from somewhere just behind him, laughing at him. He looked around but never saw anything except inmates still pounding on the windows. With his heart skipping some beats, he turned around and saw the padlock on one of the rungs to the ladder. Taking the lock and climbing the ladder, he opened the lid to the escape hatch. He got on top of the roof, taking the lock and locking the hatch shut. Being a fairly new officer, he did not know the window did not break. It was the plate-glass glazing that protects the polycarbonate security material (Lexan) from scratching that shattered.

The cage officer had no training on the windows or on anything that was to be done if there was an emergency. In emergencies, the officer was to stay in the cage until he thought that he would become a hostage. There was a gas mask in the cage and the Lexan windows would stay in place as long as there was no hot fire to melt the windows. If the time came to exit the cage, the officer was to take all the keys from the cage with him up the ladder. There were keys in all four electrical panels in the cage that will turn off the power to the panels, so that the panel would be out of commission and no doors would open. That was what the officer in the cage should have done with hindsight being

20/20. What would you do in this case? WHAT WOULD YOU DO?

* * * * * * * * * * * * *

Meanwhile, the west cage also came under attack. Inmate Close was disguising his voice, yelling out through the crack in the cell door, saying, "Get out of the cage before they get in!" Browne said, "Before you climb the ladder, open lower C-7. Close the door when all the officers are in the cell. Then stay as long as you think you are safe."

The cell door opened and closed behind them.

Just then, a glass window broke, sounding like a bomb went off behind him.

Pieces of glass flew at Officer Smith's back in the west cage. Turning around, he heard a loud voice laughing. He even saw a devil's head with horns coming at him. The cage officers had no training about the design features of max. He did not understand the construction of the control cages. Officer Smith did not know, in particular, that there was glazing on the inside and outside of the Lexan window.

Not thinking, he started climbing the ladder to the outside. Opening the hatch, he saw the padlock to lock the hatch after he was out. Grabbing at the lock, another window exploded, making the cage officer drop the lock to the floor. He was not going down to get it so he emerged, standing on the top of the hatch so it could not be opened. He did not know what to do next, let alone, know what happened or where he was. Seeing the other officer on the roof, they started waving their arms and yelling.

The officer in tower three saw two officers on the max roof. He broadcast over the radio load and clear, "Two officers on top of the max roof."

The two inmates who were barricading the west front sally-port were finished and took a moment to talk. "I'm not going up on top of the roof and having to kill two officers because he won't come back inside this building. I'm not going to get the death penalty for killing an officer. How about you?"

The other one spoke up, " No, I don't want to do that either."

"So, let's go over to the other side and barricade the other front sally-port," the first inmate spoke up, and off they ran through the building.

It was around 1015 hours. The officers who were trapped in lower C-7 started talking between themselves as two of the officers in the cell looked out the door window. It was loud on the block, hearing all the inmates yelling and carrying on.

They were trying to show their solidarity toward the rioters.

McPhail, sitting on the bed, said, "Well, guys, I think we are in trouble; there is no way out of this one."

Browne spoke up, "Well, be glad we are together, all of us, and we are safe for now."

"Safe for now?" Miller spoke up. "Look out the door at the cage. They are starting a fire in front of the cage door to melt the plastic windows."

"Oh, shit!" officer Boggs said out loud. "If they get in the cage and start opening up cell doors...."

"Ditto," came from most of the guards in the cell.

McPhail said, "Think of options we have in case this door opens."

Officer Miller made a statement, and was still being calm for the occasion. "I am going to take a piss in case I don't get the chance to later! So turn your heads if you don't want to see the monster! And you all should do the same!"

* * * * * * * * * * * *

1015 Hours

That was all Captain Struble needed to hear from the tower, "Two officers on top of the max roof." Struble needed to start emergency procedures. At the top of the list was calling the duty officer who was on call this weekend. The duty officer this weekend happened to be the warden of the prison, Jack McCormick.

Mr. McCormick lived in Butte and after getting the call, was on his way from home, driving about 45 miles from Butte to the prison in around twenty minutes with emergency lights flashing. Associate Warden of Treatment (AW) Mr. Michael Mahoney was next on the list to be called. He was the first one to arrive at the prison, coming from Deer Lodge ten minutes before the warden. Mahoney was around 5 feet 10 inches, 215 pounds, a hall-of-fame running back in football for the Carroll College Saints, out of Helena, Montana. Mr. Mahoney was a gentleman and a scholar. He could have excelled in anything he wanted to do, choosing corrections, which was fortunate for the state.

With the phone in Captain Struble's hand, he briefed available officers to head over to the maximum compound. Then he called the other three individuals in the duty officer chain of command, notifying each one of them of the severity of the problem at the time. Then he called the Disturbance Control Team (DCT) members. Captain Struble was somehow accomplishing three tasks at one time; talking on the phone, checking his emergency handbook, and lining out a sergeant who was taking other officers to max to find out some information.

During the next several minutes, security staff streamed into the max yard, gathering around the max building where the two cage officers were visible on the roof. The sergeant who was dubbed the person in control of the officers outside of max told the onlookers, "Don't go in unless you're sure you can handle it!" He was speaking metaphorically, like if the front door opened and having on the proper equipment, like guns, shields, night sticks, and mace. Or, if they could get on top of the building and go through the hatches, taking on the inmates after opening the cage.

The sergeant then ran back to the command post to relay the information. The officers were discussing their dilemma. One of the older, more experienced officers than anyone in the group said, "Hey, the guy doesn't know what he is talking about. We can't go into that building without any equipment or tear gas, and no weapons. All we will do is be taken hostage and make the problem worse.

"We have no one taking command of this situation. I am not going to have all your lives on my conscience." That day, there had to be an angel on that officer's shoulder because the arrogant inmates inside were waiting and ready for that to happen. The cage officers who were still on top of the roof, Smith and McCaughey, were yelling that the max inmates were rioting, that they were attacking the cages.

The officers who were on the ground had a new task on their mind, telling the officers on the roof, "We need to get you down from there. Do you see any way down from up there?"

McCaughey told him, "I don't see any way to get down except to hang from the top of the roof. Then I will let go and you grab for my waist before I hit the ground, to slow down my fall, hoping that I don't break my legs." McCaughey put his right leg over the foot-high ledge that surrounded the outside of the flat roof.

Then, bending his back and turning the front of his body facing to the inside of the roof, he put his left knee on top of the ledge, with his hands grabbing firmly to the ledge. Then, using only the muscles in his arms, he slowly lowered his body down to the full extent of his arms, with only his hands hanging on. "I will yell 'Ready!' when I let go, okay?" said McCaughey. Pausing for what seemed like a lifetime, he heard an "Okay, we got you!"

McCaughey's feet were about fifteen feet off the ground. His hands were getting tired of holding on. He whispered to himself, "Help me, God," and said out loud "Ookaay!" letting go his hands, keeping his eye open as he fell to the ground so he would know when to bend the legs as he hit the ground. The officer did exactly what he was told, taking some of the stress off McCaughey's body by slowing down his fall. When he landed on the ground, both officers fell backward safely.

McCaughey was all right, with just a little pain in his legs.

A voice from the ground said, "Come on, Smith, it is your turn!" So Smith looked around and saw that there was no other way down; he was not going to wait for a ladder.

One more time, Smith said, "I will say 'Okay' when I am ready. McCaughey, are you sure you are all right?"

"Yes, I am fine," said McCaughey.

Smith looked around and there was black pungent smoke coming out of the two escape hatches and yard. Smith yelled down to the people on the ground, telling them what was going on. Smith said, "Do you think I should stay up here and watch what is going on?"

A sergeant on the ground yelled to him, "No, get down here. If the inmates can get out of the yard, then they can get on top of the roof and throw you over."

There was no more hesitation from Officer Smith. He was crawling over the ledge, slowly lowered his body to the length of his arms. A second later, the officers on the ground heard him say, "Okay!" He hit the ground harder than his cohort, but out of his mouth came, "I'm okay, I made it." If it wasn't for the problems inside of the building, they all would have laughed.

★ ★ ★ ★ ★ ★ ★ ★ ★ ★ ★ ★

1015 Hours

The shift commander was Captain Struble; the wheels were turning in his mind. *What do I do? Do I recognize the information for what it is? That the trapped staff were temporarily safe. The officers are not yet hostages. Or do I think ahead that once the inmates' attempts to break into the control cages prove successful, they would then have control of the staff that I mustered in this morning. Also, the PC inmates are in danger. The marauding inmates have the ability to release all of the other maximum inmates plus death row inmates that are housed on B-block.*

Do I dare to rush a decision to put a large pirating force together to save the building, or do I put a large amount of chemical agent into the two control cages through the roof hatches or send officers with firearms in the front door of max or down into the cages that might prevent a complete inmate takeover of the building?

The shift commander was experienced and had been through other inmate disturbances in the past. *But shit, I can't do any of them because of the policy that only the duty officer or higher can approve firearms or tear gas inside the compound. The staff who are here do not have the experience, preparation, training, or equipment to take on this peril*, Struble was thinking to himselfz.

Just then, the maintenance supervisor came into the command post.

"Erv, did you want me to turn off the power to the max building?" Neilson said as he came in.

"Whoa, Carl, I am glad you are here! Can you do it?" asked Captain Struble.

"I will try the panel in the back room that is a security safe-guard, turning off the power to the east and west cages." Carl and Erv went to the back as Carl took out a key for the sophisticated electronics board. Carl put the key in the lock and turned it. Then he threw the power override switch for the west side of the max building cage console.

"Erv," Carl said, "I don't know if the power will come back on when I turn the key back to get it out, because I need the key to turn off the other side of max cage. We have not been trained on the panel. The only one that will know is the high-five in control of the prison."

Erv said, "Do you have another key over at the armory?"

Carl shook his head and said, "Yes; I will be right back."

It was no longer than five minutes, and Carl was back turning the second key on and turning the switch off, leaving the keys in the panel.

"Erv, that should do the job." Carl was smiling as he said it.

"I hope so," said Erv. Back to the command chair, Captain Struble went.

Around 1020 hours, the two cage officers told everyone on the ground that the four floor officers and the sergeant were locked inside the cell on lower C-7. They were all right when the cage officer left the building. Between ten and twenty-five officers were present at the max site. Randle Chase, Bobby Thatcher, and a few others officers went over to the other side of the building to locate the officers inside the cell. The window was too thick to talk back and forth unless you were yelling at the window; then all the inmates would be able to hear them.

They talked to them through the window with paper and pen that the inmates left in lower C-7.

Chase asked them if they were all right. The answer was, "For now. The inmates are burning the cage door, trying to melt the door window."

Chase said, "I will tell the command post and get back to you." Then they left.

The officers on the east side of the building where the PC block was were trying to talk to the inmates. Inmate Davison, with fear in his panicked, oversized eyes, was living on the PC block that was on the east side of the max building. He was yelling through the window in his cell, telling the officers that inmates were trying to break into the cage; that if they did break in, then the PCs would all be dead. Other staff also observed inmate Hornback in his cell, appearing bloody and beaten. Other staff officers were at the front door looking through the glass. But on the side of the door corridor where there are windows that could see down the east-side hall, they were watching inmates breaking into the counselor's office.

Also, the officers looking through the front-door window could see inmates beating on the control-cage windows with mop handles, fire extinguisher, and phone dolly. Plus, the officers at the front door windows could see both cages with fires in front of the doors but could not, for sure, know how many inmates were involved or who they were.

A call from the command post came over the radio, saying, "All staff around the max building return to the command post immediately."

Arriving at the prison was Associate Warden Mahoney. He did not assume command of the institution, but worked in parallel with Captain Struble. He concentrated on events inside max, leaving, for the meantime, Captain Struble concentrating on taking care of the rest of the prison. Erwin Struble asked AW Mahoney if the security safeguard panel was working, if it was turned off the right way.

Mr. Mahoney said, "Erv, I am sorry to say that the controls have been shut off since February 4 of this year. Two logic boards in the fire alarm system failed.

"Maintenance staff were unable to get the contract service firm to fix the electronics. There has been some history of bad feeling between them and us. The contractor out of the Ohio firm was called many times, but would not return our calls. In May, our maintenance staff asked the warden for assistance, and he wrote a forceful and firm letter to the manufacturer and the contractor. We were having more problems in Close Unit III at that time, so maintenance took the two circuit boards out of max and put it in III. No response was forthcoming from the contractor, so here we are."

Two days after the riot, the contractor came from Ohio and fixed the electronics panel. (I can only assume that the firm was included in a lawsuit.)

As a result, the maximum security building was without a fire alarm system and the auxiliary features, part of the logistics board, was also disabled. These included the smoke evacuation system and the command post power override switches for the control consoles, as well as three external doors at the maximum building, plus an auto print system which allowed the shift commander to monitor and receive a hard copy of the status of all those systems and alarms. If, in fact, there had been a serious fire at max instead of a riot, there is a high likelihood that many more lives would have been lost than what will be lost today.

* * * * * * * * * * * * *

After going down the line of people to call, Captain Struble ordered for two perimeter vehicles; also, two officers in each tower, which would open up tower 2 that, at the time, was not being manned.

Mahoney encouraged two staff members to take an AR-15 rifle and a .357 revolver to the lower C cell of max and break out the window in lower C-7 where the staff members were trapped. Then two officers were instructed to cover the hostages with the weapons from outside.

The officers broke out the window in lower C-7, but the cell was empty. The inmates in cell lower C-6 were banging on the window to get the panic-stricken officers' attention. They were yelling to the staff outside but could not make themselves heard. They wrote a note to the officers, saying that the staff members were in the lower C-block shower room, which has no external window. The staff officers asked them why there are three inmates in the same cell. They wrote that all the doors were open to all the cells and blocks!

The officers yelled from the outside, "Are the officers all right?"

Up to the window came a note saying, "We don't know be-cause we are staying in this cell to protect ourselves."

Two other officers had been sent on a reconnaissance mission to enter the basement underneath the max building after re-trieving the keys from the main control room. With a fast walk, the officers went around to the back of the max building where there was a metal grating built into the ground, with cement poured around the grate. Standing over the grate was an intake air flow making loud noise coming from the basement. It was the sound of the furnaces and air going in. To the left of the grate were the back door and the trailer known as the "death trailer." The trailer was a small mobile home about 12×60 feet, old, made about in the '70s, then refurbished; made into three rooms with a table in the middle room. The executee was watched behind a window, the three executioners with a plunger in their hands, ready to squeeze the plunger and, metaphorically speaking, relieve the state of one dilemma. On the other side of the inmate, through another window, were the witnesses and ac-cusers of the accused. The trailer was going to be used to execute inmates who were on Montana's death row block, presently held on B block. The death sentence was reinstated in Montana when the legislators pleaded for a change in 1987. From 1949 to 1991 there has not been anyone executed by the hands of the State.

One of the two officers opened the basement door and went down the stairs.

There was no need to be quiet; there were no inmates who could hear them down in the basement with the humming coming from the furnace. Most of the sounds came from inside the building on the east side, so the officers went over that way first. Maneuvering around pipes, heat ducts, and air vents, they made their way to the heart of the ear _____ through standing water dripping from the cracks in the seams of the floor. Under the blocks of D, E, and F, there were eerie sounds—yelling, screaming, pleading, hollering cries that will haunt those two men for the rest of their lives. Acrid smoke was coming out through the ventilation return ducts; the smoke made the officers gag. The officers put their shirts up high enough to cover the mouth and nose. After hearing all that could be tolerated, they went to the other side of the building. On the west side of the building, there was still water accumulating on the floor and smoke just as bad as the other side, but there were no voices that made the hair stand up on the back of their necks. As a matter of fact, there were no sounds coming from the west side. That was long enough for the assessment. The officers went back out to the fresh air and sunlight, and away from purgatory. The two officers ran back to the command post to report all information to the shift commander.

Warden McCormick arrived at approximately 1040 hours. He went straight to the command post. Mr. McCormick was a wise, intelligent, middle-aged man about 6 feet 2 inches tall, 185 pounds. He was admired and respected by all who were around him. He was known as "Smiling Jack." He had no problem with having people follow him through his endeavors. As he entered the command post, he waited on, asking questions of Captain Struble and Associate Warden of Treatment, Mahoney, until the time that he could be briefed on who, what, when, where, why, and how things came to be. After an intense briefing, the warden assumed command clearly and decisively.

Mr. McCormick asked, "Erv, have there been any problem coming from the low-side and or high-side units?"

Erv said, "There hasn't been any problem coming from the rest of the units as of this time that was reported."

McCormick said, "Blow the siren and get as much help here as we can. Call the sheriff's office in Deer Lodge, let the sheriff know what is going on and we need help. Put a road block at ranch 1. Get hold of the Highway Patrol Office in Helena, and have as many of them park around the outside of the perimeter fence as possible. Have someone call all staff in to help. Have someone keep calling the max phone numbers to try to contact the inmates and try to keep the inmates from getting too excited. Ask them what their demands are at the time."

Captain Struble spoke up, "Sergeant Dan Jones will make a good hostage negotiator until one gets here from Helena." Dan Jones was standing outside the door at the time; Struble motioned him into the room.

McCormick said, "Dan, go into the parole board room, get on the phone to the cage numbers in max. Try to talk to the inmates, ask them what their demands are. Keep trying until you get them."

Struble delegated sergeants and officers to the high side as the warden flipped the switch to the siren. It was between 1045 and 1100 hours when the siren bellowed out. The siren in the past has been sounded for short intervals to let the surrounding area/town know there was a problem. Also for all employees to call and find out what was going on and to come in if needed. Usually, the siren would sound out for a test once a month for a short interval, but today, the siren was constant for approximately forty-five minutes.

The officers left the secured area, headed for the high side. After going through the high-side gate and around the corner by the high support building, ten officers and a sergeant could see the entire high-side compound from the kitchen to the south. In front of them were Close I and Close II. The high-side recreation yard was to the northeast on the left side of Close II. Close Unit III was down the sidewalk and to the left of the recreation yard. Inmates were going to the kitchen from Close III. Inmates were also coming back from the kitchen to Close II for lunch. There were 100 or so inmates in the recreation yard.

As the siren bellowed through the Deer Lodge valley, it was hard to hear anyone who was standing beside the officers. So the officers went in a group, cutting across the grass to intercept the inmates on the sidewalk that led between the three units, stopping all the inmates going to chow and moving faster the inmates who were returning from chow.

The inmates were asking questions of the officers, "What is all that smoke coming from the max building? We told you there was going to be a riot but you didn't believe us."

"Move along! Go back to your units and lock down. This is a drill," one officer said.

"Drill, my ass. We haven't eaten lunch yet, when are we going to eat?" said another con.

"This is just a drill. We will feed you as soon as the siren is turned off like before." The same officer was yelling at them so they could hear over the siren.

The inmates started back to their units.

The officers still had the high-side yard to clear out. On the way back to Close Unit III, the inmates stopped and started talking to the inmates in the recreation yard. The officers sensed there was going to be a problem with inmates in the yard as the officers slowly walked together as a unit over toward them.

The officers, not showing any aggression toward the inmates, said, "Move along back to your unit. The yard is canceled." The inmates did not move, so the officers stopped.

The sergeant spoke to the group of officers, "Stay here while Jeff and I talk to the inmates alone."

"Do you think that is a good idea?" asked one of the guards.

"No, but I think if I talk to a couple of the older cons, they will lock down," said the sergeant. So the two of them walked over closer, then stopped. The sergeant yelled out, "Pet and Randy, come over here for a minute," as he waved his arm in a gesture to have them come toward them. The inmates grouped up as they started talking among themselves. A little time later, inmates Pet and Randy came to talk.

"What is going on, Sarge?" said Pet.

"The siren is going off so you know that we are doing a drill. So everyone, back to their unit," said the sergeant.

"Don't bullshit us. We know that max is rioting. You know that we are to help them start a riot over here to be united," said Randy.

"Yes, you are right." Speaking truthfully, the sergeant kept talking. "You see the smoke coming from the roof of max? Look behind you. There are highway patrol cars getting into position around the perimeter fence. What will it gain you if you riot also? Max inmates will bargain for you even if you don't riot.

"If you are grieving that we are not treating you right and the officers in the max cages are saying that things are slowing down already, you will be out here just causing trouble," said the sergeant.

Randy said, "Your two cage officers went out the top cage hatches; we saw them."

Sergeant explained, "No, that was two other officers checking out the inmates in the max yard from the roof."

Pet said, "We could take you officers hostage if…."

He was interrupted by the sergeant, "You could, that is for sure, with all of you out here, but you know what that means. I don't need to explain it to you, do I?"

"We will go back to talk to the rest of the group. You will find out what our decision will be soon enough," said the two the two cons and they walked back to the mob.

As the two officers walked back to their group, the sergeant got his radio out and called, "Command post, this is high-side sergeant."

Two seconds later, a response came over the radio, "Go ahead, high-side sergeant."

Get your weapons ready to storm the high-side recreation yard, but don't show the guns unless I call you back."

"Ten, four, high-side sergeant," came a voice over the radio.

Then the sergeant told the officers to stay still unless the inmates started coming for them; it was only five minutes later, but it seemed like over an hour.

The inmates went from their group and started back to all three units. Officers started backing up away from the sidewalk, giving the sidewalk to the inmates so they could go back to their units. All the high-side inmates went back to their units with some smart-ass comments as the inmates walked by, but the officers did not say anything back. And that dilemma was over. The officers were grateful, and started back to the command post.

* * * * * * * * * * * *

1015 Hours

The fires were started on the outside of both cage doors. They piled coats, orange jump suits, towels, and anything that would burn halfway up the door.

Things were going as planned for the inmates. Dark black smoke was going through the max building and in the cages, out the top through the hatches.

Then came the sprinkler heads turning on with a constant spraying of water. The water concentrated around areas where the detectors identified the smoke. On came the water in front of the cage doors. At first, the fire was so large the inmates did not think the water could put the fire out. The inmate lieutenant was on the east side, helping out at the cage.

On the east side of the building, the officer went out the top hatch, leaving the cage unattended. The glass windows were all broken around the hexagonal cage, but the Lexan on the inside of the glass windows was still intact. This tired out the inmates for a short time, banging on the windows. The fire was going good for the first ten minutes, starting to melt the Lexan in the door, but the water sprinklers were starting to put out the fire.

The lieutenant of the inmates said, "We need one brother to climb the side of the cage wall and look through the false ceiling to see if there was any room between the metal pipes and heat vents to squeeze between them and get inside of the cage.

The inmate who volunteered was helped up to the three-foot window ledge. That made him tall enough to grab the ceiling tiles that were already getting soaked from the sprinklers. He ripped pieces of tile down then pulled himself up into the ceiling, crawling slowly from one brace to another brace and/or pipe that was running vertical to the ceiling. He had a good look around the outside of the cage. Minutes later, he came back to the opening in the ceiling. Before coming down from the ceiling, he reported to the lieutenant that there was no way in from the ceiling. Exiting down was a lot easier than going up; he just brought his body through the opening with his hands holding onto the metal ceiling brackets, then lowering his body slowly down until he was hanging with his hands overhead stretched out. His feet were about two feet off the floor, so he just let go. He landed on the floor while bending his knees some to take the shock out of the drop.

One marauder yelled, "The water is putting the fire out! What are we going to do?"

The lieutenant spoke up, "Get a mattress from the laundry room; no, get two mattresses, and hurry!"

The inmates at the east cage did not know what was going on with the west cage, but figured that it had to be in the same predicament. The sprinkler was like a challenge to see which side would get into their cage first. The officers were already out of the cages and on top of the roof. The lieutenant was wondering why the two brothers did not bring the cage officers to him. He noticed that the brother never came on this side, so maybe they were still in the process of getting the officers. If they do not have an excuse for getting the officers, then he would deal with them later.

The fire went out, and the entire pile of clothes was soaking wet. But that was not a problem. The mattresses were there already waiting and were kept out of the water until needed.

The lieutenant spoke up, "We need more dry material to burn. You guys get some more clothes from the laundry room on this side, anything that is dry and will burn." There was no problem starting a fire because all inmates had matches and cigarettes

The inmate lieutenant said, "Go get the gurney from the other electrical door, and make it fast." One minute later came the gurney,

The marauders piled more clothes in front of the door and put a mattress over the door, blocking the water sprinkler. Starting the clothes afire one more time, the fire started picking up but was not getting hot yet; the moisture in the air was keeping the fire down. Smoke was so bad that the inmates around the cage had to cover their mouths and noses with their bandanas, taking them from their heads.

The fire went out one more time, and most of the marauders was about to give up, pulling the mattress away from the door.

The lieutenant commanded, "Go get the K-cylinder from the infirmary, fast! And you run fast to the sergeant's office and get the two-pound coffee creamer!"

A response came from an inmate, asking, "What is a K-cylinder and what are you going to do with the coffee creamer?"

The lieutenant said, "Stupid, the K-cylinder is the oxygen bottle, and you don't need to know what the creamer is for. Now, run!"

Minutes later, the inmate came back with the bottle, and another marauder was right behind him with the powdered creamer. The lieutenant put the bottle on the stretcher. He could see that the K-cylinder was too low for the cylinder to be across from the window of the door. Taking a mattress and putting it under the K- cylinder, he leveled it at the right vertex for the Lexan window. It was placed in front of the door, and water was running off the top of the gurney.

The lieutenant gave more orders, saying, "You two take a mattress and block the sprinkler water from the K-cylinder."

The lieutenant pointed to another inmate brother and said, "You open the lever to the bottle about a quarter way open, and start the gas with a Bic lighter."

The inmate stuttered a little when he said, "Wh…wh…why don't you want to start the fire?"

The lieutenant said, "Because I told you to, that's why."

The inmate did what he was told to do because he had no choice. The rest of the inmates backed away as the bottle was opened. The Bic lighter was flicked to ignite the flame that went to the front of the bottle. All the marauders, including the one who was putting the flame to the cylinder, turned their bodies away from the unexploded cylinder. Some of the inmates went around the cage for shelter. They all closed their eyes and held their breath for the unknown. The guinea-pig inmate was relieved when the bottle did not blow up, and a blue flame came on.

The creamer was thrown on the plastic window that was on the cage door.

Creamer stuck to the bulletproof window. The lieutenant's plan was working; the Lexan was melting away from the door.

"Wait a little while longer, then I will take a mop handle and try to poke a hole in the glass," said the lieutenant. The Bic lighter was getting hot for the marauder to hold onto. The flame was going, so he took the light away from the K-cylinder.

The flame went out, and the lieutenant slapped the kid on the head, saying, "Why did you stop with the lighter? It was burning a hole in the window!"

"The lighter was getting hot on my fingers, and I thought that it would stay lit if the flame was going," answered the confused inmate.

"Oxygen needs another agent to light it; it won't stay lit by itself. Get a glove," said the lieutenant.

Another inmate standing there watching had a glove. He was as surprised because it was all new to him also. He handed him the glove and stepped back and watched. The flame was started again and more creamer was put on the fire constantly, keeping the window hot with flakes of creamer. As the creamer was administered, tiny sparks would fly from the window into the air.

So the lieutenant was handed the stick, and then said, "Someone come here and keep putting the creamer on the fire while I make a hole in the glass." The lieutenant took the stick and pressed against the glass; the stick went through. He pulled the stick out some, and started turning the stick in a round motion. The stick started on fire but that was not a problem. He kept turning the stick until the stick was getting short from burning away.

About five minutes went by, and it was 1030 hours. With stammering onlookers, the lieutenant asked for another wooden mop handle on the floor beside them. He took the wooden mop handle and stuck it through the Lexan, holding the metal end under his arm into his arm pit for leverage, and moving the handle around the hole as the hole was getting bigger and bigger. However, the wooden handle caught fire from heat of the plastic, and he had to ask for another mop handle to finish the job.

The proud voice of the lieutenant said, "This one should do it. The hole in the door is about a 6-inch by 6-inch; that should be big enough to open some block cells so they can get out and help us have fun. Okay, guys, take the mattress and the gurney away," said the lieutenant.

The polycarbonate Plexiglas was on fire, but the flame went out the minute the water hit the window. That cooled the temperature of the blackened door of the cage. Then an inmate went over to the door with a stick. The inmate tried to open the cell doors from the outside of the control door with a mop handle. It was like a compelling board game; having to put the end of the stick on the rocker switch, getting the right angle to push down on the left side of the switch. A couple of doors came open, but it was slow. Then they tried putting the mop handle on the left side of the switch that was on one of the three control panels. Then he would lift the mop handle up against the Lexan glass, making the stick push down on the button switch.

Another inmate tried to put the stick through the hole in the door with his arm through the hole, trying to open doors off F-block. The F-block panel was to the left of the door. The stick was put on a rocker switch, opening one of the cells on the block.

The lieutenant watched them trying to open doors, and he was silently laughing.

He only let them amuse him for a short while, about ten minutes, before the lieutenant chose the cage door to start a fire under, to burn a hole through the Lexan. He looked in the cage from a side window and saw the key was left in the door. Because if the key was not in the door, then he would have to burn a window on the side of the door, big enough to crawl through. The lieutenant was growing tired of the young marauders.

* * * * * * * * * * * *

1033 Hours

On the east end, doors were opening and closing. Inmate Ron Nida was a PC on D block, upper D-1. He was sleeping late from watching television the night before. Nida's door opened, and that instantly woke him up. The door was still opening and shutting as he was getting up. Chip Davison was calling him through the vent in lower D-1.

The cells in max and also the Close Unit III building had a fresh air vent over the toilet. Each vent was shared by the cell next to it and the two cells below. This was how inmates communicate, by talking in the vent; it was known as the telephone.

Davison said, "Get up and look out the door, Ron! We're going to be killed if that sally-port door opens.

Ron asked Davison, "Where are the guards?"

Davison spoke up, "The riot must be happening, like McFarlane said was going to happen. The guards must be dead or taken hostage. I don't see the officer in the cage, but the smoke is so bad the water is spraying down from the ceiling. The officer could be in there, but I can't see him."

Ron said, "My door is opening and shutting, so I will go out and get something to protect us, like mop handles. I will shove one under everyone's door."

Nida's door opened again. He stepped out onto the tier and ran down the stairs to talk to Davison again. Then Nida went up to the cell where the swampers' supplies were, and started breaking mop handles. Then he went to each cell door where a fellow PC was living, and the door did not open. He shoved a handle to the PC inside. Next, Nida and some of the protective custody inmates out of their cells started stacking shelving in front of the stairs to the sally-port door, as a barricade.

* * * * * * * * * * * *

1040 Hours

"Out of the way, guys," said the lieutenant of the inmates.

As he got closer to the cage door, two inmates moved away from the door. The lieutenant reached through the melted plastic window with his left hand to the right of the door handle. Feeling around, he finally felt the key in the door. It was almost out of reach for his arm, but he put his arm all the way in up to his shoulder.

His body was facing the same way as his arm, to the front of the door. The lieutenant turned the key clockwise a quarter of a turn until the key would not go any further. The door did nothing; it did not open. There was no click or anything to give him any notion to push on the door to open it.

The lieutenant. was thinking to himself, *Shit, did they lock the outside lock on the door when one of the brothers wasn't watching? The last time coffee was brought to the cage from the Rat swampers, they left the dead bolt unlocked.*

All that the lieutenant heard was the water coming out of the sprinkler head.

If that was not going on, then you would have heard a pin drop on the floor because all the marauding inmates were watching without a sound. The inmate lieutenant turned the key, this time counter clockwise, which did not make sense to him. But this time, the key turned hard but it was still turning. He heard a click from the lock, synchronizing the key to the lock. It worked for the lieutenant. He pushed with his body inward to open the door. It opened with all onlookers cheering, knowing that the cage has been molested. All the cells were being opened on all three blocks—D, E, and F on the east side of the building. Inside the east cage were all sorts of things the inmates could use, like a bent bar that was made to be a wrench to open doors manually in case the power went out; a gas mask, and three wooden sticks with a leather strap on the end. The sticks had a strap to wrap around the wrist to hold onto, called a nightstick, for guards to quell disturbances. Plus two spray canisters that were not much good to the marauders. Also in the cage were belly chains and leg irons. The belly chains were made to fit around an inmate's waist. The chain had a lock to cinch it up tight to anyone's waistline. The leg irons are bigger handcuffs with a smaller chain attached to a built-in swivel. When the iron is around the ankle, it allows a person to have a half-walking stride. Those chains were a planned takeover item and a necessary gold mine.

One belly chain was used in the cage to secure the escape hatch from opening.

That was accomplished by putting the cuff around the ladder rung, double wrapping the belly chain around the lid hatch handle, then back through the cuffs to make it tight. Then the lock was locked around the stair rung to complete the task. Now the escape hatch was secured on the east side.

Next was the yard door to secure. It was anchored shut in the same manner by taking the belly chain, placing two cuffs around the stout round brass door handle, then the belly chain was stretched to the bars in the window. Last, the lock was locked around the bars and secured. This anchored the door some, but it still needed to be locked with a Folger Adams key. The Folger Adams key was always left in the cage so that the guards could get to the yard fast if needed be. The key was already at the door because most of the inmates knew which key it was and where the guard hung the key on the wall of the cage. The yard key locked the door to the yard, and now it was secured.

The inmates watched time after time where and which key fit the yard door, so it was not a surprise that it took no time to secure the door. The back door was next. It also was secured in the same manner as the yard door. Putting the cuffs round the brass handle and chaining the door shut by stretching the chain to the bars where the electric door window that seals off the back hall from the east side. The lock was locked around the bars and secured to the back door. Because the back door was already locked shut and the door swings out, there would be no way to open the back door from the outside. This was one of the only plans that the marauders had that the administration would not think of when or if they tried to take back the max building.

Kenny Allen was looking at the keys left behind in the cage when the cage officer went up through the roof. Looking at the keys for the doors, it came to him that maybe these keys will open the door to the west side cage. Without saying a word, he started running to the west cage, yelling "I got the keys, I got the keys!" all the way down the back hallway and over to the west cage.

* * * * * * * * * * * *

1035 Hours

The inmate lieutenant opened the door to the east cage with only the turn of his hand to the left. The door was pregnable only at this time because the outside deadbolt lock was not locked, so the officers could get into an exit with ease.

Inmate Kenny Allen was telling everyone that would listen, "All the keys are here with night sticks and mace canister. There is a gas mask, and the keys are left in the control panels."

Someone else started opening all the cells on D, E, and F blocks. Allen thought for a minute and said, "Hey, guys, these two keys might open up the cage on the west side," as he smiled with anxiety setting in. Allen ran from the east cage through the back hallway to the west cage, yelling, "I got the keys, I got the keys...." Allen, with others, brought both keys over to the west cage. One key was the deadbolt key for the outside of the cage door. It was a big and brass Folger Adams key. The other was a smaller key about three inches long. That was the key the lieutenant used to unlock the door from the hole in the door on the other side.

Allen said, "I will try the smaller key first to see if they bolted the deadbolt," talking out loud. "If we don't get in, then I will try the big key."

It turned out to be a smart move by Allen because it would have taken more time to figure the keys out. The door came open with the first try of the smaller key, which says that the deadbolt was not locked. Inside the cage was like giving candy to a baby. There were handcuffs, belly chains, leg irons, all the keys to every door in the max building except for office doors. The keys in the cage were mostly Folger Adams keys. There were cuff keys that opened any cuff, belly chains or leg irons. The keys were still in the electrical panels, ready to open up the cells on the detention A-block; B-block was housing the death row inmates and C-Block was where the officers were trapped. The keys to open up the outside of max doors were in the cage, but they were not so precious, because the marauders were not looking to escape the building. The marauders were out to kill as many PCs as they could, plus kill other inmates who were hiding out in max for the same reason that the PCs were housed in max. But the inmates who were hiding out on regular population of max did not want the same status given to them as the PCs. All the cells started opening one by one, freeing the whole population in the max building, even the PCs on D-block.

Again, on the west side of the building, the marauders went by their plan and secured all outside doors and hatches. First, the escape hatch was chained and secured, then the yard door was chained and secured in the same manner as the east side yard door. All block doors were opened and the main sally-port door was open on both sides. The front door was secured in the same manner as the yard doors. Now, the marauders were safe inside a fortress of steel and concrete; nothing getting in and/or just as important, no one getting out. There was one inmate still in the yard, locked out of all the trouble—old man inmate Ray.

* * * * * * * * * * * *

1035 Hours

It was quiet for a change, no beating on the west cage, no pounding on the infirmary door. Quietness is an eerie sound for a takeover of a building. Inmate Powell got off the washer, stepping in an inch of water. In the dark laundry room, he went to the door, looking out the window. The smoke from the cage area was dissipating; he could actually see the cage now. Inmate Powell backed off from the window, detecting with his peripheral vision that someone was coming from the back hallway. It was inmate Cox walking by, carrying a mop ringer in his hands, headed for the cage. Cox took the seven-pound ringer bucket by the handle and swung it at the cage window, holding onto it. Inmate Powell sat back down in the dark because there were more marauders close by.

The voices stopped at the laundry door, and one said, "Who is in there?" with someone else saying, "The swampers."

Someone else said, "Well, let's kill them," a fourth voice said, "We have already tried getting to them. Be careful; they have bleach and they know how to use it."

They forced entry on the door, but that lasted about fifteen to thirty seconds because there was no play in the door. It was not going to open even if the nine inmates pushed against it.

The talking started up again with one inmate saying, "I heard we can't get through the door. Don't the rest of the rats live on D-block?"

Another inmate said, "Yeah," with a happy sound to his voice.

Someone else said, "Well, let's go get them!" That was the last of them for now.

The pounding and the sound of glass breaking was still going on at the west cage. The laundry room was a two-person fortress that was impenetrable. It would not allow anyone to enter, but on the same hand, it was a death trap.

It was hard to tell how much time elapsed inside of that dark hole. But then the two of them in the laundry room heard it plain and clear as a marauder went by, saying over and over again, "I got the keys, I got the keys, I got the keys."

The PCs in the laundry room knew it would be calamitous for all the inmates in max and for the five officers who were detained on C-block.

"What keys do you think they have, Chuck?" Powell asked.

With a low voice, McFarlane said, "It could be only three choices; keys that I don't know about in the counselor's office. Those keys won't do them any good if there are some. The keys that the sergeant has on his ring, which I don't think they got to the officers yet; or the last choice which I am afraid is the right one. They have the keys from the other side; the cage keys, which I don't think the prison would be so dumb as to have the same keys to fit both cage doors."

＊＊＊＊＊＊＊＊＊＊＊＊

1035 Hours

The cell doors started opening all at once. Officer Miller looked out the door and saw an inmate opening the cells from inside the cage. Two inches of water covered the floor in the cells after the door was opened. Earlier, the officers blocked the water from coming in with a towel and clothes the inmate had in his room before he went to the yard.

"What are we going to do now?" all the officers said simultaneously.

Browne was the only one who had an answer, "Get that heavy cotton mattress on the bed and bring it with us. Our only hope is to lock ourselves in the shower stall because, if you look at the inmates around the cage, they are ready to take us on. They have weapons and there are more of them than us. Before we get in the shower, get the mattress wet and we will put it against the bars on the inside of the grill gate. Lock the padlock to the inside so they cannot break the padlock. Let's go."

There was no arguing or discussing Browne's plan because there was no other plan. They were at the full mercy of the marauders in the open. They did not want to leave the block because it was for sure that they would have been killed for trying to escape. The shower was to the left from lower C-7, at the other end of the block. There are two showers on C-Block, one on each level facing to the right if you were looking from the control cage. The officers chose the lower shower because it was the closest and because they would have to bypass inmates coming out of their cells and down the stairs from the upper shower. That was the last time they had a choice on anything that day. On the way to the shower, the officers made it there with no delays or interference coming from the inmates trying to stop them. But there were plenty of eyes burning through them, watching every move they made. Inside the 3-foot by 5-foot shower, five large officers stood with the mattress between the bars and bodies. Without asking, each officer figured out why Browne wanted the mattress soaked in water. It was in case the inmates tried to burn them out. But what Browne didn't let them know was when the mattress was wet, the cotton would clump together; it would be harder to penetrate the mattress. But as Browne and the rest of the officers knew, it would be only a matter of time that they would be out of the inmates' grasp. The time span on how bad the inmates wanted to get to the officers would determine the durability of the officers' small shelter.

As they were caged in the shower, Browne started to think out loud, "You know, guys, this was a better idea than we thought." He was not taking any of the credit because the credit could be short-lived.

Browne said, "With us not being able to see what is going on out there, we are not a threat to them and they know where we are at all times. They will try to negotiate with the governor because I'm sure this will get to Governor Stephens.

We do not know how long we will be in here because when riots happen, it usually takes three days or better to negotiate. Oh, if they start poking sticks at us to try and stab us, try to grab the stick before they pull it back. Pull the stick out of their hands; that will give us some more time before we will have to give up."

"Give up?" said McPhail, "I don't think we should give up no matter what."

Browne stated, "No, we don't give up until the last possible time that one of us gets hurt. Then we will have to give up."

Browne kept talking. "If the inmates start a fire outside of the shower to smoke us out, then I think we should start the shower and keep it on. That will take the smoke away from the shower and smoke up the block. If they break out the hollow cement block that the latch is in, then we will have to give up because there is nothing we can do. But I don't think they will think of that, I hope and pray."

The officers were more stunned than scared inside the shower. To this point, they have not been harmed or threatened. The inmates on C-block came out of their cells running to get out of their so-called dungeon. Running for what and where and why, only to prove that they are the barbaric and ignorant people that society proclaimed them to be.

Bobby Close was leading the pack down the stairs and through C-block to the block door. As he got to the door, he stopped, moved to the side and let the other inmates race by him. Close looked around, seeing the officers going to the lower shower stall. He locked the grill gate behind them. Paul Allen was coming down the stairs, but Close stopped him.

Close said, "Paul, you stay here and watch the officers in the shower room. Get two more inmates that you can trust and make sure the officers don't leave the shower."

Inmate Paul Allen interrupted Close, being young and ignorant, "But Bobby, I wanted to go and help take out my hate for the last year I have been in here."

Close started talking, "Kenny didn't want you involved because you only have a short time left in prison. Your mother would be upset with Kenny if you were involved, so do your job by watching the officers in the shower. If they try to leave, have one of the other brothers threaten them with clubs, but don't you do any of the talking or threatening. Do you understand me?"

Like a shy kid and with his head down, Paul Allen said, "Yes."

"Plus, Paul, take a blanket from a room and hang it over the shower door so they can't see out," said Close.

Paul Allen went down the cement stairs and talked with two other inmates who were hanging around the block. "Hey, you guys," he said, "help me watch the officers, and we can threaten them if they start trying to come out of the shower. I will get a blanket and put it over the shower door so they can't see out." The three went over to the shower with a cotton blanket and draped it over the shower door frame.

One of the two inmates started mouthing off, "Stay in that shower or we will beat those cop uniforms off you!"

"Stay cool, we don't what any problems and we are not going out of this shower," said one of the hostages.

Close looked up the stairs where he lived, and saw inmate Nelson looking out the open door next to him. Remembering that Nelson was trying to tell the cops about their plan to cause havoc in the max building, Close yelled out to inmate Spray and some others, "Spray and you guys stay upstairs. We need to take care of some business."

Close ran back up the stairs and talked to the group. "Nelson was going to tell about our plans, so let's beat him up so he won't do any talking." Off they went to Nelson's cell, where a small skinny kid was trapped in his cell. The mob started beating on him. Close stayed back, watching the rest of them kick and punch Nelson until he was down on the cement floor. He was curled up in a ball, trying to protect his head and body from the blows. Blood started coming from his head and face, then all he felt was pressure on his hand that was on the side of his head. At last, his head got fuzzy and he passed out.

The mob stopped and saw blood from Nelson's head after one of them jumped on him. One of the brothers said, "Let's go and see what's going on on the other side of the building."

So they all left as Close stayed there for a minute. Even though Nelson couldn't hear him, Bobby Close said, "That will teach you to come to max and snitch us off!"

* * * * * * * * * * * *

1030 Hours

Bobby Close ran down the stairs off C-block. He turned to look where the officers were and if there were still brothers watching them. Everything was okay on the block except the water was still coming from the sprinkler heads. It was getting humid on the block with smoke from the fires that were set by the control cages. Close's heart was beating fast at this time; excitement was building inside of him.

In came one of the brothers who met Close on the stairs, and they were discussing something that could not be heard by anyone around them conspicuously, the officers in the shower. Charlie Miller was looking out from behind the mattress standing on the inside of the bars and the blanket.

Wild and Cox came over to the shower the officers were in and said, "Give us the keys to the building or we will burn you out of there and cut one of your heads off to give to Warden McCormick!"

Sergeant McPhail said, "I can't give you my keys, I will get in trouble."

Inmate Close instigated a conflict by coming up behind the two brothers, and said, "Those officers haven't done anything to us so you will not harm them."

"Are you telling us what to do?" Cox demanded to know.

Close retorted, "I'm just saying that those officers are just doing their job, so don't cause a beef with them."

Officer Browne spoke up and said, "Pete, give them the keys. We are already in trouble. Take off the key to the shower lock and give them the rest of them."

Sergeant Pete McPhail handed the keys to the front of the shower. Browne handed the keys to inmate Wild. That stopped the inmates from getting into a fight between Close and the two inmates, Wild and Cox.

Wild said, "I'll bring back the keys after we're done with them."

About fifteen minutes went by, Wild was back to the officers with the keys and said, "Here are your keys back." The only key missing was the cuff key that was on the sergeant's ring.

Inmate Close ran out of the sally-port doors past the control cage, looking around and down the back hallway to the east control cage where the rest of the brothers convened. They were feeling freer than they had been for years. Close was getting debriefed by the lieutenant as he was looking onto D-block where the PC inmates were looking back at them, with mop handles and other weapons by the sally-port door that was still closed. The sally-port door was blocked with debris from the PC's block to slow them down and make it an advantage for the PCs.

1040 Hours

The cells that protected each inmate from one another started opening up. The D-block doors were opened and the PCs looked out their door and wondered what to do next. Vern Baker yelled out over the sound of the commotion outside the block, "Let's get together and fight these guys off. Come on, guys, there is plenty of mop handles and other weapons we can defend ourselves with." Vern Baker was a stout man doing time on the PCs' block. He was an even-tempered person who would normally be lifting weights in the gym, staying away from trouble. But he got in debt playing cards and losing a lot of money. He tried to pay it back, but that just got him into more debt, having the debtors coming after his hide and wanting to keep a piece of it. The PCs would go to the high-side gym to work out five days a week early in the mornings. But after enough threats from the high- side yard workers, most or all of the PCs would not go to the gym.

Seven out of the eight inmates on D-block were getting ready for a battle, so it seemed. They picked up mops, mop ringers, put on extra clothes to take a blow and went to the block windows that faced the cage. At a standstill, the PCs were acting confident, yelling and banging on the windows. They knew that only part of them could get through the sally-port at one time, making a battle which would have been even odds or even a slight advantage for the PCs. So the marauders waited until more inmates would be coming from the other side of the building, and a better plan.

Inmate Watson was the only Black inmate in the max building. In a so-called white prison, being black was a problem with the white supremacists, the Aryan Brotherhood. Because if he did not fit in with the marauders, then he was as good as dead. Watson, a muscle-bound inmate who was bigger than any white guy in max, at that time was a problem for the white supremacists. *Before sundown, he will be killed, muttering to himself under his breath*, thought inmate Langford.

Watson was eager to help, so he went to the east cage and started running the doors. He had watched the control officers from his cell, switching keys on the panels to open more than one door at a time. He tried the key that said 'override shutoff switch' and turned it off, then tried the sally-port doors on E-block with both doors opened at the same time. Then Watson opened the sally-port doors on F-block. At that time, he told the rest of the marauders who were trying to figure a plan to get at the PCs.

"Hey, bros, I have figured out the override switches for the doors," said Watson.

Some of the inmates listened, with others not too impressed. At this time, there was at least one death-row inmate standing there, wanting to see human blood spill on the floor. This was inmate Terry Langford, who was in prison under a death penalty for the 1988 execution-style murders of Ned and Celine Blackwood near Ovando, Montana. Langford wanted to be a mountain man like the books he read; that epic mountain man from the middle 1850s and after. He left the big city and robbed people to get to Montana, and found out that there were no wilderness areas left where he could just live off the land. Plus, his short time trying to live off the land proved that he could not handle the unforgiving outdoors. After starving on his own, he went to the ranch at the foot of the Bob Marshall Wilderness. He killed the old couple that would have given him a meal for free. There were also unsolved murders that lead to Langford from his journey to Montana, but since Langford was not going to leave the Montana State Prison, the other states did not want to prosecute because it would cost thousands of dollars. The murder files are still open and still no closer for family members.

Inmate Watson went back in the cage to look around, thinking, *I have to do something to show those guys out there that I am one of them.* Looking at the panels one more time, he did not know what the buttons were for under the plastic see-through hatches that were over two switches on three of the panels. He lifted one of the plastic lids up and pressed the button on the panel that was for the F- block. Pushing the rocker switch made a clicking sound in the cage, different than the sounds of the water sprayer outside the door. Watson looked on the block and could not see anything that it did, so he pressed the other switch after lifting up the plastic lid. He heard a loud click of something happening but could not see any difference. Watson looked on F-block and nothing seemed any different. Then there were inmates coming through the side doors between F and E- blocks. It was the fire escape doors that was on each and every block. "Hey, guys," Watson yelled outside the cage door, "I know how we can surprise the PCs on D-Block Inmate. I know how to surprise the rats and to get on the block. I will open the fire escape doors when you are ready to go rushing on the D-block upstairs, and the downstairs fire doors."

Bobby Close walked over to the cage and was listening now, and said, "Do you know how to open up the fire doors, Watson?"

Watson, getting the chance that he was looking for, said, "Yes! Come here and I will show you how it works." Inmate Close and a few onlookers watched as Watson gave him an example on E-block. Even when the fire door was opened by pressing the switch, it made a click sound as to release the door lock.

Close said, "So, this will work on D-block also, Watson?" Watson knew that Close was not asking a question. If the fire doors did not open when the marauders wanted them open, they would come hunting to kill him.

After a short pause, Watson said with confidence, "Yes, it will open the fire doors from E-block onto D-block."

Then Close said, as he walked out of the cage, "This is what we're going to do: Ten or so go on E-block. Half of us will go upstairs to the fire door. Half will go downstairs to the fire door. I will wave my hand to Watson in the cage and yell 'Okay' in case he cannot see me, then he will hear me over the speaker. Watson will open the fire doors onto D-block. The rest of you keep standing here looking like you are coming on D-Block from the sally-port. This is when we will confront Davison about snitching us off. Are there any questions?"

The onlookers just nodded their heads, and yelled "Let's get 'em!"

The PCs on D-block saw ten or so marauders head into the sally-port that was the same one for blocks D and E. Vern Baker and Skip Davison were the two biggest guys on the PC block. They were the two closest to the sally-port, ready to battle to the death because they knew they were dead any which way. The Devil had waited long enough; the PCs would not need to dance much longer, anymore.

The inmates at the two fire doors waited on E-block for the doors to pop open.

They portrayed a large pack of bloodthirsty wolves against a springtime herd of deer that had shed their horns, while the deer are trapped at the bottom of a cliff with the left side of the cliff facing toward another cliff, and the right side facing a stone wall that is too high to jump. The only options for the deer are to kill themselves over the cliff to the left or fight off the bloodthirsty wolves all at once, dying with a fight, doing no good just yelling out for help and letting the wolves devour them without trying.

These were not your ordinary wolves. They were the misfits of their breed, banned from a clan because they were inbreeds and dense to the laws of the pack. So these carnivores were rejected from their clan, and found that there were others seemingly the same and they banded together. But it did not stop there. The brothers at the fire doors in the max unit were still set apart from the other max wolves. These wolves were not there to feed for substance; they were there for the joy of the slow kill. The wolves would go from one victim who was cornered, and take turns not to kill them outright. But when the prey was down, defenseless, they would start eating on the buttocks and the thigh muscle to watch the victim's eyes slowly die, then go to the next victim, their nerves running at a peak like they accomplished something good, which they never have and most probably, never will.

* * * * * * * * * * * *

1045 Hours

Inmate Bobby Close and the rest of the brothers were standing on the opposite side of the fire doors, where the unsuspecting PCs on D-block were stuck unaware.

Inmate Close lifted his hand; waving it, he yelled, "Open the door!" It got quiet for one second, then a loud, echoing high-pitched sound came from the upper fire door on D-block. It was like a garishly high-pitched sound that an electric door bolt makes when the bolt is electrically opened; it was metal against metal. That sound opened the top fire door, and Close was holding onto the door handle when the door opened. Next, the inmate in the cage, Watson, opened the fire door on the bottom level but this time, the sound was almost unheard because of the yelling and screaming sounds that the marauders and the PCs were making at that time from the top fire door opening seconds before. But when the first fire door opened, that sound will always be remembered in the minds of the inhabitants who were directly involved that day.

The marauding inmates stormed onto D-block while the PCs were stunned for just a couple of seconds. Then, like mice running away from the proprietor's cheese in every direction, the PCs went scrambling. Cell UD-8 was checked over rapidly by the first storm of marauders. The group was composed of Gleed, Close, Gollehon, Turner, Cox, Cook, Langford, and Joe Joe Millinovich. Most of the PCs ran back to the upper cells. Four of them ran to upper D-5—Holliday, Evans, Nida, and Hornback. The four PCs were thinking in numbers they might be able to fight them off. They tried to shut the door to the cell but it was locked open. Once a cell door is open all the way, it locks open; the door will not close until the cage officer closes it. So, there, the four PCs were trapped in a room together with not but one of them with the personality to fight for his life; that one was PC inmate Ron Nida.

At about the same time the upper fire door opened, the lower-level fire door opened, but this time the sound of the door was hardly heard or for that matter, it didn't matter because the PCs were already running to hide themselves from their killers by running away, which was fruitless. Ritchson, Robert Wild, Lopez, Nevens, Spotted Elk, Kenny Allen, Seelye, and more were at the lower fire door.

Inmate PC Ernest Mazurkiewicz, thirty-two, was serving fifty-eight years for robbery, deliberate homicide, and use of a weapon. He entered Montana State Prison in March 1990. Mazurkiewicz was one of the eight PCs left on the block, but he did not run to his cell on the lower tier LD-3; he ran into upper D-6.

Inmate PC Vern Baker, twenty-four, was serving time for burglary, theft, bail jumping, escape, and tampering with witnesses. He had been in prison since February 1986, and he went into UD-4. The six PCs who went to the upper level wanted to get away from Skip Davison.

Edmond (Skip) Davison, thirty-three, was serving thirty-five years for rape, aggravated burglary, and carrying a concealed weapon. He entered Montana State Prison in 1979. The other PCs thought the max inmates would have wanted only to kill Davison because he was the most despised for snitching out the biggest heavy in the prison. The marauders were coming for Davison now. The PCs were thinking that the marauders were rioting because if they killed Davison, then Gollehon and Turner would have a hung jury if no one would testify against them in the upcoming trial. Tomorrow the trail was starting, for killing Pillegi in the high-side yard.

Davison ran to his home in LD-1. There was nowhere to hide; they were going to find him eventually. So Davison just paced the cell floor with the worst being inevitable; it just was a matter of how soon the marauders would find him.

Davison was thinking, *If I fight, maybe they will stop beating me if, during that time, I keep telling them that I will not testify in court against them. That's what I will try to do. But if they kill me, then for sure, I can't testify against them.*

Outside Davison's home, he heard a voice yelling, saying, "Here he is! Davison is in lower D-1." Davison picked up his broken-off mop handle and faced the cell door, ready to meet the Devil's advocate. His heart was pounding fast and his breathing was uncontrollable; anxiety was taking control of him.

The inmate who found Davison was one of the biggest troublemakers the prison had at this time, inmate Seelye. Seelye was a transfer from another prison, where they had a lot of problems with him. After Seelye was transferred to the Montana State Prison, he was still getting written up constantly. He was always getting the rest of the inmates to start trouble on his block. He knew how to stir up trouble, before Seelye would back away from the trouble. He would then let the dumber inmates take the blame, and there will always be thick inmates. Seelye was not audacious; he was just plain and simple trouble-maker. He was in the yard when they escaped, and one of the first to take over D-block. Seelye thought he would just be present on the block, watching the carnage that was starting to happen. He was looking through the lower level on D-block to see what was to steal. Also, Seelye was demolishing anything that could cause trouble for the State of Montana without proof that he did it. This inmate is recalcitrant and invariable to society and furthermore, to life itself.

Seelye found an inmate in LD-7, but it was not Davison. He tried the door to the cell but it would not open, so he figured that after most of the excitement was over, the marauders would be back to take care of PC Willson.

Seelye yelled out, "There is a rat in LD-7, but it's not Davison, and his door is blocked closed." So Seelye went down the line of cells until he came to the last cell on the lower level, cell

LD-1. Seelye backed away from the cell so as not to have Davison running after him. Seelye was allowing time for the other marauders to run down the stairs and over to him because Davison was bigger and stronger than Seelye, but that was not the reason he backed off. Seelye was not afraid of Davison, even if the odds were not equal, with both of them having an equalizer. It was not his fight. He did not care if this man lived or died. Seelye was an out-of- state transfer that just wanted to cause problems. There was no need for him to get hurt for nothing. Furthermore, he matriculated from prison college and considered that if he came up with an injury, then after it was all over, the investigation could figure that he did the killings. So as a defense, he stood back and just waited until the rest could take over, and he would fall back and watch the recreation.

There was one last PC on D-block; his name was Dan Willson. He was a social loner, did not like being on the PC block, but he owed too many debts on the high side of the prison. So, inmate Willson had no choice but to become a PC or he would have landed in the hospital for slipping in the shower over and over, or become a sex goddess for a cellmate. Willson was a con; he knew his way around a prison, how it worked and where the loopholes were.

When the riot started with the marauders pounding on the cage windows over forty-five minutes ago, inmate PC Willson was figuring how he was going to stay alive.

Chances were that anything he did would not stop the marauders if the riot lasted for days.

Willson was thinking to himself, *The cell doors on the high side would jam if you forced the door off its track and wedged it shut. I could take a toilet bowl brush handle and pry the door up at the bottom of the door were the track is, and make it fall off its track.*

So that was what Willson did, while the rest of the PCs were trying to figure out what they were going to do when the doors opened. Willson got down on the floor and held the brush handle close to the bottom, prying up and out. Willson found that the door was heavy and it only came up a quarter of an inch before he gave up; the door was too heavy with not much leverage from a small stick. He sat back on his bed for awhile, trying to figure it out. He knew that the technique was right, so why did it not work? He thought and thought.

Then, Willson was thinking, "If I put on my gloves for hand support and I lift with my legs, I can get that door up over an inch and drop it down off its track. If that doesn't work, then I will go and help the others on the block and fight alongside them."

He got down on the floor like before, but this time got into a squatting position like he was weightlifting. He put the stick at the bottom of the door, lifted up with his legs as hard as he could. *It was lifting the door a little bit more*, he was thinking in his mind. The door was high enough now, so he canted the stick out a little to his left and dropped the door down; it was off the track and jammed shut.

Willson let out a silent yell, knowing that he did something great. Willson tried to open the door, shoving at it with no avail. But that was good; he knew that it would be hard to get the door open from the outside. But that was not good enough for Willson. He did not want it to fail, so he called Nida to his door, yelling, "Nida, Ron Nida, get me a mop handle and bring it to my cell, would you?" A few minutes later, Nida was at the door with a mop handle. He put it through the food slot in the door.

Nida asked, "What are you going to do with the stick, Dan?"

Willson answered, "I got the door off the track. Now I am going to put a stick behind the door so it won't open."

Nida said, "What if they smoke you out of the room?"

Willson answered, "Well, I don't know what I will do. I guess I better think about that."

Nida said, "Good luck, Dan. It looks like we are going to fight them."

Willson said, "Good luck to you, Ron, and the rest." Then Nida left Willson's door and went back to talk with Davison.

Willson was back on his plan, measuring the door to the wall. Then he went to the bed and started wearing down the wood on the rough part of the cement bed slab. The slab was about a foot and a half off the floor. It was wearing the wood away at a fast pace. Then he turned the handle a quarter of a turn and started wearing that away. He knew from experience that if he tried to break it over his knee, it might not break in the right spot. The correct place was important because if it fit tight between the door and the wall, then he should be safe.

"Two more quarters of a turn and I will try and break it over my knee," Willson said to himself.

The stick was worn around the spot that he wanted to break. It was finished and looked good to Willson so, placing it over his knee, he broke it. The stick looked good from a distance. So he went over to the door and tried it in place. It was a little too tight so he forced the high end that was against the wall down to level. It was in place and seemed to fit perfectly. Now, with the peace he broke off, he started sharpening the end on the cement floor. It would take time but it would work in case they got through the door, because he knew that if the marauders got in the door, then he was dead. He figured that the rest of the PCs would die, but this was his best chance of staying alive.

He was also thinking while he was sharpening the shank, *I am a dead man if they get through the door. So I will let the water come in under the door after I get done with this shank. My hot pot will be plugged in and as they enter my room, I will drop the pot in the water to electrocute them before they get me. Then it might be over for me, so I will try and run away after stabbing one or two of them, and hopefully will kill some of them before they kill me. I don't what to hurt anyone but they are backing me into a corner.*

* * * * * * * * * * * *

Inmates Millinovich and Mazurkiewicz were fall partners with other gang drifters who befriended an Alaska man, Larry Beckwith, who was shot to death near Townsend, Montana, in 1989. Inmate PC Mazurkiewicz snitched off Millinovich, saying that he did the killing. Mazurkiewicz received a lesser sentence on his time for snitching out Millinovich. So Mazurkiewicz was categorized as a PC to max at the Montana State Prison. Millinovich pleaded guilty to deliberate homicide by accountability, in exchange for prosecutors dropping charges of murder and robbery. He was sentenced to Montana State Prison in max.

Millinovich wanted revenge on his fall partner, Mazurkiewicz, so when the fire door opened, he was looking for him. It turned out that Mazurkiewicz was the first to be found. He was trying to hide in the corner of the room next to the door wall.

Mazurkiewicz was wearing a green parka coat. He stuffed padding in the coat sleeves, ready for a fight, standing up, trying not to be seen. But he was a big guy, which made hiding impossible. The marauders looked inside the room, first not seeing him. Then one of the marauders, with a quick turn, looking to his right by the toilet and sink, saw Mazurkiewicz. The marauder thrust a mop handle at Mazurkiewicz and yelled, "Here is one rat!" Mazurkiewicz gave a high-pitched scream as the mop spear went jabbing at his arm. The rest of the marauders pushed past the first cell so they could join in on the slaughter. He was boxed in a corner to the wall. Mazurkiewicz at first tried to defend himself by moving to the door, but there were more of them out on the walkway. Screaming blood-curling cries came from Mazurkiewicz; the cries could be heard over the sound of all the yelling of the marauders on D-block. The sprinkler water head spraying gallons of water throughout the max building was causing a lot of problems for the marauders.

There were two inches of water on the floor, and the sound-proofing material on the ceiling was sagging down. The air was at 100 percent humidity.

Looking for PC Davison, the upper-level scum had Mazurkiewicz now by the arms and the neck, shoving him out of the cell door. The marauders were shoving him over to the four-foot metal rail made of an inch-square tubing of steel. Two more rungs of metal tubing horizontal to the walkway landing served as supports for the walkway rail. Mazurkiewicz was fighting for his life. He knew that the odds of 7-to-1 were fatal. More onlookers were standing by to stop him if he somehow fought free.

So Mazurkiewicz was yelling and pleading to the scum at the top of his vocals, shouting, "Please, don't kill me! I didn't snitch-off Joe Joe, I didn't do it. Joe Joe, stop them! I will do anything to-to-to get you out of here. It waaaasn't me who snitched you off, I was caught in the middle of it. You have to b-believe me!"

Millinovich said, "You ratted me off, Mazurkiewicz," said Millinovich, struggling to do his part in lifting Mazurkiewicz up in the air. Millinovich wound an extension cord around his neck, trying to strangle him.

"My lawyer told me you were the one, and now you will die for it," Millinovich stated the obvious.

Mazurkiewicz was heavy, and it took all seven inmates struggling to lift him as he was squirming for his life. He was trying to free himself just to talk them out of it, but to no avail. Grabbing hold of him, he went up to the rail, squirming.

Mazurkiewicz was lifted and thrown over the rail, falling through the air, as a high-pitched yell, "Heeellll!" came out for one second, falling about twelve feet to the unforgiving concrete floor. As he was falling, Mazurkiewicz's arms and legs moved fast, trying to beat physics or to restrain his landing. The force landed his face and body to the stone floor. His facial bones were smashed, with the nose, both hands, and wrists broken. He landed on his hands and legs, but the centrifugal force canted his left leg out and broke it from the hip.

Mazurkiewicz was not dead yet. He was moving around, screaming with pain.

But inmate Langford, with cold, hateful eyes, a man who loved to be in on the kill, jumped into action. Langford put a smirk on his face before he grabbed a fire extinguisher from another inmate. He ran down the flight of steel stairs, turning to his left, then went down more concrete stairs to the lower level where Mazurkiewicz was trying to get up. Langford took the fire extinguisher in both hands over his head like a club. Then, hard as he could, he swung down, smashing the back of Mazurkiewicz's head in. After Langford saw the blood oozing out of Mazurkiewicz's head, he swung again. This time, as everyone on the block was watching, the fire extinguisher broke the cranium open and blood and brain matter splattered, covering Langford's face and clothes. This thrilled the marauders, with everyone's adrenalin pumping at its limit.

Millinovich was yelling at the top of his lungs, "Yeah, yeah, that will teach him to snitch off anyone else, yeah!"

Then Close and the others came down the stairs to get into the killing of PC Davison. Other marauders who were down on the lower level went upstairs because they found five more of the PCs.

The UD-3 was a jackpot for the ineffectual marauders. There were four PCs in the cell, and inmate Nida was at the door, with the others behind him not lending any help. Nida was a medium-build man, about 5 feet 8 inches, 165 pounds. His time at the prison was about over. Not only that, his life was about over but he had less than one year before parole, not knowing why he was on the PC block but probably he owed some debts to other inmates, and he was a snitch. So, instead of being punked-out or playing more inmate games, he went PC to wait his time out on D-block until he got his parole. Nida had a mop handle stick to defend himself, and gripped it with both hands to poke at someone. He was in a defensive position; he thought that would ward off the marauders. Inmate Wild, a sexual deviate, stopped in front of the door of UD-3. He came at Nida with a fire extinguisher and pulled the trigger. The powder came spraying out onto Nida as he closed his eyes.

Nida did not see the fire extinguisher coming at his head, but he jabbed with the op stick out in front of him. The stick caught the arm of Wild, leaving a gash on the right forearm.

Wild took both hands on the fire extinguisher and swung it at Nida's head, hitting him on the left side of the temple and jaw. Nida was knocked out before he hit the cell wall, and then plummeted to the cement floor. His head hit the floor on the right side, with a twisting turn from the blow that knocked him out cold, or was it the cement floor that slowed his heart to a rest beat. Ron Nida's body was lying next to the toilet, and on the floor to the right side of the cell, blood was oozing out from the gash and lump on his head. As the bootless marauders were leaving what looked like a lifeless body of inmate Nida, they were going toward the other PCs in the room.

Holliday, a federal transfer from Indiana, was sitting on the bed. Ernest Holliday, thirty-eight, was serving forty years for conspiracy, extortion, and robbery. He arrived in max two months ago. Holliday looked at the wall of marauders at the door. He did not have a weapon or anything to protect himself. There were two bodies lying on the floor. The first one was dead from who knows what, and the second body was lying next to the first but halfway under the cement bed; he also appeared dead. Nida was out of the way on the floor, and the marauders entered the room, talking to Holliday.

Holliday spoke up. "I didn't snitch anyone off or tell anyone nothing of the upcoming riot. I was told about it beforehand from guys in max. And I have AIDS, so it would be best not to make me bleed. I am telling you guys the truth. Guys, don't hurt me, please."

As they were talking to Holliday, they were kicking and poking at the first body on the floor. It did not move or breathe, so one torpid marauder said, "This one looks dead and it is Hornback, our favorite PC that everyone would love to kill. It looks like he was smart and killed himself, with all that blood on him."

Before they checked the other body next to Hornback, another marauder spoke up and said, "Holliday, who in max will tell us about your story, if it is true or not?"

"Tim Owens," Holliday had no hesitation saying his name.

"We will ask Terry about this," said the leader of the group. Gleed and Wild ran down the stairs and over to where Terry Langford was beating on Davison.

Langford, because he was on death row, had a high status in leadership. Wild yelled to Langford because he was busy having fun killing.

Langford came over to him and said, "Yeah, what!"

Wild told him about Holliday, and Langford said, "Go get Timmy Owens and bring him to Holliday and ask the questions in front of him so if you think one is lying, then kill him and if both are lying, then kill both of them."

Off and running, Wild and Gleed went to get Tim Owens of F-block, to bring him back. Inmate Owens was in his cell room, trying to stay out of the riot, but that was not going to happen.

Wild said "Get up, Timmy! You're going over to D-block and talk to PC Holliday."

Owens got up and said "What is going on? I what to stay out of this."

Gleed said, "You're already in it, so get your clothes on or we will drag you over to D-block.

Wild said, "Holliday said that you know him from county jail, and you can tell us that he has AIDS."

"He told me he has AIDS," said Owens.

Wild was acting crazy and hyper. He grabbed Owens and lifted him up and said, "Get up, you're going!" It took seconds for Owens to get his clothes on, and off they went back to D-block.

As they were on their way back, more inmates were on their way over, looking at what was going down on D-block. There was a stereo cranked as loud as it would play, found in one of the PC's cells, and placed on the cement stairs on the lower-level day room. The fire alarm was still going off, but it was not as loud on the blocks as it was in the hallways. The sound-proofing insulation on the ceiling was wet and sagging. It was humid on the block, with water two inches deep on the lower level where the drains kept taking gallons of water per minute on all six blocks. Above the noise of the stereo were the yelling, crying, frantic screams of PCs from upper and lower, pleading for their lives. It was unbelievable and indescribable, the horror that was going on inside the building. But for the marauders, it was the most heart-racing thrill they were experiencing and would ever experience.

Davison was getting kicked, stabbed, shanked, and beaten every way they could think of to torture him. He was blocking his face with his hands, trying to protect his face. He was pleading, "Please stop, I will not testify in court. I am sorry, please stop." This was taking place outside of his cell in lower D-1.

Inmate Close took an extension cord and wrapped it around his own hands.

Close left more than enough cord between his hands, about seven inches. He moved behind the body of Davison, forcing the cord around his neck. Close lifted Davison against the front of Close's body, choking him. Davison was pushed to the wall. Blood from Davison's face, hands, and shirt pressed up against the bricks was painting the wall. Then Davison slid down to the floor. As Close was strangling him, another marauder took a sharpened piece of metal with a rag wrapped around the end for a handle, and stabbed Davison in the chest. Davison held his hands up to his throat, trying to breathe to prolong the last of his life.

After all that beating, Davison was still hanging onto existence. He put his hands up under the cord, trying to relieve his airway enough to gasp for air. Langford saw that Close was having a hard time, so he handed a pair of scissors to him. Close twisted the cord tight around the neck and held the cord with one hand, and reached for the scissors from Langford. Langford was grinning, knowing that Close wanted to kill Davison himself. Taking the scissors, Close jabbed a hole in Davison's throat.

Blood came spurting out of the entrance wound in Davison's neck. Close took the shank from his throat, and even more blood sprayed out. Again, he stabbed; this time, Davison was going limp. Close was covered with blood all over his body. He let Davison fall to the floor. As he fell, blood was coming out of his mouth and words from his lips, trying to say something, but all that was coming out was bloody bubbles. That was not enough; Close kept on cutting his throat and then after that, he got up from the floor, jumped up, and came down on Davison's head as hard as he could, breaking his face and jaw. Davison was dead for sure, but other marauders kicked and stabbed at him. They took their turns beating him, just to make it look good in the presence of Close and Langford. His eye was hanging out, and someone said to others as he was pointing, "Is that where his eye is supposed to be?" as they all were laughing.

Upstairs, at the same time that Davison came out of his cell and was getting beaten, UD-4 Vern Baker was found. Gollehon and Turner wanted to mess with Baker, but they did not what to get hurt, and they knew Baker was big enough and crazy enough to hurt them both.

So Gollehon said, "Baker, come out of that cell or all of us will come in with sticks and kill you the hard way!"

Baker was ready to fight, but he thought about it and said, "Okay, I will come out and I will hang myself."

The marauders did not think they heard him correctly, so Turner said, "You are coming out and we will let you hang yourself, Baker. So, get on with it!"

Baker said, "Do you have a cord I can use?"

Gleed, who was also there standing, said, "There is one right there on the floor."

The cowardly marauders thought Baker was going to trick them, so they were watching Baker closely as he picked up the cord and wrapped it around his neck.

Baker tied the cord semi-tight to his neck and then tied the other end to the top rail on the upper landing. Vern Baker was climbing the rungs on the rail as he was thinking to himself this was not the way he wanted it to end. He was tired of this life the way it was turning out, and was ashamed of the crimes he had committed. He was wishing that things turned out differently for him, that maybe if he listened more in school or if there was more family love and less abuse in his life, maybe that would have gotten him on the right track.

It was harder than he thought to kill himself; each step up was like climbing a mountain. He was telling himself that it would be over fast, in seconds. As he lifted his leg over the rail, he found he could not do it. But just then, two thugs grabbed him and pushed him over the rail. He did not have time to say anything or even grab his neck. With a fast and hard thump from his waist hitting the landing, and his neck jerking upward, it started strangling him. For about two seconds he was suffocating, dying; then the cord broke and down he fell to the lower concrete floor. He was still suffocating; the cord was still tight around his neck. Panic was in Baker's eyes. He landed on his feet and dropped hard to the floor, taking his hands and trying to loosen the cord around his neck. His face and head were turning purplish black, and his eyes were bulging out as he tried to take a breath. Finally, his hands freed him as he lay gasping for air, fighting for life. Two marauders ran down the stairs, grabbing him and making him go back upstairs and do it over. Baker could not walk; he had to be helped up the stairs. This time, death was not questionable; he had no choice but to hang himself. He wanted to live but after hanging once, he was too weak to fight them off, even though he was stronger than two of them together. One of the devil's advocates gripped the cord that was still around his neck, keeping pressure on it so the blood would be restricted from his head, keeping Baker weak. The other inmate guard had his arm through Baker's arm, forcing him to climb the stairs.

As you can see, the marauders were role-playing in their minds, trying to justify that what they were doing to the PCs was right. They were psychologically playing the good-guy/guard, taking the bad inmate to his execution when they knew in their minds they should be the ones being executed for their crimes against society.

Meanwhile, inmate Nida became conscious again. This time, inmate Ritchson had thrown him down on the cell floor and was cutting his neck with scissors. The first cut was difficult; he had to use both hands on the scissors to make the cut through the neck. Starting by the Adam's apple, he broke through the skin; blood was coming out, though slow at first. Then Ritchson took another cut, and blood sprayed him in the face and upper body. The smell of hot coagulating human blood spraying on Ritchson's face was getting him sick.

Nida, at this time, gave up. He could not move and his mind was thinking, *That son of a bitch, he's cutting my throat! I can't feel the cuts, just the sound of the scissors tearing my neck open. Please, stop! I don't want to die, please, please!*

He was thinking to himself, *Why couldn't I have died when I was knocked out? At least, then, I wouldn't know that I was dead. Now, I will die knowing and being awake to the end. Stop cutting my neck, you animal! He can't hear me. I don't even think my mouth is opening. Please, God, help me get him to stop. God, I don't what to die! Please, God, give me one more chance to live!*

It was hard penetrating the thick skin as he turned the scissors to the other side of the neck, because the cut was up to Nida's jawbone. Ritchson started cutting again; this time, more blood was pumping from the gaping hole in Nida's neck.

Ritchson's hands were clotted with blood. Now, all Ritchson could see was Nida's eyes losing life, and a haze was coming over them. Ritchson had enough cutting, he was finished. He was a little sick from the sight of what he had done, so he got up and was leaving when he said, "That rat is dead!"

Langford, who was watching, said, "Just to make sure, I'll give him a whack in the head." Langford had the cell door wrench that was taken from the cage. He hit Nida on top of the head and instantly, Nida was knocked out. Langford put a large bump on the side of his head. Blood was now clotting on the floor next to the toilet.

The smell was a warm pungent odor, the same as killing a deer and cutting the throat to drain the warm blood.

Holliday, during this time, was ecstatic seeing a person next to him being slaughtered, and watching another person being hung outside his door. He saw Vern Baker being dragged up the stairs and going past his room, knowing that he was going to hang him again. This time, two extension cords found in cells on the upper level were already waiting. The cords were doubled. Baker did not have much fight in him, and after hanging once, he knew hanging was not easy and his life will be over for good. He tried to run when they put the noose around his neck, but his legs where too flimsy and weak. His arms were built twice as big compared to his attackers, but nothing would move; Baker's body was drained of energy. The marauders had to lift and slide him up the four-foot rail because he did not want to die. Over the rail he went, stopping in midair with a jerk of the neck on the cords. His chest was enlarging but his lungs were not. This time, the cords did not break and his lungs were not getting any air. Baker's body began convulsing, jumping; his hands went to his neck, trying to break the cord, trying to breathe, trying to yell, trying for one last chance to live and do something to better his being alive. His last thought was, *God, I am sorry for my sins. Please, forgive me.*

There was no third chance in life for Vern Baker. His body stopped jerking; then, his hands fell to his side. Next, his mind gave up and then the last beat of his heart pumped. It was an end to a troubled life and then he was raised up.

Meanwhile, as Holliday was watching the ordeal on the landing, Tim Owens was escorted to the cell. Owens looked down and saw a bloody body on the floor by the toilet and two more bodies—dead bodies—on the floor by the bed.

Owens was asked questions about Holliday during his time at the county jail.

Turner said, "Did you know Holliday, and what was he in the prison for, and what did he do to get on the PC block in max, and does he have AIDS?"

Owens answered, "Yes, I knew him in the county jail. I didn't know what he did to get sent to the hole or prison, but he said he has AIDS."

"Okay, get off D-block or we will let you stay longer," said Turner. Owens did not waste any time. At a fast walk, he went through the fire door onto E-block and then walked straight through E-block onto F- block, back to his cell. Then he started breathing normally. He sat on his bed just thinking.

Gollehon told Holliday to get up from his bed and told him they were going to tie his hands up and take him away to talk to Tony. This was a trick, and Holliday knew it, so he said, "Please, please, I beg you don't tie my hands. I didn't do nothing.

"If you get my blood on you, you will get AIDS. Please, please, I will do anything you want, just don't kill me."

"Get up. Get up, you, rat, we are taking you to Tony!" said another.

He got up, careful to step between the two bodies on the floor. That was suspicious, so they jerked at Holliday's arm and brought him to them, wrapping a cord around his wrist behind his back. Holliday would not stop pleading. Of course, a no-good murderer will lie to you, anyway! So Gollehon and Turner put a cord around Holliday's neck and started pulling in opposite directions. Holliday did not fight much for his life. It took only a couple of minutes to kill Holliday. Others were holding his arms still until he collapsed.

"That was not long enough, Doug. You seen how long it took Baker to die. Keep the pressure on longer; make sure that rat transfer is dead," said Gollehon.

They threw the body over Nida; they did not cut his throat because they were afraid of getting AIDS. Holliday's body was not harmed in any way after they chocked him to death.

As Gollehon and Turner were killing Holliday, other marauders checked the bodies of Hornback and Evans on the floor. They kicked hard, thrusting downward at Hornback. He did not move or wince. So the marauder went on to the other PC, kicking him in the side of the stomach. Evans moved; he turned over and put his hands on his side and groaned. "Ohh," went Evans, trying to catch his breath.

Other Marauders ran over to him and started to beat him, taking mop handles and sticks, stabbing him.

Evans started pleading, "Please, don't kill me! I haven't done anybody wrong. Please, I will do anything not to die."

Evans' attackers told him, "You're a rat, and you will hang for it."

Two marauders brought Evans out of the cell, making him jump over Holliday to get out of the cell. They tied his hands behind his back with an extension cord. He was waiting for them to cut down Baker from the rail before he was to be hanged. The marauders had it in their minds that if they hung a PC, it was justified because hanging was by judge and jury finding them guilty of the number one prison rule: Never rat-out another inmate. Life, to this kind of person, means nothing. To take a life means nothing, but for someone to try and take their life means everything.

Evans was pleading to stay alive, trembling from head to toe, waiting by the rail. Inmate Cox kicked PC Hornback again after he was lying there for several minutes after the last time he was checked. Hornback was, in all likelihood, the most abominated inmate at the prison. The officers alike despised Hornback the same because of his crime. He was a small inmate, in prison for child molestation. While he was in prison, Hornback was raped by other inmates. When his time was up at the prison, he told a counselor that he was going to rape a child again. Hornback's sentence was up, and there was nothing the state could do to keep him locked up. He got out, went to Kalispell, Montana, and watched the kids for weeks in a park. He saw a boy who was playing alone in the trees by a stream. He went over to him and raped him; made the boy go through unspeakable pain and torture, then when he was done taking all the boy's amour-propre away from him, Hornback killed the boy.

So this was a prize for the marauders.

Cox yelled out, "Hornbitch is alive!"

Hornback got up and tried to run away. Cox, with others, stopped him and through all the noise on the block, you could hear Millinovich say, "Keep Hornback for last, we will torture him." Then the rest of the marauders yelled, "Save him for last, torture him!"

Hornback was trying to stay alive. He did not want to die and, especially, not to be tortured. Cox and the gang took Hornback and lifted him up. They were on the upper tier walkway trying to put Hornback's legs through the rungs of the rail. Hornback was screaming and kicking for his life. His legs were placed sideways in the rail with both legs together. Cox jumped on Hornback's legs at the knee.

Hornback bent his knees, hopefully to keep from breaking them. Cox was not that big of a man but when he landed on his knee, it gave a loud popping sound that made the marauders laugh. Crying like a teenage kid, Hornback was escorted by Cox to stand in line with Evans. Hornback could hardly walk, publicizing the agony he was going through. He was bent over holding his knee, thinking for the moment; he knew that if he was next and last to die, it will be hell.

Gary Evans, twenty-six, was serving twenty years for assault, theft, criminal endangerment, and escape. He came to prison in March of 1991, just six months beforehand. He was told to fit between the rails and hang himself. But Evans did not want to die, and he would not kill himself. He was not going to make it that easy for them to kill him. Furthermore, he was too big to fit between the rungs. Evans was shaking uncontrollably as the murderers were picking him up and throwing him over the rail. Close and Langford were helping because it was taxing tugging Evans, as he was trying to fight for life. Up and over the rail with two cords around his neck, he helplessly fought in vain for life. Jerking violently, his attempt to breathe stopped. Then the legs stood straight, and the neck was separated from the purple head with the mouth open wide.

Hornback saw that Cox was helping throw Evans over, so he ran to the stairs. Others saw him run, and yelled, "Cox, Hornback is getting away!" Cox started running for him but Hornback had one thing on his mind, and that was to stay alive any way he could. Down the metal stairs he went, hobbling on an injured leg that was so painful, but his mind blocked out most of the pain. Hornback ran to the landing of D-block door, through the sally-port that was open, and now there were more marauders running after him. Out in the hallway, he looked at the best way to go, to the back hallway or to the front hallway. There was no time to choose. He saw the hallway to the front door open, but that was blocked with debris from the counselor's room and the supply room. So, hobbling as fast as he could go, Hornback's only chance to survive was to make it to the front of the building where there were windows to the outside and, hopefully, there will be someone to see him and get him out of this hell.

Now Cox was right behind him, trying to grab his shirt, but Hornback jumped under a counselor's desk that was piled in the hallway. Through the back of the desk, he went scrambling to fight to the top of the barricade. As he was going over, Cox had his shirt, trying to pull him back over. That little person fought for his life to get this far, and things were not looking good for him because Cox was lifting him back over the barricade. Then Cox looked up, and there was someone coming in view of the front door window. Cox let Hornback go because if he were identified by anyone, then he was going to be stapled to the cross and that would mean the metal gurney table for lethal injection, the death penalty.

Hornback was role playing. He started talking to the guy outside the window, "Don't shoot me! I am one of the inmate PCs that the max inmates are trying to kill! Don't shoot! Get someone here to open the front door. I will come out with my hands in the air. Don't shoot!" Hornback was pleading.

Cox stopped and was contemplating. *Two brothers can put something over their faces and cover up the rest of the body that has tats, and go get that load-mouth punk-ass bitch.* As Hornback was still talking to someone outside, Cox was thinking again. *All Hornback would have to do is rip the cover off our face, and we would be caught. But if we wait until dark, Hornback will have no chance in hell.*

So Cox and the other two brothers went back to tell the others what happened.

Hornback saw that they left, and stopped talking. Hornback put on a good show because the officer left early on in the conversation, and Hornback was out in the sally-port talking to himself. Most of the time, Hornback was putting on a good act to save his life. But it was not over for Hornback, yet; nighttime will come.

One of the flunkies was cutting the extension cords that held Evans up on the rail to the upper landing, because the ones who were doing the killing left D- block and went to F-block to shower the blood off. Most of them went through the cells on D-block to find clothes to fit. It was standard policy that if the inmates in max had their own sweats, then they could wear them to yard only. So it was an easy change, taking the PC's sweats with new, to them, tennis shoes. Inmates were strolling around max like they owned the place. There was still more pillaging going on throughout the building. In the back hallway was the inmate property room that held all property for inmates who came into max when they got rolled-up.

That room was broken into, and everything in it was ransacked through. Inmates were looking for anything they could steal from another inmate, or information about other inmates. The counselor's room had a fire burning with all the files on every inmate in max. They looked through the files, viewing for clues that an inmate could find about other inmates to bulldog them for money, sex, or whatever; it would be determined by how much the account was worth. An account was worth anything that an inmate was trying to hide from other inmates.

Something that has to be established is an inmate generally has no ethics. They were taught at an early age to throw out all morals and live to satisfy themselves.

At this time, in the riot, they were kings of their environment. They were doing the dance with the Devil which they will pay for the rest of their lives the hard way.

Back on D-block, there was only one PC who was untouched—the inmate still in his cell, LD-6. Wilson became vigilant again when Lopez, Nevens, and Gleed tried to force the cell door open. They were trying to lift the door and push it back, but it would not budge an inch. Then one of them went into the control cage and tried the door switch, while the other two pushed back on the door.

It was not opening, so they kept the rocker switch on in the cage. After awhile, it heated up and the relay shut down the door, so there was no power to the switch. This stopped the inmates from exceeding in their plunder, but Wilson was doing everything he could think of to stay alive. He offered them cigarettes and coffee just to stay away and quit trying to break into his cell. The three took the bribe, knowing that someone else will take their place where they left off; especially, when the three tell others to rout him out of his fortress.

Four lifeless bodies were lying on the dayroom floor of the lower level of D-block, in a pool of crimson red blood. Wild was hacking at either Evans' or Baker's throat with a half-sharpened shank, as another marauder was holding the head to the side with his foot. All the marauders who were involved with the killings and the ones who were just onlookers thought they had to beat the dead bodies up after they were lying dead in the pool of blood. Mostly, this was done by ones who had to look like killers so they were still brothers with a code of silence.

This way, if they were seen around the dead bodies by the killers, then they could be trusted. Go figure!

Arnot was an inmate doing time in max, and he was worried about a friend he had on D-block. While on his block, he had already heard stories about the killings, and who they killed. Arnot was thinking to himself, *This is going to get me into trouble checking on my friend, but it does not matter because I am not a gang brother to anyone in max.*

He was in prison for some small petty-ass crime, doing a dime with a nickel dropped to the side if he could hang loose and do his own time. It was hard going, being on the high side of the fence in Close Unit I where all the inmates wanted to do his stretch for him. But that would necessitate Arnot playing con games, and most likely picking up a longer stretch. He wanted to go back home, so he figured if he was going to stay out of trouble, then he was going to be forced into doing time up in max where he had a cell to himself and could do his own time. He got caught with some weed in his cell, and was classified to max.

Now, all he was thinking about was to find his friend and say some last words by his side.

As he went out of his cell, he saw inmates destroying state property, breaking windows that faced the blocks. The windows were just like the cage, Plexiglas in the middle and glass on both the inside and outside. The middle would not break, as hard as the inmates tried, but it was leaving broken glass all around inside of the max building floor. Arnot was astounded to see the destruction done to max, seeing the burnt cage and debris throughout the block and down the halls; seeing the barricade at the end of the hall in front of the sally-port to the front door, with smoke coming out of the counselor's office.

His eyes had to look into the hallway on D-block first, Arnot not knowing if he could get up enough guts to go any closer to find his friend. Arnot saw four bodies on the floor; there was no way he could tell if one was his friend. The corpses looked like they were a mile away. *There was no way this could be real*, he thought. He knew that it was not a question of if; his legs already were doing the walking. Now, through the sally-port doors, he went slowly down the cement stairs and over to the first corpse. Looking at the bloody, beat up body, it was not his friend. On to the next one that was in the same gory shape; the body was bloody and beat up, with another cord around his neck, like the first body. The third body was not his friend; he could tell from ten feet away because the body was too large.

The last body was over by itself. Walking slowly over to the body, it was hard telling who it was because the body was face down. He went over to it and, in the water, bent down and looked at the bulging-out eyes and broken face, and saw down his neck with the jugular and windpipe torn open. This was not Nida, it was Davison. Arnot could see that none of the bodies was his friend. This confused him; there were now more bodies to look for, but where? So he looked around and saw lower D-6 cell closed, and someone in it pointing a finger at him, gesturing him over to the cell. He walked through the ankle-deep water under the metal stairs that go to the upper level. He kept walking to Willson's cell. Willson knew of him from talking to Nida, so he was going to tell him to look upstairs.

Willson said, "I'm sorry, Arnot. I heard Nida screaming upstairs and I didn't see his body fall downstairs, so I know that he is still upstairs somewhere; I don't think you will find him alive. It was totally hell in here, and I think there is more to come for me."

"I hope not, and thanks for the info," said Arnot, as he started walking away.

Up the stairs he went, to say his good-bye to Nida. On the upper landing, it was forbearing to semis that to his right from the stairs was where Nida would be from all the blood from the walls around UD-4 and UD-5. Looking into cell 5, there was blood splattered on the walls, bed, and floor. All the personal items and clothes were in disarray, and blood on everything. There were two bodies on the cold cement floor, with one over the other one's legs. Arnot could see Nida under the body, with his neck cut open and blood pooling around him. Arnot moved the lifeless body of Holliday over by the one-piece sink-toilet. He could see that there was a little life in Nida's eyes, so he started talking to him. Nida could not talk, but he wanted Arnot to sit him up on the bed; Nida pointed to the bed. Arnot took both his arms, and putting them under Nida's armpits, lifted him up onto the bed. Nida was sitting with his back toward the wall and his chin was down, tucked to his neck.

Nida was dying slowly, but Arnot could see some warmth and tears in his eyes, letting him know it meant a lot to see someone he cared about before he died. Arnot sat by him and said, "Keep your neck down and don't give up. I will give you a towel to put under your chin to stop the bleeding. Whatever you do, if someone comes to the door, keep your eyes closed and try not to breathe so they can't tell if you are breathing. I cannot stay here or they will kill me too, so I will be back later to check on you. You will live and we will hang out again, you will see. So long, friend of mine!" Arnot did not believe the words he said to Nida, but it was the best that could be done for him. He left the hellish cell and walked back to his block. Walking into his cell, he was sick inside his stomach, throwing up in his washbasin.

Inmate Wild was on an adrenalin high, feeling the same rush a sports hero feels after a game and scoring the winning point. He stepped into the west cage where the colored Watson was stationed. Watson was twice as developed in muscle as Wild. Wild had guys backing him, standing behind and all looking at Watson. Wild spoke up, "You black bitch, you let Hornback go down the hallway, didn't you, black bitch?"

Watson turned and faced the gang of three, and said with a controlled voice, "I didn't know it was my job. I was opening doors and watching the front door to see if someone was coming in. Cox was right behind him, with others following close behind, so don't blame me for that."

Wild was trying to get Watson to fight him, saying, "You, bitch, you are a bitch, Watson, you pussy, bitch motherfucker!"

Watson said, "Take it easy, I'll get him after the sun goes down."

"You better, or your black ass will be hanging up."

Watson did not say anything as Wild left with his cronies. Going back on the F- block, he was still on a high, thinking he was invincible. He went to a cell were an inmate was trying to hide out from the whole riot takeover. The inmate was in max for escaping the prison weeks ago. He was a young, small-framed guy, and did not fit in with the max crowd. Wild was a homosexual, and was looking for someone to defile. At times, correctional officers would shake down Wild's cell and would find a dildo that he would stick up his rectum to fulfill his desires. His sphincter is so worn out he cannot hold back a bowl movement.

The kid was perfect for the picking. Wild entered the cell, with his cronies again standing behind him. Not much was said, but Wild and his gang started beating him until the boy's fight was out of him. The victim was told they would kill him if he kept fighting back. Two of the marauders bent him over, forcing his face into the bed with his back and ass up in the air. Wild pulled his pants down past his hips and another cut the pants off the boy with his sharpened piece of metal shank; Wild had his penis erect from the thrill of the rape and getting excited like a man would be stimulated from a voluptuous horny naked wanting woman. Next, he gripped his hands on both sides of the boy's waist and upper legs. As the victim tried to move around but unable, Wild forced himself through the sphincter muscle and on into the rectum. Blood was coming from the anus, from the potency of Wild shoving his penis brutally in and out until climaxing inside of the victim.

Pushing away, he hurried up and pulled up his pants and zipped them while saying, "If you tell on me, I will kill you or I will have someone kill you, is that understood?"

The boy could hardly talk, but got out the word, "Yes."

Wild and his fall partners left the cell. The boy just lay on his bed in a prostrated and fetal position, crying, hoping that this day will end with the guards taking back max and he will still be alive. Or should he just say 'The hell with it all!' and sneak up behind Wild and kill him with a shank. The boy knew that his life will be over after that bastardly animal is dead, because his cohorts will take revenge. But he did not care to live now.

"If I wait until it is dark out, then I can get around, eluding others in the dark, and jump him as he rests." The boy would have only one chance and that would be to the throat.

Wild was finished, but his cronies, with Gleed running the show now, decided to have some more fun, as they would call it.

Gleed said, "Hey, let's go to a rapist's cell and show him what rape is about."

The insane thing about it was that Gleed was in max for rape, himself, of a younger lady who worked at a store by Swan River Forrest Camp. Gleed and another marauder went to the cell of an inmate who had raped women at least three known times. All the women were brunettes, and after the first one that he got caught with, he was put in prison. While he was in prison working on the prison ranch, the inmate went to the ranch house where the supervisor lived, and told the ranch wife and daughter that he had to rape them because other inmates were going to kill him if he did not rape them. The two got away and the inmate was sentenced for attempted rape charges. That was when he came to max, and Gleed went in his room with another inmate, held him down and someone else pulled his pants down while Gleed took a mop handle and shoved it up his ass, causing multiple problems. After the riot, the inmate got out of prison. He took care of his daughter who was in a wheelchair, as she could not take care of herself. The inmate raped her many times, bringing him back to prison. Hope he never gets out of prison again....

Back on D-block, Willson in lower D-6 was being harassed again; this time, it became more serious. The door was being forced up and down and back and forth. Willson was holding the stick, braced against the wall and door, in place.

This time, Willson said, "Stop! I won't say anything about anyone who came on the block, I promise. Go get Bobby Close and ask him to come here; he will stop all of this, you will see."

One of the marauders said, "What do you have to give me, to go get him?"

"I have more coffee and candy and tobacco. If you get him, I will give it to you all," said Willson.

∗ ∗ ∗ ∗ ∗ ∗ ∗ ∗ ∗ ∗ ∗ ∗

1130 Hours

The time seemed to go by slowly for the two PCs in the laundry room. They were not complaining because, for some reason, the marauders were staying on the east side of the max building.

A while later, inmate McFarlane said, "They are finally coming in!"

Inmate Powell's senses perked up. He was thinking that McFarlane was insinuating that the inmates were coming back to break the door down. "What do you mean 'They are finally coming in'?" asked Powell.

McFarlane said, "I smell mace; the guards are coming in."

Powell jumped down from the dryer, picking up some towels to put in the crack under the door. He was sprayed in the face with a shot of mace. The mace was sucked under the door like a flame. The marauders crept up to the laundry door, spraying the mace all around the door and frame; the mace canisters came from the west main cage. The marauders thought the two PCs would have to come out if the mace were sprayed in the laundry room. It was common practice for inmates to try gassing the PC out of the room. Officers used the mace pepper spray to get inmates out of a cell by spraying the cell with gas, about two or three spurts through the food tray door. Then, when the inmate has had enough, he is instructed to come to the door with his hands behind him, place the hands in the food slot, then get handcuffed behind his back. After the inmate is out of the cell, he is brought over to the shower, where he can wash the mace from his body. This method is the most humane; better then taking five officers in the cell with night sticks and beating the inmate. So the marauders tried gassing them out.

This burned McFarlane's and Powell's eyes and throats; breathing was difficult.

They tried breathing into a wet towel, a half breath into the towel and a full breath out. It was difficult, but without asking each other, they thought it was better to die in the room than be tortured to death. Powell was calming down, sitting back down on the dryer. He was hyperventilating, going weak, but after a few minutes he started breathing better. The inmates ran out of spray. Even though his breathing was increasing, the eyes and throat still burned. The two PC s in the laundry room had no idea what happened on the east side of the building. All they could figure was the whole max building was taken over by the marauders. They knew that none of the PCs came over to the west side of the building, or they would have seen them. All inmates Powell and McFarlane could assume was that the PCs were taken hostage or they were dead, with the latter the most probable. So, what they were going through in the laundry room was hell, but they were still alive.

Everything was quiet for a few minutes. Then suddenly, there was a very hard bang against the glass window in the door. Both PCs jumped a foot in the air.

Inmate Powell said to McFarlane, "Here we go again!"

The window was hard to break; it must have taken eight to ten blows from a fire extinguisher to break the window with wire mesh in the glass. After breaking the window, a hose was inserted through the door, pulling the trigger. Instantly, the room was filled up with powder. The oxygen was depleted from the laundry room and filling up with powder. The PCs closed their eyes and instinctively closed their mouths.

Powell heard McFarlane say, "Here," as Chuck threw a clean wet towel, hitting his chest. Powell put it over his mouth and tried to breathe. Nothing; Powell could not breathe. Starting to panic, he was hyperventilating again. He jumped up and started to climb on top of the dryer, getting a quarter breath then another quarter breath, then a full breath, so Powell started to settle down again. He got off the dryer, sitting by McFarlane where there was more air down lower on the floor.

They did not give up, so the marauders left. The vent in the ceiling was bringing fresh air in. That was the definite thing that saved the two PCs so far in the laundry room.

Fifteen minutes later, footsteps came back to the laundry room. It was time for fireworks because nothing else drove the PCs out of the laundry fortress. Lighter fluid from Bic lighters was shaken and dumped out onto McFarlane's head that had a wet towel covering him. More gas was dumped onto the washer, dryer and clothes that were on the shelf. It did not take long to find out that it was gas because a lit piece of paper was thrown in the room. The flame landed on McFarlane's head. Inmate Powell could see McFarlane's head on fire. Taking a towel, he put out the flame out that was burning the wet towel on McFarlane's head.

There were more flames on the washer and on some clothes. These were easy to put out but had to be smothered to stop the flame; it worked. The fire was better to deal with instead of dealing with suffocating. The marauders had no idea that the two PCS in the laundry room could not have gone longer if there was any more fire extinguisher powder taking the air out of the room.

It was an unspoken teamwork between McFarlane and Powell. Inmate McFarlane's job was keeping pressure against the dryer with his back and feet on the door. That kept the marauders guessing. Inmate Powell's job was dealing with anything that came up, to defuse the problem. With the window broken out, light came through. It shined a two-foot streak across part of two walls inside the laundry room. This was how the two PCs could see people going past. The shadows were being watched like a television.

* * * * * * * * * * * *

1145 Hours

Inmate Bobby Close was back on C-block, hanging out after he was all cleaned up and had clean clothes on. As he walked onto the block, he let his presence be known to the officers in the shower room. Close went down to a cell on the lower level and hung out there for some time. Then he went upstairs to his cell. Everything was still in place; nothing was touched or out of place. He brought back a keepsake that he could remember Davison by. It was a cassette tape that he did not have, from the '70s. It was the Queen Band songs—songs of power and control; now, every time he heard them, they would make him remember this day. Next, inmate Spray came to Close's home and stopped outside of the cell until he was invited to enter. Spray was another sexual deviant and homosexual. He wanted to get off by getting a blow-job from the cute young boy next door to Close.

So Spray asked, "Bobby, will you stand by while I get a blow job from Nelson? That way, if he thinks about biting my cock, you can hit him over the head with this pipe and kill him. That will make his mouth open so I will not lose my cock. I know that he will not try anything with you here."

Close took into the scam, walking out of his door. Spray went in Nelson's room as Close stood guard at the door. Nelson was lying on the bed curled up in a ball, trying to live through the beating he received an hour ago. Aware that someone came into his room, Nelson got up fast from lying down and was ready to fight, but before he could swing his fist, he was knocked down on the floor with a riot stick that was taken from the main cage. Spray did not want to kill this young cute boy, he just wanted to let him know not to fight any more.

Spray said, "Now, Nelson, you are going to give me a blowjob or I will kill you right here."

Nelson understood what was going to happen if he were to live. His body went numb. There was no thinking of anything; as his hands and body trembled, his mind went blank. Spray was satisfied. As he zipped up his pants and left the room, Close was out in front.

Close had to earn some brownie points, so he went down the metal stairs from the upper landing and stopped, looking at inmates Cox and Ritchson harassing the guards again, threatening them to not look out the blanket, and if the water kept on going off, they would take one of the guards out of the shower and throw his head out the front door to get the water turned off.

Close said, "Leave them alone. They are doing nothing to harm anyone, and they can't shut the water off."

This got the two brothers hot, and they asked Close, "What are you going to do about it, stop us?"

Close was going over to the two brothers when Charlie Miller said, "Whoa, guys, don't start anything! We will stay behind the curtain. Just don't start fighting. We will give you the officers' cuff keys, as you have threatened us to give them to you."

That stopped them, and off they went, all three talking as they were going out the block door with four more cuff keys. The officers could feel the tension tightening around them each time someone came around the block that was not housed on the block. Inmate Close and the other two marauders left C-block and went over to B-block.

B-block, which held the death-row inmates, was also loud. The music was blaring to the top of the speakers and that was where everyone hung out with the sergeant officer's thirty-two-cup coffeepot sitting on the landing of B-block. That was where the brothers grouped together to make new decisions.

Two brothers walked on B-block with a new stash of candy that they got from PC Willson.

Walking over to Close, they said, "Bobby, PC Willson said that he wanted to talk to you, that you would tell people to leave him alone, that he is all right."

"Can you guys get to him?" asked Close.

"No, he is locked in his room and we can't get the door open," one of them said.

"Well, I will go see him and tell him he is safe for now but tonight, we will get in that room with a bar," said Close. Then Close and the two other inmates went walking back, talking about a plan for tonight. Down on D-block, Close went looking at the bodies on the day-room floor. He was elated at his victory over the ones he killed or helped kill. For his booty, he took a cassette tape from each one lying on the floor dead so each time he would play the tape, it would bring him back to how they were killed. It was Bobby Close's trophy case selection.

Willson was happy to see Close coming down to his home. There was no formal greeting; it was business to convey, "Ha, Bobby, please tell these people to leave me alone. Let them know that I will not tell on anyone or I have not snitched anyone off."

Close said, "Well, Willson, you haven't done nothing to me, but I can't talk for everyone else. But I will try to keep them away from you for now if you have more canteen to give."

"Yes. Yes, I do," said Willson. Willson handed Close more candy and coffee and cookies through the food slot in the door.

After Close got the cookies, he said, "But you know that if these guys want to get to you, I can't stop them and not even God Himself can keep them from getting to you."

"Please, Bobby, do your best to stop them, will you?" questioned Willson.

"Yes, I will," said Close, and away he went.

Willson took a deep breath of air and sat down on the bed. He was thinking, *God already has saved me from you, you assholes!* Then he just sat there thinking, "How long will they stay away? I better try and rest before the next wave of problems comes this evening, after they have had time to rest."

Plans back on the party block of B-block were being made to hide keys and destroy everything that was conclusive evidence. The officers' cuff keys were distributed between the marauders who did the killings. Ritchson kept his cuff key in his pocket, and figured when the riot was over, he would swallow his key for later when he was being transferred from the prison; the key would break him free. Wild took his cuff key and went to his cell and cut away the rubber caulking from behind the sink about an inch. Then he placed the key behind the caulking and then, taking a piece of gum that was chewed and moist, placed it in the crack, then pressing the caulk to the gum. When he was finished, there was no trace the caulking was tampered with; just a cut in the rubber. Another cuff key was taken to the hallway by the west cage. Cox climbed up the outside of the cage wall with help from another inmate, and climbed into the false ceiling. He maneuvered through the metal beams to a location in front of the sally-port of B-block and C-block. He placed the cuff key and a wire shank that was sharpened to a point on the ledge of a metal beam with a piece of gum sticking it to the metal beam. Another cuff key was boiled in hot water. Then he put it in plastic. He was going to wait until the guards took back the building, then place it in his mouth and swallow it for later. Then, when he had a bowl movement, he would screen through the shit and find the key.

Bobby Close had the last key. He was going to gamble on the odds. It is in a man's nature not to stare at another man's penis or under his scrotal sack. When a guard strip-searches an inmate, he will do his job fast when it comes to the private parts. Cons know this and use it to their advantage by placing contraband up their ass or under their scrotum. Close took a key and went back to his room, placing the key under his scrotum and then, taking a small piece of duct tape that he saved for probably a year; he got the duct tape from a maintenance crew who was working on the block one day. Inmate Close talked the employee out of a piece of duct tape to tape up a picture of his family. He saved the duct tape under the cell's cement desk for just this occasion, then a few days later, got a piece of Scotch tape from an office to hang his picture; the scotch tape was legal for him to have. The duct tape would secure the key in place for a week, undetected by the guards.

An oxygen bottle was on B-block and everyone hanging around tried to figure out what to do with the bottle.

"Can you blow it up and half the building at the same time without killing me?" asked one of the inmates.

Langford spoke up, "No. Oxygen is pretty much a safe gas. It has to have an igniter to blow anything up. Even if you have an igniter, it still won't blow up; it just lights a flame."

"What if you break the top off the K-cylinder, what would it do then?" somebody asked.

Langford said, "I don't think it would blow up, but it might act like a projectile that will shoot like a canon. Just break the pipe off by dropping something heavy on it, and the cylinder will shoot out from the back end. But I am not sure that will happen. All my resources thought that is what will happen, but who knows?"

"We can put it on the upstairs landing and when the cops come in, if we're not ready to give up, we can kill maybe four or more cops," said Langford.

"That sounds like a plan," someone said.

∗ ∗ ∗ ∗ ∗ ∗ ∗ ∗ ∗ ∗ ∗ ∗

1150 Hours

The phone rang in the command post office where one of the lines was left open for the inmates to call back. There was a muffled voice that sounded like the same voice as last time, with other voices in the background, yelling.

"You're going to have to shut the cage door so I can hear you," proclaimed the sergeant. The sergeant listened to the caller and said, "Could you hold on for a minute? I will inform the warden what you have said."

The caller vented, "Fuckin' do it fast, you, you pig."

Then the sergeant muffled the phone and repeated the message to the group of hierarchy standing by the phone, "They said they have the PCs and the COs. They want the media at the fence with a camera. An inmate will come out and throw a list of demands over the fence."

McCormick spoke to the sergeant and said, "Tell them we will get back with them."

The message was delivered, and the demander yelled, "You better hurry or we will kill one of the old guards and throw his head to you!" The phone was then slammed down from inside of max in the main control cage.

At about 1155 hours, Warden McCormick had the sergeant call back to the cage, and he said, "We will allow the media person if we can surround the building. We want to keep this isolated only to the max building."

Then the sergeant added his own words, "Please stay patient. We have the TV media person here, and he has agreed to go alone into the max compound and take pictures and retrieve the paper of demands so we can end this as peacefully as possible. But to do this, we have to bring in the fire truck to the back of max but just inside of no-man's land."

The sergeant went quiet; there was a silence on the phone. He could hear faint sounds, but nothing else. It was almost five minutes before the perpetrator was back on the line. It was so quiet in the command post, with hearts beating a little higher than normal while waiting breathlessly for the caller to answer. This time, it was a little bit quieter; the door was closed to the cage, and all was said from a different muffled voice, "Your demands are justified," and the phone was hung up.

1156 Hours

The warden asked for some of the DCT team to have high-band radios and call signs: Micu #37, Mays #1, Sgt. Perry #2, Tower Eagle II #23, Commando Tower I. Mahellich call sign #36 spotting scope outside fence from main control, high- band #77 outside of max's back door, MSP #3 Mahoney, Alpha #1 DCT team, Warden McCormick when or if he goes out to the max site, Alpha #7.

Warden McCormick talked to the constituents that he picked to manage the riot in the BP (Board of Pardons) room across from the command post. McCormick said, "Mahoney, you are in charge of the DCT team, organizing with Micu, Guthrie, and Hanson. You work with Micu and Charlie Strong. You stick to Micu's back pocket at all times. I want at least two people in the towers at all times until further notice. Micu, in your estimation, what do you need to take back the building?" asked the Warden.

Micu answered, "I need twenty DCT members, with some of that twenty for support factors. They can help the team get in the building, such as a key man, fire truck driver, a man to climb a rope to the top of the building to be our eyes from there, four or six CS gas canisters (irritant similar to tear gas).

"Take extra equipment for all contingencies," commented the Warden. "Captain DeYott, have the infirmary up and going over procedures and policies." Then the warden asked if there were any comments.

Mr. Mahoney spoke up and added, "The broadband base will be set up in the BP room and the call sign would be Base Command. There are seventy rioting maximum security inmates, the worst that we have at the prison, but of those seventy inmates, by the national average, only about ten percent or a little more are causing the problems. The rest of the inmates housed in max are just trying to survive and wait until we come in to take the unit back. There are a lot of scared people inside of there, so keep your finger off the trigger until you are forced. But do not hesitate to shoot if the need arises, because you are going into the unknown. So at the utmost, do not be taken hostage. Retreat if you must, or evacuate inmates where you can.

* * * * * * * * * * * * *

1300 Hours

It was before 1300 hours when the DCT team got on the back of the old fire truck. Carl Nelson was driving, with Joe Rainville sitting on the passenger side with a fireman's axe and a crowbar, to do what with was uncertain, but for now it was for safety. Driving around the perimeter fence to the warehouse, the fire hoses were taken off the truck. This took some time because no one who was helping wanted to be overworked because they were going into an engagement ready for battle, knowing the outcome was unknown. Scary and fearful was the job at hand and there was no backing down; it was a mission with courageous valor.

1330 Hours

The hoses were off the truck, and they drove to the guard station where there were two officers standing at the building. In general, it was called the back gate entrance or the guard station, where one officer was inside the building locked into a room with switches to open and close gates and doors into and out of the main complex. But before the guard station officer opened a gate, he would call to the command post to get clearance to proceed. The officer on the floor was to shake down inmates and vehicles coming and going through the doors and gates. This sounded like an easy post and safe, because you were working on the outside of the prison with only inmates who were classified medium and minimum custody. The back gate was hectic during the day, with over 100 inmates going in and out, and trucks from the laundry and the warehouse bringing in supplies.

Years in the past, there had been two separate incidents. From the high side of the fence, there was an inmate who was working in the kitchen inside the main compound about thirty yards from the guard station. Well, each day, the warehouse truck would come in the compound through the guard station and park behind the kitchen dock. The inmates from the kitchen would unload the supplies of milk and food from warehouse trucks, then load the truck up with the plastic containers of milk crates left from the days before. Inmates have nothing to do but watch the officers do their job and find loopholes in their performance, figuring out how to get around the officers to do the devil's work.

So, one day, William Whitney was bringing in the milk, and he backed up to the loading dock and got out and went inside with the paperwork for the milk and other supplies. The truck was left unattended because there was no guard watching the truck. An inmate named Todd was watching the routine for weeks to see what was going on. Plus, Todd had escaped from jail twice before. While Whitney was in the kitchen doing his job, Todd got in the back of the truck while other kitchen workers piled the plastic boxes around him, and there were enough boxes to fill the back of the truck. So Whitney started the truck up and pulled away, far enough so he could shut the two doors to the back of the truck. Then he hopped in and went through the two gates as they opened to the guard station. After the truck was out of the compound, the truck stopped and Whitney got out. The guard from the back gate was Officer Eble. He was too busy to shake down the truck properly, so he asked Whitney if the truck was okay. Whitney replied that he was inside the kitchen and did not know for sure if it was clear. Whitney opened the doors to the back of the truck and, with Eble by his side, looked in the back with a truckload of plastic boxes. Eble said he could see through the boxes, and told Whitney that he could leave. Whitney drove to the prison dairy, which was about a mile up the road from the main compound but still on prison property. He turned off the truck and went to the back to start unloading the boxes. While he opened the doors, inmate Todd jumped out of the truck with a knife, trying to put Whitney in the truck. But William was not having anything to do with being locked into the truck. Todd ran off into the trees, and Whitney went into the dairy and reported an escape. Todd was gone for maybe six months. Eble lied in his board hearing, that he told Whitney to shake down the truck, and got a month off without pay; Whitney also got a month off without pay for doing his work and taking the blame. Last but not least, a day before an escape was planned, a gun was found in a fish aquarium at the high-side library. The methodical plan took in about four inmates from the high side. They were going to check out of Close Unit II to go between the low-side and the high-side fences into the chapel for weekly study group. The bible study was after dark, about 1800 hours. The inmates were going to kill the two guards at the chapel, and take their uniforms and wear them. Then two inmates dressed in officer's uniforms were going to walk down toward the back gate, and the officer would let another officer through the walkthrough gate. Then they would walk into the door of the guard station at the back gate of the building. The inmates were going to kill the guard and open the gates, so the other two inmates could come into the back gate. There were keys on the wall, and all the inmates knew that there were keys for the vehicles parked outside the gates. They were going to take all the keys and use two cars or trucks and escape.

But the plan was stopped when an inmate informant told where the gun was and who was involved, which was God's blessing for everyone. So, who said we don't need snitches in a prison? By the way, the biggest snitches are among the heavies, looking to save themselves or for better privileges.

The DCT team was out walking around the fire truck, just trying to relax until the phone rang inside the guard station. Finally, the phone rang; it was the warden, and Micu was the recipient, saying, "Yes, Sir." Then a few seconds later, "Yes, Sir; we will do it, and I will let you know what is going on over the radio on channel 2, and you said that Alfa #7 was your call sign; is that correct?" Then another pause, "If you would, Warden, Sir, get someone to bring the keys to the back of max." Another pause, then, "We're off." Micu hung up the phone.

Out of the guard station he came, informing all the DCT team to "reload onto the fire truck and to put the large green canvas over the top of everyone so the inmates will not know for sure what is going on and how many of us there are.

Meanwhile, Wolfie gave me the rope with three prongs on the end, to grab the wall about a foot above the roof, and two canisters of gas. I put the canisters under my blue sweater and tucked the sweater in so the canisters were hidden; that way, I did not have to carry them.

The sun was beating down and sweat was forming around the helmet, underarms, and the pit of the back, but no one complained. Silence was deadening; not a sound from anyone, but above the silence was the sound of the motor, and now the inmates from Close Unit I and II were yelling out their windows to the back of the building. Not a word was heard by the DCT team from the taunting and yelling from the inmates standing by their windows to the sober faces on the fire truck. One gate opened to the compound then closed, then the next gate opened and closed after the truck came through, stopping at the high-side gate.

Joe Rainville got out of the truck with the keys to the gate. He opened the lock and then pushed the two large gates open. The fire truck went through and stopped inside the gates while Joe shut and locked the gates, then got back in the truck. The green tarp was too small for all of us to fit under it, so two of us dressed in plain clothes were at the end of the truck, not under the tarp. I looked around as we went behind Close I and II. I remembered I still had my checkbook in my back pocket from church, and that I had to get rid of it before I started climbing the rope. Why that came to mind, I do not know, but I did not want to lose it anywhere around the building. Next, we were behind the Close Unit III building and again, the inmates were yelling and beating on their windows. Close III was built at the same time as max and built in the same manner, so the windows did not open and were narrow and long. But that did not stop the inmates from making an uproar. The fire truck had to stop again while Joe opened the two gates and shut them after we were through. The area we were in was known as the no-man's land. It was a vacant lot about an acre wide and two acres long. Nothing is inside the area except for grass.

It was there in case of emergencies like the one at hand.

Still under the tarp, the truck was at the max gate. A cool breeze came by, and shivers went down my spine and my stomach knotted up. With all that was going on around me, I felt an eerie feeling as the hair at the back of my neck hair stood straight, and hatred was coming over me. I felt it was time to pay back the inmates for destroying the inside of the max building. I wanted to take my frustration out on the useless max inmates. Then it came to me to do my job and let the Lord take care of the rest.

Rainville opened the two gates and shut them. We were behind the max building. The tarp came off and all jumped out. Going over to the front of the truck where Carl Nelson was standing, I asked him if I could leave my checkbook with him and he said, "I have a pile of things from other officers; just put it with them in the cab seat of the truck." Taking the rope in my right hand, I shielded it from the inmates looking out the windows from the max building, and went to the west side of the building where there were no windows, just a two-story concrete wall.

∗∗∗∗∗∗∗∗∗∗∗∗∗

1310 Hours

At 1250 hours, an apparent method to a plan was pretty much finalized. A call was sent to the west control cage, letting the inmates know that the penitentiary was sending a media spokesman into the max complex, as they requested. For no circumstance was the spokesman to go inside of the building, just videotape from outside the building and if the inmates wanted to throw out a list of demands, he could pick that up and get it back to the command post.

Jim Pomroy, acting administrator of the Department of Corrections, was appointed acting director less than two weeks before today, and his background was in community corrections; he was not familiar with the prison. Be that as it may, he was roped into a pursuit to keep his job to walk toward the front door and around the front part of max, showing his stage of a momentary diversion. The warden needed a person who was unknown to the inmates, and Mr. Pomroy was *that* person. The purpose was to keep the inmates interested in getting their moment of fame on TV instead of watching the fire truck going to the back of max. Mr. Pomroy was at the prison for just a short while when asked, then handed the camera and was being briefed as he was walking to the max gate.

The time started ticking at 1310 hours as he walked through the max gate alone.

He kept walking slowly to the front of max with the video camera to his face. He stayed on the sidewalk and was looking down at times to make sure of his footwork so that he did not fall off the concrete sidewalk and twist an ankle. Mr. Pomroy came to the front of the max building and saw a bloody, beaten person dressed in khaki clothes. Not knowing what to do, if he should stay there at the front door or get away from the door, he chose to leave.

He had a radio on him, and after retreating a ways from the building, he called on the radio and said, "Base command, this is the reporter in front of max."

The base command post answered, "Go ahead, reporter."

Mr. Pomroy spoke, "There is a person at the front door of max who is bloody and beaten. He is wearing khaki-colored clothes and is very scared."

The base command post answered, "Do not go near the building any more. Stay back as far as you can to see the top of the max roof, and video things from there. Is that understood?"

"Roger, base command, that is understood," said Mr. Pomroy.

Thank God, they didn't want me to go back to the front door, Pomroy said to himself. He was thinking, *When is that fire truck coming? How did I get this job and why did I ever go to college to get a degree in corrections? I thought I would be at a desk and give orders, not have my life threatened. But that is why I got into corrections; it was to make a stand in penology, to keep people that need to be in prison, like those that are in max, and for a better, safer life for people on the streets.*

Boy, look at all the law enforcement around the outside perimeter of the fence.

Local police are here and all with their lights on the top of the vehicles. The towers have men with rifles on the gun ports at the top of the tower and a sniper on the mound northeast of max on the perimeter road. I am safe, I think, out here. I wish they would get going with that fire truck. It was coming from the back side of Close Unit III, but I don't see it anywhere. Lord, I pray that all these gambles go well, that no more people get hurt and that my days from now on go better than this crucible ordeal.

* * * * * * * * * * * *

1330 Hours

The DCT team was hopped up and at the same time, each one was scared to death. But there was no turning back and no one would have said they were afraid, because it was a man thing to have no fear. I walked around the building to the west, and there I was facing the wall of concrete and steel fortress. From the sidewalk to the top of the wall, it was twenty feet or better.

Throwing the anchor and rope was easy, as I said to myself, "Just grab the end of the rope with my left hand and twirl the rest of the rope with the hook in my right hand and...and...and throw it uuupp. There, that was easy! Okay—now, how do I climb this rope to the top? I have only climbed ropes that dangled from a ceiling in a gym. Oh, boy, I really opened my mouth this time, didn't I, jackass. Well, I have climbed ropes using my legs as a stop on the rope and I have climbed without my legs, just my hands, but that was over ten years ago. Okay, here I go pulling myself up and wrapping my legs around the rope to rest. My knuckles are rubbing on the cement wall. This isn't working."

I jumped down about ten feet to the ground, hoping that they don't need me yet on the rooftop already, because it did not happen. I thought for a minute; I had seen on TV movies that the ninja climb walls with their feet to the wall and hands on the rope. I did not have a better idea, so I tried this. It was hard but it was working; slowly, up the rope I went. As I got closer to the top, it was getting harder because the rope stayed close by the building. My tennis shoes were gripping the wall well.

Reaching for the rooftop with my left hand and arm, I pulled myself to the top.

Then there was no going back down the rope because it was either make it on top or fall to the ground. Taking my right hand on the rope and my arm hugging and grabbing the wall, I started pulling myself up. I had my chest and arms up now; I tried to hurry up because gravity was forcing my legs down. Pulling upward with my arms, now my waist was over the top, so I lifted my right leg over, and the climb was about over. The left leg came fast. I did it! I looked around, and I was the only one on the roof.

Meanwhile, at the back of the max building, they were trying each key in the back door. "None of the keys would fit; what is wrong? You try the keys, Carl," stated Micu. Carl tried the keys and could not get a key to fit.

"This is taking too long for a surprise attack. Let's try plan B and take a ladder to the top of the roof and go down the catwalk into the back part of the building," said the DCT team leader, Micu. That was quick thinking and a good plan, so Carl and Joe got the ladder and put it on the back of the building to the west end.

* * * * * * * * * * * *

I was the only one on top of the building, looking around, to find that the escape hatch was nearby. Walking over to it, I could hear voices in the cage, talking. My heart skipped a beat, knowing that this was the scariest time in my life. If the inmates knew I was on top, they could come get me, and I was not going to let that happen. I could stand on the lid of the escape hatch after I put the canister of CS gas down the hatch. That sounded like a good plan to me, so I tried to open the hatch but it would not open. The marauders must have locked it from the inside. I ran over to the other side to check it out, and it was locked also. Then I went over to the back of the building and talked as low as I could, only for the team to hear me on the ground. "The hatches are locked and they will not open." After telling Commander Micu the information, I was looking for a getaway plan in case any inmates heard me or even saw me from inside the building. Next to the back door was the death trailer, and it was only a jump away to the roof.

"That would work just fine if I had to jump, I suspect," I said, talking to myself. "It looks like a twelve-foot drop and the roof is metal with good wood support beams. I think it would give a little to break my fall. The only thing to worry about is jumping too far out and landing on the trailer, then falling off the trailer to the hard cement walkway. If that would happen, it would be better than what the inmates could do to me."

* * * * * * * * * * * *

The ladder was placed against the north wall, and up came the DCT team, one by one, to the rooftop. An alternate plan was devised that two from the team would go down from the roof to the catwalk, then down the ladder to the floor inside the yard. They would check the door that leads inside the back hallway from the chain link fence that separates the six dog runs. The two team members went down with their .357 pistols loaded. On the roof were three shotguns watching each door in case of an ambush. The team member who had the key to the door was instructed to try the door and if it opened, then he would lock it back up until the rest of the team could get down there for a dynamic entry. A right turn of the key was made, and it opened the lock. A rush of adrenalin came over him. Then he took it one more step to see if the door would come open all the way. There was no chance that an inmate could be hiding behind the door because there was a window in the door, and the team member looked both ways and down inside the door.

There was no one around the door, but the door did not open because it was chained shut. The team member looked at Commander Micu, and taking his hand with his palm down, brought his hand back and forth to his neck, with his head shaking from side to side, indicating there was no entry through the catwalk. Commander Micu waved them back up to the roof. With the entrance team gathered on the roof, Micu asked if anyone had a suggestion. One said they could break the window in the door that leads down the catwalk. Another person said "We could pry off the lids to the escape hatches and drop the gas down, then go down a minute later." Another suggestion was to go back down the ladder to the front door and go through the door with a key and then through a barricade to C-block where the officers were.

Commander Micu asked, "How long will it take to break the hatch open?"

An answer came back, "We can have it open in less than five minutes."

"Let's get to work, guys. Open up both hatches and gas them as planned."

Four DCT team members went to the east cage hatch with a crowbar and wire cutters. The west cage was being hacked at with a fireman's axe. Others were also trying to pry up the hatch, but it was not working because the best tools were at the other end. In two or three minutes, the east cage hatch was opened and the CS gas was dropped down and then the hatch was closed again, with a gun watching the hatch.

The west cage was next and it went fast, cutting the belly chain with the wire cutter, then throwing my CS gas canister down the hatch. Then the hatch was shut for some seconds. Then Commander Micu tried to look down the dark hole with his gas mask on but he could not see inside. The sun was shining brightly, so that made it impossible to see down a hole until your eyes adjusted to the darkness. Finally, his eyes adjusted and he could see to the bottom of the cage, and no further.

So with no thought for his own safety, Commander Micu told the team, "Stay together. We will get about five men in the cage before we head over to C-block and find our officers." In most cases, the commander will stay back to command, but this was not done because there was no formal training in this circumstance, and Micu was a born leader, taking control; "Do as I do and we will get through this," was his motto.

After one more look down the hole, he pulled his gun from the holster and with his finger on the trigger, he turned to face the metal ladder with one hand on the gun and the other hand on a metal rung. The DCT team members had a hand on him right by the hatch, ready to grab him if he was pulled down from a would-be marauder. Micu kept his body close to the rungs and pointed the pistol down the ladder, taking his hand off the rung and catching the same hand on the next one down. He could hear voices close to the cage, or was there someone inside the cage? He lowered his leg to the next rung down and then a hand in the same manner as before, then waiting down on the third rung until his eyes adjusted again. There was no one in the cage; Micu could see clearly enough through the CS gas smoke. He stepped down another rung and let go of the upper rung, swiftly grabbing the next bar down. Now he was halfway down the ladder, and could see that the door to the cage was shut. Inmates were running back and forth, going where, he did not know. Micu kept on going down the ladder in the same manner, still hearing voices coming from the cage. Now, the voice was singing.

"What is going on?" Micu was asking himself. On top of the roof, one of the team members was on his stomach, trying to look down the hatch, with his .357 pistol pointing down away from Micu but to the front where he figured the door was to the cage. To the DCT team that was on the top of the graveled flat roof, it seemed that it was taking forever, standing there waiting with the silence, hearing a fly buzzing by as they waited their turn to enter the hatch.

Commander Micu was finally to the flooded cement floor. He kicked the two CS canisters out the cage door and shut the door again. He figured out the voice that penetrated the smoke was a radio talking about the riot and at times singing songs. Micu waved to the second member who was watching him, and he yelled through the gas mask to come on down. Micu kept his eyes forward out the door window, ready for something to happen unexpectedly. There were still inmates running around, but none were trying to interrupt the coming advance.

Robert Young was the next one to start the descent down the ladder. He was equipped with a revolver; as well, he was trying to maneuver the rungs in the same grace and manner as Micu— one step with his foot, then swiftly letting go of his hand and grabbing the next rung down the ladder. This was going fine to the halfway point of the ladder, when his hand slipped from the rung and down he fell to the pooled-up water. He fell on his back with his head hitting Micu from behind, and a loud thud sound came out of his mouth. Pain shot down to his feet as Young lay there momentarily, as Micu helped him up and yelled through the face shield, asking, "Are you okay?"

Young answered, "I think so," and Micu left it at that.

Robert Morani was already on the ladder, headed down when he saw DCT member Young fall, but it was unclear what happened. Morani was equipped with a short-barreled shotgun that was manufactured to disperse a crowd of people dead or wound away to the ground. He was forced to climb down the ladder in the same manner as the other two, but he had the shotgun pointed down, and his finger was on the trigger. He was still blinded by the sunlight and hearing voices from below, and not understanding what was being said, just noting that Young fell off the ladder.

What has happened down below? Morani was thinking. *Did the inmates take Micu and Young hostage? I can't see a damn thing, and what are the voices coming from the cage. I hope I don't have to shoot. Please, God, let this plan work.*

Down another rung he went, then by the power of sight, he could see that Micu and Young were all right. Morani yelled up the ladder and said, "Call Alpha 7 and have him turn off the power to the building; there is too much noise hindering us down here!"

A member of the team called, "Alpha 7, this is Afa 12. Turn off the power to the max building."

"Alpha 7 copies," came a reply that only radios with channel 2 could hear.

Seconds later, the power was off and the building was somewhat dark inside. The only sound inside was alarms coming from the basement and filtering through the floor. There was still light enough to see, but it gave the illusion of doom and despair in the pit of hell.

Jerry Guthrie was the fourth to head down the ladder with his pistol in his hand.

He was able to maneuver the ladder faster than the others because there was more communication from below, telling him it was safe to come down. The team was now piling into the cage faster than before but, systematically, they were in defensive tactics; every move was thought out before doing it or they would not get another play. It was a constant fourth down; no mistakes, no turning back.

There were seven DCT members in the cage now, and it was time to make a move to C-block. The sprinkler head was outside the cage door and as each one of the team went through it, causing some inconvenience to the troops, making their helmets and face shields wet and hard to see through; not to mention the gas mask that was sweaty and sticky on their faces. They left two team members to guard the back hallway in case of an oncoming attack from D, E, and F side. Two team members were watching the front hallway as Commander Micu and six others made their way, walking slowly around the outside of the cage to the sally-port of C-block. Two of the troops were stationed at the sally-port with shotguns, watching both blocks.

Where were the marauders? each of the team members was thinking to himself. *Not one inmate has tried to stop us.*

What was going on and getting more obvious was that the marauders were not organized with a takeover plan this early in the game.

Charlie Miller was already yelling out behind the mattress, "We are in the shower down here."

The hostages who were barricaded in their tiny fortress unlocked the metal grill gate door to the shower. They were in that cramped space for around three and a half hours. It was long enough to ponder their lives before, during, and if it was going to be their last day alive on earth. The unknown will change their way of making decisions for the rest of their lives. A big weight was lifted off their shoulders as they came out of the shower looking totally drained of energy. Micu did not have to say anything to the hostages; they were coming toward him.

Micu looked around the block, pointing his pistol as he turned, and yelled with the gas mask still on, "Stay in your cells, gentlemen, and don't move. We will get you out of here as soon as we can."

All the inmates stood in their own cell doorways, smiling. Bobby Close was just leaning against his door with his arms crossed, acting calm and cool, his bandana on his head. He was not smiling, but a slight grin was on his face. Each inmate acted as if they were angels just coming home from parochial school. The hostages came to Commander Micu, and he asked, "Is any one of you hurt?"

The five answered no.

"Is this all of you in the building?" asked Micu. He received an answer of yes from all of them at once, but he still had to ask the question again in another way to make sure there were no mistakes.

"Are there any other staff hostages somewhere else in the building?"

"No, let's get out of here," one of the hostages said.

"We will take you through the front door. Let's go!" said Micu.

During this time as well, most of the inmates who lived on A, B, and C blocks were at their cell doors, waiting to see what was going to happen next. The marauders were not organized; they did not figure a takeover plan. Locking all the exits to the building with chains was ciphered complete because in riots in the past, they would negotiate for days to get the hostages back and/or with the building or prison back.

Before the prison was built, it was designed to house inmates in different units instead of one building in case of a riot, to contain the area being assaulted.

Through the water they went, the five hostages and two team members, back through the sally-port of B and C, stopping to make sure the rest of the team knew what to do next. Micu gave an order to start on C-Block and get all the inmates to strip down to nothing and have them lie on the floor to cuff them with plastic cuffs on the hands. Keep them on the block until officers were coming in the front door to escort them to no man's land.

The assault to take back the maximum building started at 1320 hours when Warden McCormick gave the okay to go, broadcasting it over the radio. From 1320 hours, there was no communication from inside of max. It was like a time capsule left somewhere in space, with the warden on down the line. Their hearts were beating out of their chests. Each minute went by like they were hours. The warden, with a gauntlet team of ninety-plus staff, was waiting at the max gate for Commander Micu to inform them it was clear to start sending inmates out the front door. The staff was given all the equipment that the prison had to hand out. There were some night sticks, some shields, some helmets, and a lot of plastic ties that, when they were placed around, say, your wrist and cinched tight, it locked in place like a piece of metal. These plastic restraints, when used, can only be cut off to get them off, and can only be used once.

There were a lot of mixed up emotions going on by staff. Most of them were jacked up, scared, and worried for the officers who were taken hostage. On top of all that, knowing that the max inmates destroyed the max building, costing all of the staff and all the taxpayers millions of dollars. Very few, a couple, of the staff had mental issues of their own, wanting to take it out on the inmates to relieve problems that they were having at home. There was an officer who was called Silver Spoon because whenever he got into trouble, people helped him get out of trouble. It was said that if he jumped into a pile of shit, he would come out smelling like roses after the incident, but it still would be a pile of shit. Silver Spoon's father was a police officer, and it was well known that the town was being robbed, with stores losing big items like televisions and stereos and furniture in the night. The information was getting around town about the policemen robbing the stores, so the robberies stopped and there was no investigation. Silver Spoon was big and dumb. He knew that his life was fine being with the gauntlet team, but if the marauders had him as a hostage, they, in all likelihood, would have used his brains to negotiate with. Silver Spoon's family was comparable to a mafia family in a little town, but too ignorant to do any better than stealing candy from a baby.

So, there would be about three out of ninety people on the gauntlet who were getting their kicks from abusing inmates that day.

Down the hallway, Commander Micu and the five hostages went toward the front door. There were around fifteen DCT team members in max now, most of them armed with a shotgun or pistol, on guard for the hostages to make it safe to the outside of the building. Checking each door with his pistol leading the way, Micu's finger was on the trigger, looking into the broom closet, which was the first door to the right down the hall. He checked it out and saw there were no marauders. This process took seconds checking rooms, because all rooms were empty with their contents in the hallway, barricading the front door. Next were the rooms to the left, a supply room and the visiting room for inmates to visit behind glass. These rooms checked out okay. Then came the sergeant's office; it was trashed, with the desk in the hallway, but it was clear of marauders.

At this time, the inmate in the front sally-port was yelling at Micu, saying, "Help me! Get me out of here! I am one of the PCs that they were trying to kill!"

There was one more door to check before Micu listened to Hornback, who was in the sally-port. The door was on the right and that was the staff bathroom, and a mop room to the front of the bathroom. Micu looked to see if it was clear as he was looking at the inmate in the sally-port. He told the inmate to get down on the floor and stay there, but inmate Hornback was excited to finally see an end to his ordeal.

Hornback was still standing, trying to explain, saying, "I am one of the PCs, and they were trying to kill me. I just want out of here."

Micu stated, "I don't care who you are, get down or you will be a dead inmate."

The hostages could not breathe from the CS gas in the hallway. They were starting to choke, and eyes were tearing up.

Browne told Micu, "We can't stay here any longer, the gas is killing us. We're going back on the block until you get the front opened up."

Micu nodded his head and said, "Okay," as he had his pistol pointed at Hornback. Back the hostages went to the sally-port, and onto B-block they went to get some cleaner air. They did not want to go back onto C-block because, psychologically, to them it was a step in the wrong direction. On B-block, they were told to go to a cell and they would be locked down until the front door was opened, but none of the hostages were about to be locked down.

Browne, after coughing and choking, said, "Let us go through the cage and out the escape hatch." So that was the next plan, and back through the sally-port they went, wading through the water to the cage, with the sprinkler still spraying the door of the cage. There was even worse CS gas smoke by the cage, but that did not stop the hostages from going in the cage and starting up the ladder. They were all trying to hurry and get out to the fresh air. But for the last two hostages, it was choking them. They put their mouths over to their arm and tried to breathe into their shirt sleeves. They waited it out until it was their turn to climb the ladder. Choking but still relieved that he was going up the ladder, Dale Browne was always thinking of his companions before himself.

On top of the roof, I was watching the hostages coming out of the hatch one by one. It was a relief seeing them alive, and I kept on asking them if they were all right. As they came out of the hatch, each of them bent over, taking deep breaths trying to clear their lungs.

It was 1339 hours, and Alpha 1 called on the radio, "All officers on the roof."

That was to let everyone know what was going on, but everyone knew because the staff could see from the max gate. Nineteen minutes from the time the DCT team went down the hatch, the officers were freed. It was time to move closer to max, and Warden McCormick with his men was jogging toward the front door of max. The walkway was a good quarter-mile jaunt from the gate, but it was good to burn off energy that was looking for a release. McCormick would wait until he got the okay from Commander Micu before he would open the front door of max. I could see the troops coming from the gate, as did the DCT team member that was on the roof with me.

He said, "The gas is making me sick, Boog. Is it getting to you, also?"

"It's not getting me sick, but it does stink, Paul," I replied, answering his question.

Paul had a shotgun, and his job was to watch the one inmate who was in the recreation yard. All I was thinking at this time was, "Thank you, God, for saving my fellow workers and especially for the life of my friend, Dale. But, Lord, will you do one more favor for me? Please, let my brother Bob be okay. I know that he has done wrong, but let him live to change his life around, to honor you and humble him to bring others to you, I pray. Amen. And I gave the sign of the cross, in the name of the Father, Son and Holy Spirit. Amen.

Commander Micu was talking to inmate Hornback as he was lying on the floor in the front corridor.

"All the PCs are dead. I think I am the only one left," said Hornback.

"Where are the bodies?" Micu asked, talking through the barricade.

"They're on the day room floor of D-block. Get me out of here before they come to get me!" pleaded Hornback.

Commander Micu and Sergeant Garrison tried taking the barricade down, but it seemed too daunting and too physical a task for Micu; his mind was at a rush, and there was more excitement on the east side of max. That was what Commander Micu lived for, to be in control and to have the upper hand, and with his pistol, he had both. So he went back to the cage area and informed team members that he was going to the east side of max; he would take Garrison, Guthrie, and Spangberg with him. This was not recommended by the team before; they were told to stay together and clear one side, then the other. Breaking apart the team could cause confusion and/or trap part of the team from well-organized marauders just looking for a mistake, to kill ever more and then that would be their fame of glory.

Down the back hallway, the four members went checking all doors for problems.

The laundry room was the first room to the left. It looked shut, so they went through the electric door that was still open. Looking to his left again, Micu scanned the infirmary room. It was demolished and torn to pieces, but no inmates were inside. While Micu was checking the infirmary room from the doorway, Guthrie was checking the storage room next door. The storage room was trashed but clear of inmates. Next, Micu checked the outside door to the catwalk that was on the right. The door was chained and locked shut, so he proceeded to the max storage room to the left, with the rest of the team behind him. Micu looked inside; this was the biggest room in the back hallway. Shelves were tipped over and boxes were everywhere in the room, and some in the hallway. It was a disaster, but only spending seconds on the room from the doorway, he lead the team to the back door where it was chained shut and locked to the electric door bar to the east side.

Through the electric door, they went while Alpha 7 was trying to get in contact with him. Outside, they were being deprecated against riot, not knowing what was going on inside; tension was off the chart.

Warden McCormick was thinking, *Why did I jeopardize the lives of more people? Come on, Micu, answer the radio.*

The next room was the east side laundry room. It was trashed also, but clear of inmates. Looking down the hall to the east cage, inmates were running back to their blocks and leaving D-block through the fire doors and the sally-port corridor. The four team members hurried past the cage to the corridor of D-block. The way was clear so they went on the block, and the sight they saw was unspeakable. While the four-member team was investigating D-block, two inmates from down the hallway ran past D-block on their way back to the west side of the building. Four inmates were in the counselor's office, looking for information to extort other inmates for money by looking through files. Through the back hallway they went.

Then the four inmates met others from the DCT team.

They were stopped at gunpoint, ready to be shot, but the DCT member demanded, "Stop where you are! Where are you going?"

The inmates answered, "A-block. That is where we live." There were no team members on A-block, so he let them go as he followed them around the corner of the west cage to the block.

That was the third one who came over from the other side. I hope Micu and the others are okay, the team member was thinking to himself.

This was the longest nine minutes of Warden McCormick's life. From 1339 hours to 1348 hours, there was no communication coming from inside the max building.

But, finally, there came a voice over the radio, saying, "Alpha 7, you can open the front door; this is Alpha 1.'

There was nothing the four-member team could do on the east side of max, so they went back to the west side. Hornback was freed when the door opened, but he was handcuffed and brought out to see the infirmary crew that was coming up the walkway. The barricades were broken down and some of the debris was shoved back into the sergeant's room. This gave the warden a chance to send in more men to help get inmates stripped and cuffed. The CS gas was so strong inside the building that they called for more gas masks. The C-block inmates were first to be stripped and cuffed and brought out. For the most part, all the inmates were glad that it was over. Inmate Bobby Close was putting on a façade, talking to the officer as if he knew nothing happened on the east side of max.

Alpha 1 asked for the water to be shut off, so the warden called maintenance to shut off the water, and a minute later, the sprinkler heads stopped pouring rain down on them. Now, they were totally in an offensive formation. It was just putting in the time doing a job as instructed, as the stress level went down a notch.

There were now four or six more officers helping inside the building, to strip the inmates and flex-cuff their hands behind their backs. The job was performed by telling everyone on the block to strip down to nothing then lie face down on the floor in front of their cells with their hands on their backs behind them. Then one officer would flex-cuff the inmate while a team member with a pistol stood by, pointing the gun at the inmate's head. This got the inmate's attention, and was working well on C-block. Next, the officer would take the inmate by the crook of his arm and help him up, escorting him over to more officers to line them up. Then when there was a group of inmates, run them off the block and down the hall to exit by the front door. There was plenty of staff running them through the building and out the door. The ironic thing about the procedure, which was necessary, was the glass that they broke from the windows on the blocks was the glass that they ran barefoot through to get out of the building.

This was where Silver Spoon came into the picture. He was knocking inmates who had their hands cuffed behind their backs down, or slapping them on the bare back just to show them he was no better than them. By mentality standards, Silver Spoon was below inmate standards. Everything was happening so fast, and Silver Spoon and two others had on helmet with face shields, so the inmates could not identify the narcissists. We are a humane society where you show inmates the right way to do things in a calm manner, if applicable, and only use force to the point, degree, and bearing to subdue an inmate. It is a fact that if you show aggression, then a person learns aggression, as a high percentage of the inmates have dealt with from childhood.

The team went to B-block next, which was the death-row block. The inmates were given a direct order to strip by their cells and then lie down on the floor face down. *This was not going as smoothly this time*, thought team member Geech.

Some inmates were following orders, but some were watching inmate Langford, and he would not get down. Langford had a grin on his face, and he was going to test the waters to see if Geech could stop him, or see if there were real bullets in the gun. Geech told the whole block again to get down, and most of the inmates on the block were down at this time, but Langford was still standing by the rail on the upper level. He was stripped down to nothing, but he would not get down on his stomach. Not a word came from his mouth, saying anything about any problems that he could not get down. He was just standing there with a grin on his face, staring at Geech, saying, with his gestures, that it was Geech's move. What will he do or should he do?

Meanwhile, Commander Micu conveyed that things were going well on the west side of max, and he wanted to investigate D-block again. He heard that one of the PCs was still alive in a cell, so this time, all but six of the team members went on the east side of max. Security-wise, there were enough men to check all rooms and clear the hallway down to the front sally-port. As they started through the back hallway, the doors were unchained and unlocked to get the CS gas smoke and fire smoke going out of the building. The back exit door was left locked so no inmates could somehow leave through the back.

Inmates McFarlane and Powell were yelling at the guards in the black suits.

"We're in here, two PCs in here!" both of them said.

Inmate Powell was waving a white pillow sheet through the broken window in the door. The officers yelled for them to come out, and a guard with a big ring of keys walked over to unlock the door. A pistol was pointed at Powell's face looking through the window. The two PC swampers yelled through the door, "The door is unlocked!" Pushing the dryer aside so that they could get out of their fortress, Powell and McFarlane thought they would have a warm welcome receiving them.

But coming out of the door, they were being yelled at, "On the ground, get on the ground, now!" It appeared to be the barrel of the pistol talking to them. That was all they could see, but it was effective; down they went to their knees as someone grabbed Powell's arm and forced him to the floor. A female officer had the flex-cuffs and was trying to put them on as another officer had a boot on Powell's back, forcing him to the floor. He had to lift his head up to keep from drowning in two and a half inches of water. The female was having trouble putting the cuffs on, so the other officer said, "No—like this."

He took the flex-cuff in both hands and went under both wrists at once, and brought the end of the plastic through the tie then lifted the end piece, bringing the hands in the air, cinching the hands together. Powell turned to look over at McFarlane and saw he was having the same amount of fun. Powell just told himself that he was thankful for being able to feel some pain at this time instead of being dead on the floor. Again, he was just thankful. They were both lifted up by the crooks of the arms and told to run out of the building.

On the radio, it was relayed, "Two PCs coming out of the building, McFarlane and Powell. Tell officer Powell who is stationed on the roof his brother is okay."

I knew that I was a special priority because if my brother was dead, then the administration had two options: First, keep me away from any guns in case I went ballistic or in today's society, we call it going postal. They figured that if someone was watching me, then I was easy to be found. Plus, then someone would come get me and grieve with the other inmate losses. I would have not done that, but would have gone home to grieve with my mother. So, knowing that he was alive, the administration knew that I would do my job and would not think about myself.

Hearing the radio transmission, Paul said, "Did you hear that, Boog?"

I was trying to act like it was no big deal, and I said, "Yeah, I heard, thanks."

Paul said, "Well, I guess I will go down from the roof because my stomach is queasy, if you will take my shotgun and watch the inmate in the yard for me, Boog?"

"Yeah, I will if I can have your radio also." So I took the shotgun and radio as I watched one inmate waiting to be taken from the yard.

The last of the DCT team members was the cameraman, and Officer Gibb was waiting on the roof for an okay to film the inside of the building. His chance came, and down the hatch Gibb went. Finally, he will see the devil's work behind the lens of a camera.

As inmates Powell and McFarlane were running through the building, officers were standing along the hallway with riot sticks, shoving and prodding them to keep them going so they would not lose their way. Outside the front door were two lines of staff members or a gauntlet. The sun was bright coming out of the dark fortified dungeon, as inmate Powell squinted his eyes just to see. "Move it!" was heard all the way down the line, "faster!" until he reached a place that was called no-man's land. Then McFarlane and Powell were told to lie down on the ground with their faces to the ground.

McFarlane whispered to Powell, "How did you like that merry-go-round, Bob?"

Bob replied, "It got a little bumpy and swimmy at times, Chuck, but it still beats being trapped in that laundry room with you telling me stories."

They both started to grin, and Chuck said in a low tone, "Look who we are lying by, the people who were trying to kill us on C-block." Powell just shook his head.

"Strip those two inmates," came a voice, as four officers came over and took off Powell's shoes and socks. He did not have to do anything, just lie there as one officer cut the pants and underwear off him. Next, it was his shirt they cut off, so fast that the shears cut like it was paper.

Bob said, "Chuck, did they take good care of you also?"

Chuck replied, "'Take,' but there was no 'care' about it."

Hornback spoke up, "Bob and Chuck, you guys are alive! They killed my friend, Ernie, they killed my friend, Ernie! They killed my friend, Ernie!"

Over the radio was transmitted, "We need a stretcher out here in no-man's land."

Minutes later, Hornback was taken away on the stretcher.

After Hornback left, McFarlane heard a staff member say, "The only one who should have died today, didn't."

That was the consciousness of all the people who were there today, that life would be better if Hornback were dead. But there was a reason that he did not die, and that reason was for God, Himself, to know for now.

By now, the sun was beating down on the naked inmates in the yard area. Steps were being made to house the inmates from max. A plan came up to use the old max build that was being used as a reception unit. This would take some time to relocate the inmates there, but for now, it was going to be baked inmates. After a half-hour of lying around with his hands tied behind his back with flex-cuffs on, Powell's hands began to start going to sleep on him. The flex-cuffs were tight around his wrist, so to ease the pain, he would rotate from side to side, and that was relieving some of the pain, but getting the shoulder sore.

As he was lying there, to get his mind off of his hands, he started to think, *I wouldn't be here in this mess if I wasn't thinking only of my own gratification and selfishness. My family has to hang their heads and live with what I have done, where I just commit a crime and go to prison, and live like I am paying back time for my crime, but in reality, the state takes care of a screw-up and I eat and sleep on.*

But my family is the one who loses, and my daughters are the biggest losers. I hope, God, that they will forget about me if I can't change. Please, take care of them for me, God, I ask only that.

* * * * * * * * * * * *

Commander Micu led the team to the east side through the back hallway, checking all rooms and doors. Then, as he came to the east cage, he gave orders for half the team to check out the hallway down to the front-door sally-port. Micu was to bring the team medic person on D-block, and two other members to guard them as they looked through the block. Sergeant Morani and two other team members started down the hallway, seeing black smoke coming out of one of two rooms at the end of the hall. But before going to where the smoke was, they had to check out the left side of the hall, a staff bathroom and a swamper's room. They checked out okay but it was trashed to pieces, the toilet and sink broken up, and the swamper's room had nothing inside but water and broken supplies. Next was an officers' lunchroom; the table was in the hallway, barricading the front doorway. The last three rooms were taken slowly because two of the rooms were on the right side of the hallway and the third room was the counselor's room where they could see the smoke coming from. This was tricky because the rooms on the right were around a short corner, and the hallway was blocked with piles of furniture, cabinets, and other miscellaneous thing. There was a small amount of light coming through the cracks of the barricade from outside. The team was trained to anticipate these predicaments because if inmates are waiting around the corner with clubs, they could rush the gun and knock it out of the hand before it was fired.

Morani whispered to the other team members as he lifted up his face shield and talked close to their faces, "Stay by the right wall but stop before you get to the corner. Look to the room on the left and watch to see if anyone is coming out of the door, or if they are trying to ambush us. If so, then yell 'Stop!' and just shoot if they take a step our way. I will wait to the left before the door, and if there is not a person at the door, you will nod your head and I will turn my shotgun to the corner on the right." He pointed with his shotgun and looked around the corner to see what was there.

The plan was set as they started walking closer. The doorway was clear to the left but black putrid smoke was coming out of the room. A nod was given and a surge of energy came from Morani as his finger was on the trigger, turning and walking toward the right corner. No present danger was there, so Morani nodded his head to the side, and the two members went around the corner and looked into the room to the right. Morani swiftly turned to his left and was looking in the counselor's room to the left. The smoke was coming from behind a chair in the room; something on the floor and the back of the chair was burning. He could see clothes and paper burning, but what was it lying behind the chair? Morani looked around the room before he went over to the chair. In his mind, the smell was human so being hesitant, he waited a second to see where his men were. The two men were trailing behind him. He went over to the chair, kicking it to the side and finding it was some burning rubber and a pile of clothes, to his relief. Out the door they went to tell the officers on the outside of the barricade that they could tear down the wall and open it up to extract inmates. Down the hallway, the three team members went, back to the east cage looking for Commander Micu.

Out of the D-block sally-port door came a gang of inmates. With quick reflexes and a sense of reason, Morani turned around, shoving the barrel of the shotgun into the gut of the first inmate. As inmate Gleed's arms were going in the air, Morani's finger was pressing lightly on the trigger.

"Don't shoot! Don't shoot!" said Gleed. Morani's finger let off the trigger as he took a step back and let the inmates run past them to the right hallway behind the east cage and into F-block where their cells were.

Morani kept his eye on the sally-port and said, "Watch those guys behind us!"

Inmates were running off D-block through the fire doors onto E-block. Micu had his two team members watching Medic O'Neill from the inside landing by the block door. O'Neill checked first the inmates lying on the floor face down. He checked for a pulse from the corroded artery in the neck of Holliday. He was dead but still warm, as O'Neill looked up at the inmate sitting against a mattress on the wall.

His head and chin were down, pressed against his neck, and his eye were closed shut. Blood was everywhere in the room; on the walls, floor, sink and toilet, but O'Neill was not privy to it so all he saw were bubbles of blood coming from the throat of Nida. O'Neill was stunned seeing a man with blood on every inch of his body, lifeless but there was some air coming from his lungs, causing the bubbles.

O'Neill went to touch Nida on the shoulder and asked loudly, "Are you all right?" the response phrase generic to EMTs. Nida opened his eye but could not talk. "Don't move. I will get you a towel and put it under your chin so it will clot the blood. Can you walk out of here?"

Nida moved his head and neck together, trying not to move his chin up from his neck. O'Neill brought the towel over to him and placed it under his chin where there was already one bloody towel from before. O'Neill is a stout man, and was conscious of Nida's delicate, weak situation. He figured if he could get his patient up and going out to the doctors, he would have a better chance than waiting here for maybe another hour. Reaching behind Nida, he kept a hand around under his armpit, and O'Neill grabbed his other arm to lift. Nida was lightheaded; the room started turning around while O'Neill sat him back down on the bed so he could get his bearings. The cut throat did not hurt so bad, it was the weakness throughout his body that troubled Nida. Nida was holding the towel to his neck mainly by his chin, but the right hand was next to the throat for support.

"One more try," said O'Neill as he lift Nida from the bed.

Helping him walk was tricky at first; Nida's legs were stiffening up from rigor mortis setting in. It was one foot then another foot, Nida's mind told his legs as he stepped over Holliday on the floor. Outside of the cell, he rested on the landing rail by the stairs. It was slow, but O'Neill was doing everything possible to get him a doctor and a blood transfusion. If he could get him out of the building, then a stretcher could take his place. Down the stairs Nida went. His mind was working hard just to walk, but a strange feeling come over him, giving him strength. Out he went through the sally-port doors. It was time to take a break for a minute, so O'Neill rested him against the cage. The CS gas was coming out of the cage, so it was a short break, but Nida was doing better. Down the hallway they went to the barricade that was almost opened up. Clean air was flowing through max building now as Nida made his way inside the front-door sally-port and outside to life. The doctor and nurse were there with a stretcher. Two officers helped Nida onto the stretcher, and down the walkway they went to the infirmary. Nida will live to tell his story and start a new life from now on.

* * * * * * * * * * * * *

It was Geech's move in a tense predicament. If he allowed Langford to stand, then the rest of B-block, that was the death-row block, would follow suit.

Langford was calling his bluff, thinking to himself, "Do they have real bullets in the gun. Is the man more afraid of me than I am of him? Can we change this around so that we can kill more people?"

The third time, Geech said, "Get down on the floor, now!" Langford was thinking about the oxygen tank that was about two doors down on the landing to his left. He looked over at the tank and saw the heavy block that was sitting by the tank.

Langford was thinking, *Why don't they set the oxygen tank off, blow a hole in them cops?* Langford was ready to try and run to the tank and smash the pipe.

He just grinned and took a step toward the stairway, ready to find out if….

"Bang!" went the loud thwack of the gun.

A .357 bullet rang through the block and went in Langford's door about five inches from the outside of his left arm. Five inches to the right would have been dead on his heart. There was no mistaking Geech's accuracy with a pistol. Langford got down on the floor, giving in to the only thing Langford knew, and that was justice will prevail in the end. That shot was heard outside the building; no one had known what happened. Warden

McCormick sent in an officer to find out if things were going okay inside. That changed the play book from that point on. It was all offense from that time on, and all one-sided. It went like clockwork; flex-cuff them up, then line them up and run them out of the block door through the hallway, running them out the front door. This was where Silver Spoon and a couple of others used all the brains they had and still came up short. Slapping inmates on the bare back, knocking inmates down, shoving inmates into the walls, hitting them with clubs just for their fun of being thick between the ears and thinking they would get away with it. Next and last, the officers ran the inmates out between a gauntlet, out to no-man's land.

* * * * * * * * * * * *

I was still on the rooftop. Half of the inmates were already out of the building. The CS gas smoke and fire smoke was coming up out of the yard. The gas made my eyes tear up but it was not a cause to worry. Thinking to myself, I wandered how my brother Bob got to where he is now. It was a path he has chosen for himself, maybe not wanting to take it to the limit that he did by harming others, but choosing the path by dancing with the devil in his life too many times. *But why, why would he hurt his mother and family the way he did? Doesn't he realize his family are the ones who pay the price of his sins from the townspeople, and his poor daughters? Why, God, would You allow anyone to follow the devil for a moment of joy when you can abstain from sin by following Christ and having joy in life for eternity? Yes, Lord, I know that he belongs where he is now, but because you have saved his life, please, Lord, bring him down to your plane and build him up to everlasting life. And God, I know that all the inmates in max are following the devil, and most likely they will follow him to hell, but God, please soften at least one heart and let him live through eternity with You. I know, Lord, that being Catholic, I cannot believe in the death penalty, to kill a man for his sins, even though they have raped or killed. It is not for me to take revenge or even stand aside and willfully allow others to do so. That given law is so hard for me to understand, Lord, because these inmates are so evil, neither of them have remorse for their sins, and only live to continue sinning and to live only to try killing or raping again, and I mean this about my brother also. But, it is not for me to do or die or wonder why. It is for me to follow Your plan. Amen.*

It was finally time to take the inmate out of the recreation yard. Three officers, one with a pistol, came in the yard as I was watching them with a shotgun pointed in the air. The Folger Adams key was in the hands of an officer. The key was to unlock the dog-run gate door that opened where the only inmate was still in the yard from the beginning of the riot. Inmate Ray was stripped, then he was told to lie on the cement floor face down. One officer came over to him and placed one knee on his back and then picked up both wrists, putting them together. Then he took the flex-cuff with both hands and put it under the wrists and, putting the left end through the right metal tie, cinched them together. Then two of the officers picked him up by the arms and ran him out of the building. It was time for me to get down from the roof, so I went over to the front of the building and yelled down to the warden and asked if they still needed me up on the roof any longer. I told him that the inmate was out of the yard and things were clear up here. So down the ladder I went with one hand on the rungs and the other hand on the shotgun. Part of the team was headed back to the armory, so I asked if they would take my shotgun with them. After I unloaded the shotgun, they left, and I went to no-man's land.

Back at the command post, plans were contrived before the warden went to max with the extraction team. The old max building was the reception building, and plans were formulated to transfer inmates on reception to all the units inside the prison. This was a task that was not taken lightly. Each inmate had a file with their rap sheet. Rap sheet is a file that tells everything that is known about each inmate. It was a time-consuming process but it seemed to work out fine with a numbering system giving points for each crime and years that inmates were sentenced to the Montana State Prison. This and other factors figured into where the inmates were housed. The biggest factor in this hurry-up placement was if an inmate accumulated fewer points to place him in the letter units, or higher points placed him in the close units or max.

* * * * * * * * * * * * *

The DCT team started taking inmates from the east side of the max building.

Starting on F-block, inmates were told to strip and lie face down on the floor by their cells. There were still a couple of troublesome inmates wanting to show their power. Lopez and Seelye were putting on a show for the rest of the inmates on the block. While the rest stripped and lay down, these two kept on standing by their door with clothes on. They were told again to strip, but in their minds, if they acted innocent by not complying with the direct order to strip, then they were innocent of the killings on D-block, even though Lopez was wearing khaki cloths, and only PC inmates wear khaki cloths in max. Two burley officers went up to Lopez. One sprayed him in the face with pepper spray and the other officer wrapped his arms around his legs, lifting him in the air and slamming him down on the floor. Next, the first officer had a night stick and placed it through the arms of Lopez and turned the stick so that it turned him on his back. With the one officer still holding Lopez's legs, the first officer reached down to get Lopez's right arm and brought it to his back, cuffing him with steel handcuffs. The two officers took Lopez down to the stairs and handed him off to two other officers on the block. Seelye did not want any more convincing that stripping was the best way to go. He had already started stripping before the officers were looking at him. The D-block was already secured off from the rest of the blocks. The fire doors were shut and guards placed at the sally-port just inside the doorway on the block.

One last block was left to extract inmates from, and that was E-block. There were no altercations from E-block; it went smoothly for a change. Last thing the DCT team needed to do was go from block to block, door to door, slowly checking to make sure there were no inmates hiding away or whether there were more inmates dead elsewhere. Each door, if locked, was unlocked and every plumbing chase was checked. The false ceiling was checked, and a confirmed count was verified out in no-man's land that all max inmates were accounted for with fifty-five inmates in no-man's land and five inmates still inside of max, dead.

The county coroners were placed in the area of D-block to watch over the bodies. The two coroners were Mr. Jewel and Mr. Pohle.

Commander Micu and his DCT team left max after reporting to the warden. Back at the armory, the team was still running on high adrenalin, getting "Thank yous" from different State Capitol high officials present, including Governor Stephens and Mr. Chisholm, Mr. Pomroy, and others. After that, they got a shower, then filled out incident reports on what they did inside the max building. Last, before they went home, each one of them had to see a psychologist to make sure they were okay mentally. They would have to see the psychologist again within a month to make sure what they did and saw would not mentally cause them problems down the line.

Dale Brown and the rest of the hostages were reunited with their families on the walkway from max, and were greeted by Governor Stephens. They also were given a chance to take a shower and given clean clothes and interviewed by the psychologist.

* * * * * * * * * * * *

As an officer was walking by inmate Powell, he asked the officer to look at his hands that were going numb on him from the flex cuffs around his wrist. The officer came to check on Powell's wrist which was turning white from a lack of blood. So the officer said he would check on it with other officers. Later, I came to check on my brother in no-man's land. With all the inmates stripped down to nothing, it was hard to spot my brother Bob. But finally, I saw four inmates that were off to the side by themselves.

As I went over to them, I had to say something, so a joke seemed like the proper etiquette. "Boy, there sure are a lot of white asses out here. Bob, what did you do to get into all this trouble?"

Bob replied, "For once, Jimmy, I didn't do nothing, but it was quite a rush and I didn't need no drugs to get it. Ha, can you get someone to loosen these flex cuffs; they are cutting off the blood to my hands, and a blanket to lie on? The grass is like needles stabbing us."

"It sounds like you have not learned anything, Bob, but I will see what I can do," I said as I turned and left.

As I left my brother, I went over to where other guys from transportation in our department were standing. Talking to Steve Antonich, I told him that the flex cuffs were too tight on my brother's hands. He informed me it would be best to stay away from him and do not talk to anyone about the cuffs. This was a very smart thing he told me because there were others taking care of those problems, and if I got in the way of things, then I was the problem. So, staying around Steve in no-man's land, about a half hour later, we were asked to go with a couple of inmates to Powell County Hospital and watch them until we were relieved at 2200 hours.

This was a good duty because there were two officers on one inmate, and watching inmates at the hospital was easy. Taking turns, one officer was inside the room and the other officer was outside the room with a pistol. The whole east wing of the hospital was taken by the prison, and the officers who were in the hallway talked about the riot, and it seemed to bring us all together closer that day, relying on one another.

＊＊＊＊＊＊＊＊＊＊＊＊

It was probably an hour until two officers picked up McFarlane and escorted him over to the County Sheriff, Mr. Fisk, and Undersheriff, Mr. Howard. They were in the cool shade next to the max building. They cut off the flex cuffs, and while he was talking to the sheriff, his hands were free to get the blood running to the fingers. The sheriff asked him questions about what he saw and what was going on at the time he was barricaded in the laundry room. Then when McFarlane was done, the sheriff placed a pair of metal handcuffs on his hands in the front of his body. The two officers brought him back and laid him down on the dried out weeds. Next it was inmate Powell's turn to go, and he was relieved to finally have the flex cuffs off his wrist. It was shady where the sheriff was interviewing him, and life was great for about fifteen minutes until the metal cuffs were put on and the officers escorted him back to where he was, lying him down on the ground. He was thinking how nice it was in the shade, sitting down talking to the sheriff. It was like being free but he was still nervous from his ordeal. But still he felt good and alive, thinking about when he was free to do his own thing on the streets, but how stupid he was to break the law. He told himself that he was going to change, but did he come to this decision because of what happened to him in the riot? Was he really going to change or after a week or a year, would he forget about what he went through to stay alive? Was he incorrigible? Did he not care about anyone but himself? Could he quit giving in to the devil and humble himself and believe in God? That would take years to change, but he was going to try. That was all he had to do, think about things, because it was taking hours until the warden could figure out what to do with the four PCs. The sun was beating down on the inmates in no-man's land. Sunburns were increasing on all the inmates, so they would rotate from side to side then the sun was going down and, it being September, the evenings were cool.

Blankets were given to all the inmates who were in no-man's land after the sun went down. A story was already getting around that Bobby Close saved the lives of the officers who were taken hostage. So Sergeant Morani gave inmate Close two blankets because of the good thing he did. Bobby Close was thinking to himself, *Yes, my plan is working. I am going to get away with murder and be a hero on top of it. Yes, it's working. I am a genius!*

The cold would bring a chill to the bodies in the yard, but it was still a comfort to all the inmates in no-man's land because the riot was over and the state will take care of them, being more humane than how they were humane to all their victims in max or on the streets. Sometime after 1800 hours, the four PCs were moved to Close Unit III and placed in the detention cell on H block. This was the only place to house the PC inmates. Inmate Powell was thinking they would have taken them downtown to the county jail. Anxiety was high, not knowing what was going to happen to them in Close Unit III. There was no sleeping that night or, for that matter for the next week, from anxiety, which was understandable. Anytime the doors opened or inmates from Close Unit III left the building, the four PCs were up from their beds looking around to see what was going on. I went over to

Close Unit III two days after the riot, to see my brother. I walked into the unit and one of the floor officers took me to the block to see my brother. First, I went over to McFarlane's cell and talked to him and told him that I owed him one for saving my brother.

Then, visiting my brother for a minute, I said something like, "You lucked out again, Bob. I'm glad you are still behind bars."

* * * * * * * * * * *

The max inmates were finally out of no-man's land by 2100 hours. It was a rough job for the officers working in the new max building. There were bars on only three of the four blocks in the old reception building that restricted the max inmates in their cells from getting to the officers. Officers were getting things thrown on them and being spat upon, as the max inmates were still on a high from what they did in max. The max inmates were left naked and without mattresses for five days, except Z block. Inmate Ritchson on Z block was found with a cuff key, and other inmates kept harassing the officers.

Each night, there was a meeting with Warden McCormick over anything and any unit. But most of the conversation was about the max inmates. On October 9, the cage officers heard that the inmates were going to tear up the reception unit, now max unit. The inmates were going to break the toilets off the floor and destroy the cells, plus try to injure officers coming on the blocks. A meeting with Warden McCormick and five duty officers brought forth the problems at hand, given to them from Sergeant Perry, to figure out a solution to stop the problem from further disorder before it got out of control. What needed to be done was to line up the inmates they knew were causing the problems and figured did the killing, and shoot them. But, this was not the way of the United States or Montana's way of doing things.

Warden McCormick gave an order to do what was necessary just to control them, to use as minimal an amount of force as possible. Let all informed know what was going on, and bring the DCT team in to wait at the armory in case they were needed. The warden figured that the officers on shift would do the restraining, so it would be less traumatic on the inmates being restrained. The method of restraining was called hogtying or put in a suitcase.

Before anything was done to the inmates, they were told what was going to happen and why it was happening to them. Six inmates were ordered for their clothes to be removed, and then they were placed in leg irons and handcuffs, tied in a reverse fetal position for twenty-three hours.

During their confinement, inmates were released to eat and to go to the bathroom.

This would have been uncomfortable but humane, and it stopped most of the problems in the restricted max.

The Maximum Security Building was cleaned up and fixed, and the inmates went back to the max building on October 15, 1991. The inmates that the administration figured did the killings, were placed on D-block, to let them think about what they had done, in some cases, for the rest of their lives.

* * * * * * * * * * * *

After the riot, the staff's challenge was to take back control of the prison, which had been decreasing for years. An all-out shake down and relinquishing of items was completed during the time that the prison was in full lock-up. Items such as rugs and large containers of smoking tobacco, and a limit of twenty-four audio cassettes was gone through. This was a big undertaking for the prison. One unit was gone through with a big dump truck to throw the new contraband items out and take them to the prison dump. Inmates were given a chance, before throwing items away, to send them out to family. Some inmates did not have family to send home to or did not have the money to send them out, so there were a lot of things discarded. The biggest problem was the one-hobby permit. Some inmates would have $500 to $1000 in hobby equipment and almost finished hobbies, and the inmate would have to choose one hobby and throw the rest of the items out. This kept the prison inmates and staff at a high stress level, but it had to be done.

Plus, inmates were fed in their units, and stayed in their units twenty-four hours a day.

The staff industries was put on twelve-hour shifts and worked in the kitchen, making sandwiches for 1,100 inmates. The inmates were fed a cold meal in their units twice a day seven days a week. There was a step-down plan to get the prison back to normal, but this plan was not working. The inmates had no idea how long they were going to be locked down in the units, and staff was not communicating with them, so in best terms, it was chaotic for all. Recreation for the high-side compound was reduced from four hours per day to an hour and fifteen minutes per day, and education time was reduced from about fifteen hours a week to three hours a week. Some inmate pay jobs were eliminated. High-side visiting was reduced from five days per week to three days per week.

After a meeting with Mr. Chisholm, Mr. Pomroy and Mr. McCormick implemented changes in the way the prison was running, realizing that what they were doing was not working. Communication between the staff and inmates was increased by informing inmates of temporary restrictive changes before the fact.

Recreation for the high compound was changed to two and a half hours a day. Most of the inmates' programs had been restored, and education restored to its original three hours per day. There were fifty-five recommendations that the Disturbance Analysis Report Team made, and most of them were carried out.

* * * * * * * * * * * * *

The riot of 1991, September 22, was the worst in Montana's history, with five dead inmates and more than four million dollars of taxpayers' money spent on fixing the building, convicting fourteen inmates of horrendous crimes of burglary, for entering D-block where the protective custody inmates were killed. Some inmates were also charged with kidnapping for forcing five correctional officers to take refuge in a shower stall. Lopez, Seelye, and Cook pleaded to reduced charges which did not include homicide. Prosecutor John Connor, Jr. led the state defense against all fourteen inmates. The job he did was indescribable, the most remarkable undertaking and prolific work ever accomplished by a team of lawyers from the State of Montana.

(1) Reed Keith Nevins, twenty-seven, pleaded guilty on June 4, to one count of murder by accountability, burglary, and kidnapping. The murder charge was further reduced to mitigated

deliberate homicide in February, 1993. Disposition: The sentence handed to him by Judge Ted Mizner was twenty-five years for homicide, twenty years for burglary, and ten years for kidnapping, all to be served concurrently, and consecutively to his current term. He was still doing time at the Montana State Prison as of 2010.

(2) Harold Edwin Gleed, Jr., twenty-nine. Upon his litigation on June 12, 1992, he pleaded guilty to one count of murder by accountability, kidnapping, and burglary. At a February 19 sentencing hearing before Judge Mizner, Prosecutor John Connor, Jr. further reduced the murder charge to mitigated homicide. Gleed was sentenced to twenty-five years for mitigated homicide, twenty years for burglary, and ten years for kidnapping. It will be run concurrently, and consecutively to his current term. Gleed's original crime was in Ronan, escaped from Swan River Youth Camp with Tony Allen in July of 1984.

The two kidnapped and raped a clerk in a store they robbed in Evaro. He was still doing time at the Montana State Prison as of 2010.

(3) Douglas Duane Turner, twenty-one. Litigation: Turner went to trial on July 18, 1992.

He was the first inmate to face a jury on riot-related charges. Following a week of testimony in Powell County Court and nearly twelve hours of deliberation, a Helena jury found Turner guilty of five counts of homicide by accountability and one count of kidnapping by accountability. The panel deadlocked on the burglary count.

Turner's lawyer called for a mistrial, saying the state had failed to prove the underlying felony necessary to hold Turner accountable in the homicides. Judge Mizner denied that motion on September 15, 1992, saying Turner's participation in the break from the prison yard was enough to support the felony murder rule. On October 9, 1992, Judge Mizner sentenced Turner to five concurrent life terms without parole for the murders, twenty years for the burglary count and ten years kidnapping. Turner's original crime was in Glendive, Montana, serving a 300-year sentence for killing three members of a Glendive family in 1987. He went to trial for the September 1990 baseball bat murder in the high-side yard, of inmate Gerald Pillegi, just days after the riot, and was sentenced to death with his fall-partner, William Gollehon, on that charge. Turner was the youngest of the riot defendants.

Turner hung himself in his cell years later, before the state would have executed him.

(4) Benjamin Earl Cook, twenty-three. Disposition: He pleaded guilty to two counts of felony assault and one count of riot on July 30, after the State dropped five murder counts. At his November 12, 1992, sentencing hearing, Judge Mizner gave Cook ten years with four suspended for each of the two assault charges, and five years for rioting, all to be served concurrently. Judge Mizner also recommended the defendant be transferred out of maximum security. Original crime: He was sentenced to Montana State Prison in 1989 out of Lewis and Clark County on a sexual assault charge. I believe Cook is out of prison and has not returned.

(5) Brian Spray was the only riot defendant not charged with homicide. Spray pleaded guilty to felony assault and riot on July 30. The state dropped charges of sexual intercourse without consent. Disposition: At an Oct. 9, 1992 hearing, Judge Mizner sentenced Spray to ten years with five suspended for assault, and five years for riot. Both terms will run concurrently.

(6) Gary Allen Cox, twenty-nine. Litigation: Cox was the second riot defendant to go to trial. His trial lasted a week in Powell County Court before a Missoula jury. On August 6, 1992, he was convicted on all counts. On November 12, 1992, Judge Mizner sentenced Cox to five concurrent life sentences, twenty years for burglary, and ten years for kidnapping. Original crime: Cox was sent to Montana State Prison on a life sentence for the 1982 drive-by shooting of a Missoula man. He also tried killing a correctional officer in Close Unit I before he was placed in max. Cox is an out-of-state transfer, and will never get out of prison.

(7) William Jay Gollehon, twenty-eight. Litigation: Gollehon was tried before a Bozeman jury in Powell County Court from

August 17 to August 21, when he was found guilty on all counts. Disposition: On October 23, 1992, Judge Mizner sentenced Gollehon to five concurrent life sentences without possibility of parole, plus twenty years for burglary and ten years for each of two kidnapping counts to be served consecutively to the life sentences. Original crime: At the time of the riot, Gollehon was serving a 130-year sentence for the 1985 beating death of a Billings woman.

He went to trial for the baseball bat murder of inmate Gerald Pillegi days after the riot. He was convicted and sentenced to death. Gollehon is in max at the Montana State Prison, and still awaiting execution and still in the appeals court as of 2010.

(8) Kenneth Anthony Allen, thirty. Litigation: Allen went to trial before Judge Jeffrey Sherlock and a Helena jury in Powell County Court on September 14, 1992. The case was discontinued on September 16, when Allen pleaded guilty to a single count of mitigated homicide. Allen subsequently asked Sherlock to withdraw his guilty plea; the motion was denied. Deposition: On March 19, 1993, Sherlock sentenced Allen to twenty-five years consecutive and designated him dangerous offender, where he will have to do half of the twenty-five years before he is eligible for parole. Allen's original crime was in Kalispell, Montana. He escaped from Swan River Youth Camp with co-defendant Harold Gleed in 1984. The two kidnapped and raped a store clerk and were arrested at the Idaho border. Kenneth Allen is still at the Montana State Prison and is out of max, doing time on the low side and at times screwing up and doing time on the high side. Allen will be out of prison someday.

(9) Joseph William Millinovich, twenty-seven. Litigation: Millinovich was the first riot defendant to be tried outside of Powell County in Dillon, Montana. On September 21, 1992, the trial started with Beaverhead District Judge Frank Davis. The trial discontinued on September 24, when Millinovich pleaded guilty to a single count of mitigated deliberate homicide and burglary. He has afterward asked Judge Davis to withdraw that guilty plea. I transferred Milinovich to a Virginia Prison. That was an eight-day car trip, two officers,

four days to get him there and four days back. It was a nice trip back with no inmates. I believe he will never get out of prison.

(10) Daniel H. Lopez, forty-six. Litigation: Lopez went to trial before a Butte jury in Powell County on November 11, 1992. The case ended when the state dropped all murder counts and Lopez pleaded guilty to burglary and riot. The plea agreement came after one of the state's witnesses refused to testify against another Indian. Disposition: Judge Mizner sentenced Lopez on February 19, 1993, to twenty years for burglary with ten years suspended, and five years for rioting. Lopez is the oldest of the riot defendants, and has been in the prison longer than any of his co-defendants.

Judge Mizner also recommended a transfer to Colorado. Original crime: Lopez was sent to Deer Lodge in 1970 on a forty-year stretch from a Missoula County rape charge, aggravated assault, and attempted theft in Gallatin County. He was also charged with aggravated assault while in prison. Lopez was transferred to Colorado, and most likely is still in prison.

(11) Stephen Mark Ritchson, thirty-four. Disposition: He appeared in Powell County Court on November 19, 1992, and pleaded guilty to two counts of mitigated deliberate homicide, one count of burglary, and kidnapping. The state dropped three other murder counts. Judge Mizner sentenced Ritchson on February 23, 1993, to a total of 110 years, 40 years for each murder charge, 20 on the burglary and 10 years for kidnapping. Judge Mizner recommended Ritchson be transferred to Minnesota.

Ritchson was transferred to Minnesota and later transferred to Marion, Illinois.

Original crime: Sent to Montana State Prison in November of 1977, on a twenty-year sentence for aggravated assault, theft, and burglary out of Lewis and Clark and Blaine Counties.

(12) Terry Allen Langford, twenty-five. Litigation: Langford went to trial _____ 30, 1992. After a week of testimony and ten hours of deliberation, the Missoula jury found Langford guilty of burglary and one count of homicide. It was the only split decision in the seven months of riot trials.

Langford was on death row the day of the riot and was only released after inmates had control of the building.

Disposition: Judge Mizner sentenced Langford to life without parole and twenty years for burglary in a sentencing hearing March 25, 1993. Original crime: He was under a death penalty for the 1988 execution-style murders of Ned and Celine Blackwood near Ovando, Montana. Langford was executed in 1998. Langford was the second person executed after Duncan McKenzie in 1995. Prior to 1995, the last execution was fifty-two years before McKenzie's; twenty-five-year old Philip Coleman was hung in the Missoula County Jail on September 10, 1943, less than seven weeks after a murder he committed during a robbery.

(13) Robert T. Wild, thirty-three. He was charged with five counts of homicide by accountability, one count of burglary, one count of kidnapping, and one count of sexual intercourse without consent. The state dropped the rape count just before the trial December 7, 1992. Litigation: After five days of testimony spanning two weeks, and then nine hours of deliberation, a Philipsburg jury found Robert Wild guilty on all counts. The verdict was returned after 1 A.M. on December 16.

Original crime was out of Toole County in 1981 on a ten-year sentence for robbery.

Judge Mizner sentenced Wild to five concurrent life sentences but denied the possibility of parole. He also sentenced Wild to twenty years on each kidnapping count and twenty years on the burglary count. These terms will run consecutively, and are enhanced by ten years because of a persistent felony offender designation. Wild, in court, complained that the deck was stacked against him. He was right, with over 300 years to serve, playing with half a deck and a violent temper, he will lose the card game. Inmate Robert Wild is still in max at the Montana State Prison and looking for a transfer away from Montana, but as of 2010, is still waiting.

(14) Scott Richard Seelye, thirty-eight. Litigation: Seelye requested a change of venue and was set to go to trial in Helena before Judge Dorothy McCarter. He would have been the second-to-last riot defendant to go to trial. He entered a guilty

plea to reduced charges of riot and felony criminal mischief even as jury selection was set to begin. Disposition: Seelye was sentenced to five years for riot and five years on the criminal mischief charge. The two sentences will run concurrently. McCarter also recommended that Seelye be transferred to a Minnesota prison. Seelye did time in the super max of Florence, Colorado. I transferred Seelye to the super max in Colorado. We had four officers and two cars and made the trip in 11 hours, driving all night with plenty of weapons. Seelye was later sent to Minnesota and, in all likelihood, is still in prison as of 2010.

(15) Robert Dee Close, thirty-eight. Litigation: Close's trial began in Powell County Court on January 16, 1993. Close was the only inmate to call protective custody survivors and correctional officers to testify on his behalf. Four of the hostages said that Close saved their lives, and PC Willson said that Close saved his life, also. On January 22, 1993, a Butte jury saw through his scam of being innocent, and found him guilty on all counts. Judge Mizner sentenced Close to life in prison, plus forty years and no parole. I transferred Bobby Close three times to Walla Walla in Washington's Maximum Security Prison. Each time, it was the most stressful trip I have ever taken because he was always polite and tried talking quaintly, but looking at his eyes, there was no life in them so I knew each time he was transferred that my life was in jeopardy. I do have respect for Bobby Close because if his life was different and with his talents, he would have made a positive mark in life, the same as his brother Jim Close is doing. Robert Dee Close replied in court, "I did what I did and I live with it!"

(16) Robert Powell was thirty-nine years old at the time of the riot. Inmate Powell started getting into trouble as a teenager with drinking and drugs. He quit high school his junior year, and went to the Marines. He did okay in the Marines but gravitated more into the drug scene and later, in his thirties, was convicted of a rape charge and did time in prison. He got out and went to California for some time, then moved back to Deer Lodge, Montana. Powell committed another crime of

rape, abduction, and having a weapon. He was sentenced to fifty years dangerous, plus five years for a weapon. He entered the max prison the summer of 1991 before the riot. Robert Powell, as of 2010, is fifty-nine years old and is still doing time, but he has gone through counseling for years, and I have heard he found the Lord, so there is still hope for him.

* * * * * * * * * * * * *

The correctional officers' punishment and other alleged violations: All the officers were on paid leave up to three weeks, then they were given a board at the prison and received their discipline.

(1) Sergeant Donald McPhail received a thirty-day suspension without pay, was demoted to correctional officer, and prevented from receiving a promotion for a year. He was cited for failing to adequately train his staff. McPhail retired in the late '90s and has passed away since then.

(2) Officer Scott Smith was working the main control cage that day. He was suspended for fifteen days without pay. Smith was cited for failing to maintain security, failing to control all movement in the building, lack of familiarity with equipment in the cage that controls doors within the building, leaving his keys to the inmates, abandoning his post, and failing to keep doors locked at all times. Scott Smith has left the prison and is working elsewhere.

(3) Officer Michael McCaughey was working the satellite cage that day. He was suspended for five days without pay for failing to maintain security, surrendering keys to inmates, abandoning his post, and leaving doors unlocked. McCaughey is still working at the prison in the maintenance department.

(4) Officer Charles Miller was working as a floor officer the day of the riot. He was suspended for fifteen days without pay. Miller was cited for leaving security doors open and unattended. Miller has had more than one back surgery from the fall he took on C-block that day. He went back to work but

years later, received a medical retirement, and is doing fine now.

(5) Officer William Boggs was working as a floor officer the day of the riot. He was suspended for five days without pay. Boggs came back to work and retired after the turn of the millennium.

(6) Officer Thomas Olson was working as a floor officer on that day. He was suspended for five days without pay. Olson was cited for leaving security doors open and unattended. Olson never came back to work after the riot.

(7) Officer Dale Browne was working as a floor officer the day of the riot. He was taken hostage and survived the ordeal. He was suspended for fifteen days without pay.

Browne was cited for leaving security doors open and unattended. Dale Browne is still working at the prison and, on occasion, works max but most of the time, works a set schedule. After the riot, Dale Browne's personality has changed. He will not talk about the riot and lives a life of an eccentric. Dale is working on twenty-six years as of 2010. He is the only officer taken hostage who is still working at the Montana State Prison.

(8) Mr. Michael Micu was the Commanding DCT team leader on that day. He showed real heart that day, and dynamic leadership throughout the riot. Mr. Micu has climbed the ladder of success and earned the status of being call Mister. He was, at the time, a lieutenant and two months later, he took the captain's job away from Gurkie. Then he went to the training officer and from there to the prison investigator. With thirty-plus years at the prison, he is now the state investigator, traveling throughout the state. But with two divorces under his belt, his demeanor has changed to being somewhat polite. Mr. Micu would not be, in my opinion, a person you would elect to an officer because he would still screw anyone over to get his way, and now he is even better at politics. Mr. Micu has done well for himself, not going to college and for the wages in Montana has upped his status to high-middle class. Prisons in general need all kinds of personalities, but overall, a correctional officer has to have a strong will not to give in to inmates' scams. Mr. Micu was the right choice to lead the assault

on the max building because with a gun, he was in his domain. Mr. Micu does well working by himself, but to place him into a public office would be a screwing for anyone under him.

(9) James Powell was just one of the 100 people who were trying to bring the prison back from hell. It was the scariest and most confusing day of my life. I cannot imagine what it was like being one of the PCs killed that day, or the PCs who were not killed that day. The inmates who did the killing believe they had accomplished something great only because they will never do anything good in their lives. I feel sorry for them because their families pay for the wrong they had done. Inmates who commit crimes and go to prison, do not get to see the good in life that God has given us. So, their punishment for not following God's plan is to not see the good that God has given us. But there is hope for all and that is why I do not believe in the death penalty. God's hope is to change each one of us to follow Jesus' path and become like Him.

I worked for the prison for twenty-five and a half years before retiring in 2005. I left the prison and went down to Nevada to work in the mines for two years. Then I came back and started at the prison under a new retirement system, and was the first to do that. A year later, I was in a car accident and am now retired again for good. I have had two surgeries on my back and still have a measureable amount of problems resulting from two car accidents. The highlight of my life was four years in high school and two daughters. High school is nothing to vaunt about; it is after high school that matters. If it were not for sports, then maybe I would have been in prison. I was born in a middle-low class family with a lot of pride. At fifty years old, I still am a middle-low class person. I wish studying came easier for me and wish that I had found the Lord early in life, then I could have raised my status up to a middle class. But I am blessed with the things God has given me and blessed for the things God has not allowed to happen to me. The status or class a person is categorized in has no bearing on who goes to prison. It has to do with discipline, child rearing, and beliefs. Life is good!

(10) Randle Chase was an officer that day, and helped take back the building. He worked as an officer for years and then went to maintenance and was fired for stealing one truckload of items from the carpenter shop. That was the only thing he was caught stealing, but it was not his fault because he learned it from his father who worked at the prison in the past. His father would steal ten gallons of milk at a time, and pigs, beef and who knows what else was stolen. This was a practice that was going on in the '50s and '60s and '70s by the upper echelon. Chase has since tried to get back on at the prison but they will not hire him.

(11) Erwin Struble was the captain the day of the riot. He was a very good captain and knew his job well. Later in Mr. Struble's career, he thought he did not have to be at work for the whole shift, but received pay for the full shift. He went night shift and was moonlighting during the daytime, coaching the baseball team. Well, he would go to work about an hour and then go home to sleep, then get up about two hours before the first shift started and come back to work. This was going on for years, and the check point officer knew about it. It turned out he got caught and had to pay back all the hours he missed. Mr. Struble got fired, and the money came out of his retirement fund. He ended up with no retirement and had to move away.

The warden, smiling Jack McCormick, was let go a year or so after the riot. Mr. McCormick learned some hard lessons that day, and probably is not called smiling Jack any longer. The Montana State Prison was on a downhill slide for the last ten years before the riot. The way to foster a prison system has changed dramatically in the new millennium. Fair, firm, and consistent is the new wave of prisons. Mr. McCormick was a good warden before the riot, and after the riot, he changed. Mr. McCormick did not believe in the people under him. There was steady pressure from Helena after the riot to change the way the prison was managed. Mr. McCormick worked for the Butte School Board, and is now running the juvenile prison at Galen, Montana.

After Warden Jack McCormick was the infamous James "Mickey" Gamble. He came from Wyoming, having a line of bullshit and could shovel it all the way to Montana's Capitol echelon. He gave himself the title of state corrections administrator over the men's and women's prisons. Gamble was going to bring the prison system in Montana out of the back woods like Moses parted the Red Sea. He gave the correctional officers more money and created high-paying jobs at the prison to get the morale up. But in return, all employees had to sell their souls to him and his way of thinking. Throughout the United States, the penitentiaries tried changing the prison system from a penal system to a rehabilitation system. While it did not work throughout the US, Mr. Gamble was going to make it work in Montana. The inmates were no longer inmates, they were clients, and you had to address them as Mr. or Sir. He had inmates as his clerks working at jobs that gave the inmates access to files that pertained to employees and other inmates in the prison. He even had an inmate clerk who took notes during meeting that no inmates should be privy to. This inmate lived up at the lake with Mickey Gamble and you were to treat him like an employee.

During Mr. Gamble's short tenure as administrator of prisons, he showed how his thinking was not working. Inmate Sattler was a pushy kind of guy who pushed his way through the system. He would get the counselors agitated and with the Mickey plan, could get an override to pass him down the line instead of putting him back on the high side. Inmate Sattler got an override to let him go to the Swan River Forrest Camp that was minimal security and hardly any supervision. He was a client that worked at the camp and one evening, Settler tried to have sex with the female counselor. She did not want anything to do with him so he was going to rape her and then kill her. Other inmates came to her rescue and saved her, but Settler caused a lot of mental and physical problems to her. She was in a neck brace for over a year. Well, that did not end the problem there. Sattler was transported to a county jail and he was put in a dorm-like setting in the county jail awaiting trial. Sattler killed one of the young men in the jail; the victim was doing jail time for something like driving while drunk. Sattler got the death penalty for the killing, and killed himself in max two or three years after. No one at the prison got fired or any time off for placing Sattler at the Swan River Forrest Camp.

That mistake was not the only one Mr. Gamble made; it was one of many that was shoveled underneath the carpet. But the last mistake was a good one. Mickey Gamble was taking three female convicted felons from the women's prison in Billings for a quaint evening fancy dinner at the Red Lobster. Becky Richards was another clerk for Mr. Gamble, and she was convicted of murdering her husband in cold blood, with forty-nine counts of theft, forgery, and deceptive practices in connection with her husband's logging business. The Red Lobster dinner was national news.

Of the two other female inmates, one was a murderer and the other was in for forgery. Inmate Richards's father-in-law was told about the reward dinner, and Mickey Gamble was fired in November of 1994. The last place he was heard of was shoveling bullshit to a juvenile prison in the State of Washington. If he was still here and did not get caught, I wonder how long it would have been before he took the inmates from the riot out to the Red Lobster on a field trip to Billings, Montana?

The next and present warden of the Montana State Prison is Mr. Michael Mahoney. He has weathered the storm for over ten years and is still going. Mr. Mahoney has started three regional prisons in the state, at Missoula, Great Falls, and Glasgow, and a private prison in Shelby. There have been two minor disturbances, one a sit-down strike in the high yard. After it was over, he sent the troublemakers to the regional prisons. That worked out fine, and now inmates are rotated around so the troublemakers, when they get back to Deer Lodge prison, are rarely a problem because there are more jobs in Deer Lodge and more time out of their cells.

Last, there was a disturbance in Close III, and Warden Mahoney fared well after it was over. No one was hurt, just a block was destroyed. The Montana State Prison is being run better than it has ever run since it was moved to the new site west of Deer Lodge, in 1979. The problem about a small town and a prison town is there is a lot of gossip. Everyone has an opinion and everyone can state his or her opinion, but to be a warden at a prison would have to be a very demanding job with little rec-ompense. Mr. Mahoney has many talents; he was a star running back in college and is a radio announcer for the local high school football team. He volunteers at social functions in Deer Lodge, and he is faithful to his wife and family. It is not bad to believe that everyone's lives are being watched, so what you do with your life matters.

* * * * * * * * * * * *

References

(1) RIOT AT MAX: Administrative inquiry into the circumstances surrounding the Montana State Prison riot of September 22, 1991. Team leader was Jeffrey A. Schwartz. Team members were Clayton Bain, Stan Czerniak, Dennis M. Luther, Lanson Newsome, John Ptaff, Jr., and Mike Schafer, 1991.

(2) *MONTANA STANDARD, BUTTE NEWSPAPER*: By W.C. Platt, Standard staff writer, 1992.

(3) *POWELL COUNTY, WHERE IT ALL BEGAN:* Powell County Museum and Arts Foundation. Historic action committee, Dorene Courchene, editor, 1989.

(4) ROBERT POWELL: Notes

(5) GARRY WEER: Notes from escapees.

The Montana Standard, Butte, Sunday, March 28, 1993—15

Prison in peril

Scott Seelye

Stephen Ritchson

Benjamin Cook

Daniel Lopez

Harold Gleed

Kenneth Allen

Joseph Milinovich

Gary Cox

Terry Langford

Reed Nevins

Robert Close

Robert Wild

14 max-security inmates face 70 homicide counts

William Gollehon

Douglas Turner

214

MONTANA STATE PRISON   PAGE 2 OF 4
MAXIMUM SECURITY UNIT
SEPT. 22, 1991 RIOT
UNDERSHERIFF S. F. HOWARD
PHOTO LOG

ROLL #2
#1 TO #6
#13 TO #15

R2 - 1   Photo of inmate Duncan Makinzie left side of face and back
                of head taken in no mans land
R2 - 2   Photo of inmate Robert Watson left hand taken in no mans land
R2 - 3   Photo of inmate Robert Watson back taken in no mans land
R2 - 4   Photo of inmate Robert Watson face taken in no mans land
R2 - 5   Photo of inmate William Frazier right elbow taken in no
                mans land
R2 - 6   Photo of inmate Gary Cox left hand taken in no mans land

#13 TO #15

R2 - 13   Right hand side of lower wall in D-Block
R2 - 14   Inmate victim lower floor D-Block
R2 - 15   Three inmate victims lower floor D-Block

```
MONTANA STATE PRISON                          PAGE 3 OF 4
MAXIMUM SECURITY UNIT
SEPT. 22, 1991 RIOT
UNDERSHERIFF S. F. HOWARD
PHOTO LOG

ROLL #3
#1 TO #24

R3 - 1     Steps from dayroom to upper level D-Block
R3 - 2     LD-7 and LD-6 door way with blood spots
R3 - 3     D-Block door way
R3 - 4     LD-8 and UD-8 door way
R3 - 5     LD-7 and LD-6 door way
R3 - 6     LD-7 and LD-6 door way
R3 - 7     Step from dayroom to upper level D-Block
R3 - 8     LD-5 and LD-4 door way
R3 - 9     UD-3 and UD-2 and LD-3 and LD-2 door way
R3 - 10    UD-1 and LD-1 door way
R3 - 11    LD-3 door way
R3 - 12    LD-3 door way
R3 - 13    LD-3 and LD-2 door way
R3 - 14    Plumbing door D-Block
R3 - 15    East control cage looking towards west control cage
R3 - 16    LD-3 and LD-2 door way with blood on door LD-3
R3 - 17    UD-5 door way with blood on door
R3 - 18    Victim on D-Block floor (Evans)
R3 - 19    Victim on D-Block floor (Davison)
R3 - 20    Victim on D-Block floor (Baker)
R3 - 21    Victim on D-Block floor (Mazurkiewicz)
R3 - 22    Inside cell upper D-Block
R3 - 23    Victim in cell upper D-Block (Holliday)
R3 - 24    Victim in cell upper D-Block (Holliday)
R3 - 25    Upper D-Block towards E-Block
```

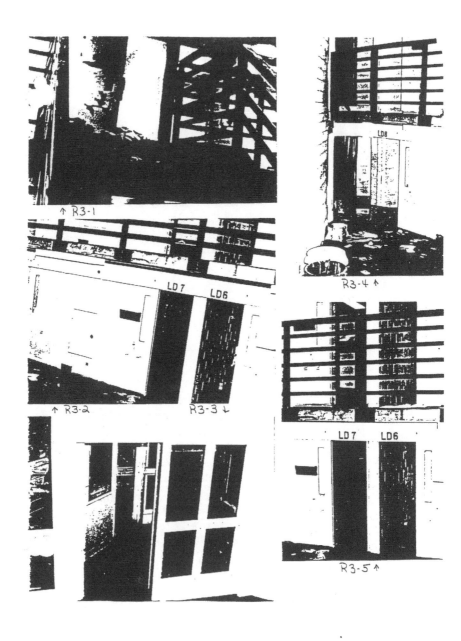

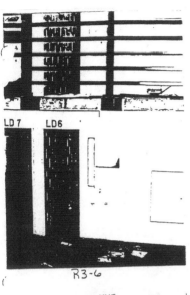

LD 7 LD6

R3-6

R3-8

UD5 .UD4

R3-7

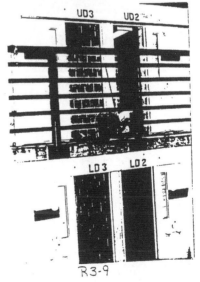

UD3 UD2

LD 3 LD 2

R3-9

R3-22

R3-23

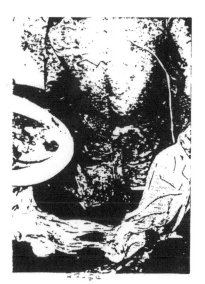

James M. Powell

MONTANA STATE PRISON   PAGE 4 OF 4
MAXIMUM SECURITY UNIT
SEPT. 22, 1991 RIOT
UNDERSHERIFF S. F. HOWARD
PHOTO LOG

ROLL #4
#2 TO #17

R4 - 2   Upper D-Block walk way towards the west
R4 - 3   Inside D-Block towards east control cage
R4 - 4   Blank
R4 - 5   Inside D-Block towards east control cage
R4 - 6   Blank
R4 - 7   Upper E-Block walk way towards F- Block
R4 - 8   Dayroom E-Block lower
R4 - 9   Dayroom E-Block
R4 - 10   Dayroom E-Block and door way
R4 - 11   LD-4 with victim on floor
R4 - 12   D-Block dayroom floor with victims on the floor
R4 - 13   From east control cage towards the west
R4 - 14   From east control cage towards exercise yard
R4 - 15   Victim Evans on D-Block dayroom floor
R4 - 16   Victim Davison on the dayroom floor
R4 - 17   Victim Evans on the dayroom floor
```

224
```

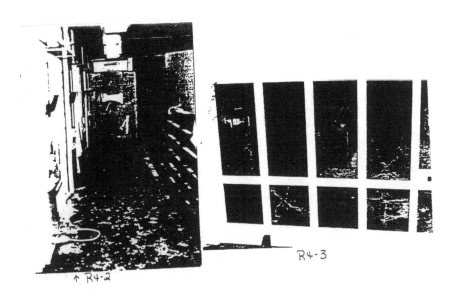

R4-3

↑ R4-2

↓ R4-7

R4-5

↑ R4-8

↑ R4-9

↓ R4-10

↓ R4-11

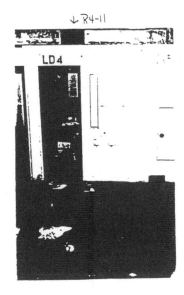

R4-12

R4-13

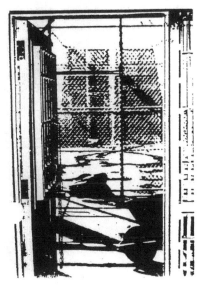

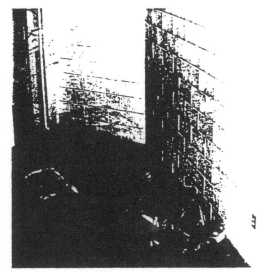

R4-15

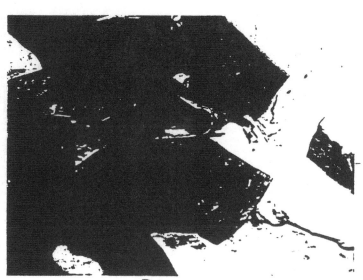

R4-17

DAILY ACTIVITY SHEET:
NUMBER: #184   9-23-91

9-22	ABRAMS, THOMAS #28595	CU-II, FS	PCMH	
9-22	ABRAMS, THOMAS #28595	PCMH	ST JAMES HOSP	
9-24	AMELINE, ALDRED #27857	SRFC	MSLA PR	
9-20	BAKER, BILLY #19556	DD, RANCH #108	ESCAPE	
9-20	BAKER, BILLY #19556	ESCAPE	MAX	TL
9-22	BAKER, VERN #23817	MAX	DECEASED	
9-22	BAUER, CHESTER #20448	MAX	ST JAMES HOSP	
9-22	BAUER, C. #20448	ST. JAMES HOSP	INFIRMARY	
9-22	CAMPBELL, PATRICK #11645	MAX	PCMH	
9-23	CAMPBELL, PATRICK #11645	PCMH	RECEPTION (MAX)	
9-22	DAVISON, EDMOND #15152	MAX	DECEASED	
9-22	EVANS, GARY #23618	MAX	DECEASED	
9-22	GOLLEHON, W. #19043	MAX	RECEPTION	
9-23	GOLLEHON, WILLIAM #19043	MAX, RECEPTION	COURT-LEWIS & CLARK CO	
9-22	HOLLIDAY, ERNEST #31285	MAX	DECEASED	
9-22	HORNBACK, ROBERT #21657	MAX	PCMH	
9-23	HORNBACK, ROBERT #21657	PCMH	INF	
9-23	MARTIN, DANNY #17977	10 DAY FURLOUGH	PAROLE TO HELENA	
9-22	MAZURKIEWICZ, ERNEST #29197	MAX	DECEASED	
9-24	NEEDLES, RODNEY #12571	UB, SCH #401	MSLA PR	
9-22	NELSON, GLENN #30490	MAX	PCMH	
9-23	NELSON, GLENN #30490	PCMH	RECEPTION (MAX)	
9-22	NIDA, RONALD #28285	MAX	ST JAMES HOSP	
9-22	OWENS, TIMOTHY #30109	MAX	PCMH	
9-22	TURNER, D. #26735	MAX	RECEPTION	
9-23	TURNER, DOUGLAS #26735	MAX, RECEPTION	COURT-LEWIS & CLARK CO	
9-20	WEEDMAN, JOHN #10603	TRANSF-WYOMING	RECEPTION	
9-24	KOEPPLIN, WAYNE	DD, RANCH #108	MISSOULA PR	
9-22	ALLEN, K. #19779	MAX	RECEPTION	
9-22	ALLEN, P. #23691	MAX	RECEPTION	
9-22	BAKER, B. #19556	MAX	RECEPTION	
9-22	BASHOR, H. #13970	MAX	RECEPTION	
9-22	BIRTHMARK, M. #22034	MAX	RECEPTION	
9-22	BUCK, M. #26520	MAX	RECEPTION	
9-22	CARTWRIGHT, N. #19880	MAX	RECEPTION	
9-22	CASTRO, R. #29971	MAX	RECEPTION	
9-22	CLOSE, R. #11744	MAX	RECEPTION	
9-22	COOK, B. #27340	MAX	RECEPTION	
9-22	CORSI, R. #25675	MAX	RECEPTION	
9-22	COX, G. #19690	MAX	RECEPTION	
9-22	CURWOOD, J. #21644	MAX	RECEPTION	
9-22	DANIELS, N. #29887	MAX	RECEPTION	
9-22	DAWSON, D. #25284	MAX	RECEPTION	
9-22	ESTRADA, E. #26434	MAX	RECEPTION	
9-22	FLYNN, D. #29960	MAX	RECEPTION	
9-22	FRAZIER, W. #23752	MAX	RECEPTION	
9-22	GLEED, H. #20550	MAX	RECEPTION	
9-22	GRANT, C. #24384	MAX	RECEPTION	
9-22	GRAY, W. #24586	MAX	RECEPTION	
9-22	HEANY, A. #21312	MAX	RECEPTION	
9-22	HERMAN, L. #19502	MAX	RECEPTION	
9-22	JOSEPH, D. #26468	MAX	RECEPTION	
9-22	KILLS ON TOP, L. #27079	MAX	RECEPTION	
9-22	KILLS ON TOP, V. #27177	MAX	RECEPTION	
9-22	KOLESAR, L. #26651	MAX	RECEPTION	
9-22	LAIRD, K. #23317	MAX	RECEPTION	
9-22	LANGFORD, T. #27638	MAX	RECEPTION	
9-22	LINN, R. #21427	MAX	RECEPTION	
9-22	LOPEZ, D. #11889	MAX	RECEPTION	
9-22	McGUIRE, M. #27957	MAX	RECEPTION	
9-22	McKENZIE, D. #13790	MAX	RECEPTION	
9-22	McMILLIN, A. #27431	MAX	RECEPTION	
9-22	MEISSNER, R. #20615	MAX	RECEPTION	
9-22	MILINOVICH, J. #29684	MAX	RECEPTION	
9-22	NEVINS, R. #22572	MAX	RECEPTION	
9-22	PEEBLES, D. #17549	MAX	RECEPTION	
9-22	RAY, R. #23220	MAX	RECEPTION	
9-22	RITCHSON, S. #10948	MAX	RECEPTION	
9-22	SAVARIA, R. #26184	MAX	RECEPTION	
9-22	SEELYE, S. #27574	MAX	RECEPTION	
9-22	SMOCK, W. #26271	MAX	RECEPTION	
9-22	SPOTTED ELK, D. #30639	MAX	RECEPTION	
9-22	SPRAY, B. #30113	MAX	RECEPTION	
9-22	WATSON, R. #26619	MAX	RECEPTION	
9-22	WILD, R. #17023	MAX	RECEPTION	

_Number: #184 cont.

Date	Name	Location	Detail	
9-22	ANDERSON, TED LEROY #26820	RECEPTION	UC, LP #801	
9-22	ANTELOPE, LAWRENCE #31489	RECEPTION	CUI-UA (REC INMATE)	CD
9-22	ARNOT, WILLIAM #27998	MAX	INFIRMARY	
9-22	AUL, THOMAS #31499	RECEPTION	CUIII-D (REC INMATE)	CD
9-22	BASIAK, SCOTT #23242	RECEPTION	CUIII-D (REC INMATE)	CD
9-22	BODILY, CARSON, #22330	RECEPTION	CUI-LB-REC OF (REC INMATE)CD	
9-22	BOESE, RICHARD #24525	RECEPTION	CUIII-D (REC INMATE)	CD
9-22	BROELL, BOYD #31245	RECEPTION	CUII-LD (REC INMATE)	CD
9-22	BROWN, ROBERT #21001	RECEPTION	CUI-LB-REC OF (REC INMATE)CD	
9-22	BUCKMAN, ADRIAN #31527	RECEPTION	CUI-LB-REC OF (REC INMATE)CD	
9-22	BURKETT, ROY JR. #31460	RECEPTION	ROTHE DORM, SCHOOL #401	
9-22	BURNS, TODD #29218	RECEPTION	CUI-UA (REC INMATE)	CD
9-22	CAHOON, SCOTT #27900	RECEPTION	CUI-UA (REC INMATE)	CD
9-22	COLLINS, DANIEL TODD #15588	RECEPTION	UC, LP #801	
9-20	CONDON, ROBERT #24577	UD, LP #801	INF	
9-21	CONDON, ROBERT #24517	INF	UD, LP #801	RPS
9-21	CONDON, ROBERT #24517	UD, LP #801	INF	
9-22	DENSON, RICHARD #21863	RECEPTION	CUI-LB-REC OF (REC INMATE)CD	
9-23	GAMBREL, J. #29255	INF	CU-I, REC CLK #814	RPS
9-22	GOFF, P. #25836	RECEPTION	CUIII-H BLOCK,DET, REC SWMPR	
9-20	GOINGS, FRANK #10207	DD, RANCH #108	MAX	TL
9-22	GOINGS, FRANK #10207	MAX	INFIRMARY	
9-22	GOSS, LESLIE, #31516	RECEPTION	CUI-LC (REC INMATE)	CD
9-24	GRANT, C. #24384	RECEPTION (MAX), TL/CD	MAX, RECEPTION, LP #801	
9-22	GREEN, ROMMEL #31450	RECEPTION	CUI-LB-REC-OF (REC INMATE)CD	
9-22	HAWKINS, LEANDER #30359	RECEPTION	CUIII-D (REC INMATE)	CD
9-22	HICKMAN, RICHARD #15821	RECEPTION	CUI-LB-REC OF (REC INMATE)CD	
9-22	HILL, CLAUDE #31490	RECEPTION	CUI-UA (REC INMATE)	CD
9-22	HOWELL, JOSEPH #10271	RECEPTION	CUI-UA (REC INMATE)	CD
9-22	JACOBSON, MARVIN #31458	RECEPTION	CUI-LB-REC OF (REC INMATE)CD	
9-21	JOSEPH, D. #26468	CU-I, LP #801	MAX	TL
9-22	KLOSTERMEIER, TERRANCE #10362	RECEPTION	CUI-LB-REC OF (REC INMATE)CD	
9-22	KADUBECK, EDWARD #30781	RECEPTION	CUII-LD (REC INMATE)	CD
9-22	LANGFORD, DAVID #28576	MAX	INFIRMARY	
9-22	LANKFORD, D. #28576	MAX	INF	
9-22	McFARLANE, CHARLES #11049	MAX	CU-III, LH	
9-20	LASSLE, R. #21104	INF	CU-I-LC, LP #801	RPS
9-22	McHENRY, CLYDE #11899	RECEPTION	CUII-LD (REC INMATE)	CD
9-22	MAIER, RONALD #31504	RECEPTION	CUI-LB-REC OF (REC INMATE)CD	
9-22	MANULA, JAMES #31096	RECEPTION	CUI-LC	CD
9-22	MARCIANO, FREDRICK #27626	RECEPTION	UC, LP #801	
9-22	MICHELL, MIKE #13543	RECEPTION	CUII-LD (REC INMATE)	CD
9-21	MILLER, J. #17749	UC, LAUND #703	INF	
9-22	O'CONNELL, MIKE #31500	RECEPTION	CUI-UA (REC INMATE)	CD
9-22	PAULSON, CURTIS #28874	RECEPTION	CUII-LD (REC INMATE)	CD
9-22	POWELL, ROBERT #20484	MAX	CU-III, LH	
9-22	RAHN, DUSTIN #30163	RECEPTION	CUII-LD (REC INMATE)	CD
9-22	RAULSTON, JAMES #31487	RECEPTION	CUIII-D (REC INMATE)	CD
9-24	REINKE, F. #21017	UA, UW #605	UA, IND ARTS #702	
9-22	REMILLARD, JAY #31517	RECEPTION	CUI-UA (REC INMATE)	CD
9-22	ROGERS, OWENS #29460	RECEPTION	CUIII-D (REC INMATE)	CD
9-22	ROMERO, VICTOR #25962	RECEPTION	UC, LP #801	
9-22	SALMINEN, RICHARD #26223	RECEPTION	CUIII-D (REC INMATE)	CD
9-22	SHAVER, JAMES #24527	RECEPTION	CUI-UA (REC INMATE)	CD
9-22	SKILVAS, STEPHEN #28550	RECEPTION	CUI-LB-REC OF (REC INMATE)CD	
9-22	SMITH, MICHAEL LORNE #28617	RECEPTION	UNIT D, SCHOOL #401	
9-21	SMOCK, W. #26271	CU-I, LP #801	MAX	TL
9-22	SMOKER, THOMAS #29306	RECEPTION	CUI-LB-REC OF (REC INMATE)CD	
9-22	ST. DENNIS, RAY #28648	RECEPTION	CUI-UA (REC INMATE)	CD
9-22	STEENHARD, TROY #27444	RECEPTION	CUII-LD (REC INMATE)	CD
9-22	STRECKER, KEITH #31513	RECEPTION	CUI-UA (REC INMATE)	CD
9-22	SWIFT, JAMES #29171	RECEPTION	CUI-LC (REC INMATE)	CD
9-22	TISKE, ROBERT #31488	RECEPTION	CUI-LC (REC INMATE)	CD
9-22	TUMBLIN, DON #23553	RECEPTION	CUI-UA (REC INMATE)	CD
9-22	WALTER, EDWIN #31514	RECEPTION	CUI-LD (REC INMATE)	CD
9-22	WEEDMAN, J. #10603	RECEPTION	CUII-LD (REC INMATE)	CD
9-22	WEIST, WILLIAM #31013	MAX	INFIRMARY	
9-22	WICKSTROM, ANDREW #31207	RECEPTION	CUII, LP #801	
9-22	WILLSON, DANIEL #19057	MAX	CU-III, LH	
9-24	WOODS, J. #18044	UA, MECH TRNG #304	UA, IND ARTS #702	
9-22	WORDEN, RICKY #15094	MAX	INFIRMARY	
9-23	WORDEN, RICKY #15094	INF	RECEPTION (MAX)	RPS

Number: #184 cont.

ON SITE:		1164		
Max:	0		TRANSFERS:	50
Close Unit I:	165		Out-of-State:	15
Close Unit III:	102		Court:	12
Reception:	50		Sup. Rel.:	3
Close Unit II:	188		Warm Springs:	12
Infirmary:	8		Galen:	8
Unit D:	131			
Unit A:	144			
Rothe Dorm:	40			
Unit B:	144		TOTAL COUNT:	1220
Unit C:	137			
Dairy Dorm:	45			
Feed Lot:	1		PRE-RELEASE CENTERS:	
Slaughterhouse:	1		Billings:	32
Dairy:	2		Butte:	30
Cow Camp:	2		Great Falls:	38
Garden Wrhse:	0		Missoula:	22
VMC:	1			
EMS	2			
Tag Plant	1		SRFC:	59

OFF SITE:		6
St. Pat's	1	
10 Day Furlo	2	
PCMH	1	
St. James	2	

MSP COUNT: 1182

COUNT OFFICER

Month-to-Date ADP: 1171

Photo courtesy Powell County court

THE RIOTERS built barricades at the entrance to the Maximum Security Unit on the east and west side of the building. Above, prison officials survey the damage.

in peril

reaction

Warden McCormick says prison got bad rap

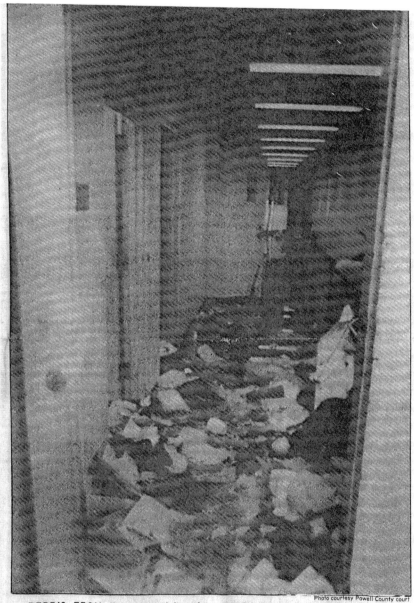

Photo courtesy Powell County court

DEBRIS FROM the sergeants' and counselors' office was strewn throughout the Maximum Security Building after the Sept. 21, 1991, riot.

MICHAEL GALLACHER/Missoulian

SLAIN CONVICT Ernest Holliday's cell is still stained with blood five days after Sunday's rampage.

Illustration by Jeanette Barnes

A GUARD IN the "control cage" in the Maximum Security Unit telephones for help during the riot as an inmate uses a large fire extinguisher to shatter the glass covering the Plexiglas. The guard escaped through a hatch in the roof.

Guards escape through roof hatches, inmates torture and murder five

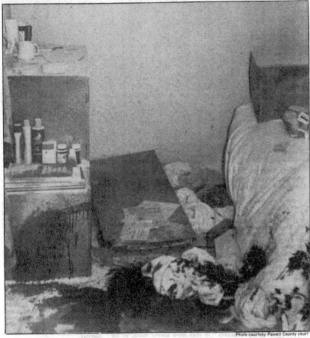

Photo courtesy Powell County court

A CELL IN THE Protective Custody block of the Maximum Security Unit is spattered with blood from the brutal assaults that occurred during the riot. Five inmates were tortured by other inmates and died.

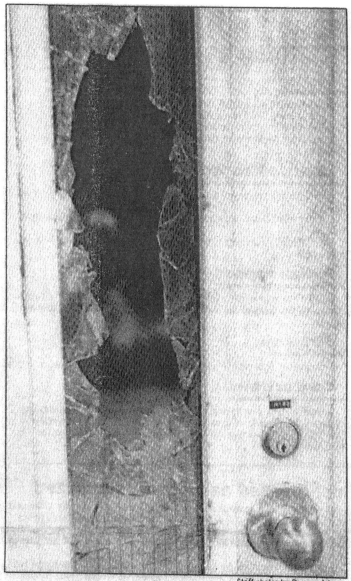

Staff photos by Duncan Adams

WHEN REPORTERS from Montana news agencies were allowed to view the state prison's maximum security unit Thursday, they saw bloodstains on floors and walls, like those pictured below in a protective custody cell, and large amounts of shattered glass. Pictured above are the remains of a small door window, which was smashed by inmates. For more photographs of the unit, see Page 5.

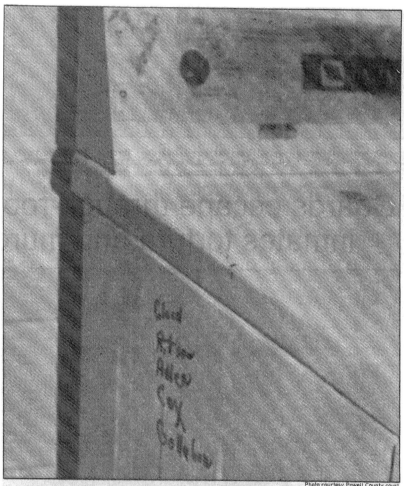

Photo courtesy Powell County court

TWO PROTECTIVE custody inmates who barricaded themselves in a laundry room did not expect to survive the riot so they wrote on the washing machine the names of five inmates they saw outside.